NEIGHBORHOOD WATCH

"A vile bag of garbage..."

- Roger Ebert

NEIGHBORHOOD WATCH

Short Stories

RAISTLIN SKELLEY

Team Hate Press

Mum,

This collection is by and large your fault. And not to say that there is any sort of blame. Fault has a negative connotation, so let's scratch that. Not fault, but guidance. Guidance, tutelage and understanding. Decades of sitting through old movies that you have seen a million times, but I was in the process of watching for the first. Withstanding my rookie misquoting and obsessive research and drilling of facts ranging from trivial to banal. But without you, I wouldn't have ever seen them and more so, there would be large portions of who I am missing from me and I more than likely would be in a far worse place. You were and still remain able to point me in the right direction of books, movies and history that will help me uncover what I'm looking for, not only to reflect it in my own writing, but what I need to see and hear to better operate in the world. I couldn't figure that shit out on my own when I was a kid, it's a coin toss as to whether I can even do it *now*.

I wrote these stories with you in my mind, because I knew if there was anyone else on the planet that would get them, besides me, it would be you. And as I wrote them, I flipped through the mental rolodex of director, story and author references that you have helped fill for me over the years. Sitting under the table at your knee as you spliced old cassette tapes, then listening, albeit and as much as I hate to admit it, stubbornly throughout my teenage years and early twenties. Because I, for some frustrating reason didn't want to hear the answer, even when I desperately needed it. Through the resentment and anger, you were able to tell more than what I wanted, but what I needed, to both hear and experience to help me get through my day to day. And you learned early on, the best tool to get to me was movies. Even in the absolute blackest of times, it was the fastest and most accurate track to get through to me. And it probably still is, though I hope I'm not the same asshole kid I was then. So, these stories, Mum, are for you.

The culmination of everything you've told and taught me, all the black nights and near pitch black days. When you split me right down to the core, this is everything that I know, am, believe in and care about. And as nihilistic and disenfranchised as the majority of these stories may seem, I know you'll see what I'm talking about. I just wanted to show you that I have learned and I have listened and as aloof as I may seem, it's not because I don't care. In trying to help me navigate this world in corporeal form, you've given me all the basic and a few of the advanced tools of my calling. The thing that makes life not so hard for me. Everything that I have done up to this point has been a practice round, a test bake, at the very best, a Danger Room session. These stories are me at my absolute bullwhip accurate and lethal. I've finally figured out how to say what I want to say, in the way I want to say it, with absolutely no compromise. And you are strung through them all, like marbling in a birthday cake. Because if I'm going to dedicate something to you, it's going to be the cake, not the run-throughs I did in the kitchen when I had no *fucking idea* what I was doing.

This is the best of what I am and I what I can do. In short, these stories are what you have taught me. And hopefully, now, you won't have to pause the movie every five seconds to explain what's happening or endure weeks long conversations about the minutia of single lines of dialogue. You can just kick back and enjoy and take comfort in knowing you're in the hands of someone who won't fuck you over or bail on you twenty minutes before the credits roll. I hope you know what I mean.

But Derek said to always end a letter with a quote. Someone else has already said it best, so steal from them and go out strong. There aren't many flattering or complimentary quotes about mothers and sons, so I picked something that I knew you would appreciate and understand. *"My Master Yoshi's first rule was 'Possess the right thinking. Only then can one receive the gifts of strength, knowledge, and peace.' I have tried to channel your anger, Raphael, but more remains. Anger clouds the mind. Turned inward, it is an unconquerable enemy. You are unique among your brothers, for you choose to face this enemy alone. But as you face it, do not forget them, and do not forget me. I am here, my son."*

I've learned where to channel my anger. And I have not, and will not, forget you.

Love,

Raistlin

CONTENTS

SURVIVOR'S PITY

{Editor's Note - This opening piece was not included in the original manuscript. It is our publisher's policy to include an introductory statement from all authors for short fiction collections. After months of negotiation, the author provided us with this statement following a warning issued by our Chief Editor threating to withhold payment and delay the publication's release. The missive was found duct taped to the front door of our publishing office, handwritten with a dying pen on blank pages torn from an electronics manual. The ink had smeared in the rain of the previous night's storm, making transcription of the letter a rather arduous task. Scribbled at the top of the page in black marker, in what can only be deduced as a post factum epiphany was this message: *TO BE READ IN THE STYLE OF EDWARD HOPPER'S* SOIR BLEU}

Originally, I wasn't sure what to say at the start of this thing. I went over a lot of works I admire to get an idea about an introduction: *Paul's Boutique, Bazooka Tooth, Sailing the Seas of Cheese, Eyes Like the Sky*. None of them were any fucking help. Don't get me wrong, masterpieces all, but none of those works are by any means a yardstick for what you are about read, so rest easy. Or uneasy, depending. Comparing this collection to any one of those works is the equivalent of comparing your best dining experience to eating Taco Bell burritos off the hood of your car at one in the morning. One involves silverware and potentially good conversation, while the other involves inhaling exhaust and watching rats and napkins blow around in the parking lot.

If I've lost you, now would be a good time to bail, because this is clearly not for you. If you now have a hankering for burritos, keep reading.

The key factor to deriving any sort of pleasure from this collection, or deciding if it's a ride you want to go on in the first place, is that these stories have no social, or political responsibility. They don't care about what makes you uncomfortable or *oogy*, and could give a good god damn about your offense. They weren't written as manifestos and they aren't fueled by left or right-wing propaganda. They were written to entertain. A shocking sentiment, I know, but honest.

Let me give you a couple examples of what I'm talking about and get a few things out the way. For one, I don't believe in any god. Therefore, none of my work is ruled or dictated by any Judeo-Christian values, Buddhist philosophy, or Scientologist rhetoric. This book is decidedly uninterested in a pursuit, praise, or recognition of a higher power. To quote a man much smarter than myself, "I believe that there is no god.

I'm beyond atheism.". If this rubs you the wrong way, then putting this book down is the first step toward gaining relief, because, once again, *this is not for you.*

Secondly, I am heterosexual. This statement is not an unskilled attempt at conservative flag-waving; more along the lines of the FBI warning at the beginning of a movie. I had to sit for *far too many years* in advanced English classes listening to socially awkward nerds dissecting the bibliographies of authors that died before my grandparents were born, and contriving ways to justify that their works were nothing more than cleverly veiled attempts to write about the respective author's closeted desires to have a same-sex lover. I'm over it. It's literary wanking at its most base and infantile level. I don't have problems with homosexuality, just please don't write a book report on how *LOV[E] + Life* or *Happy Trails* were allegories for struggles about my wanting a male lover. They're not. And if you go into this book, or any of my other work, looking for religious or homosexual subtext, you're going to be extremely disappointed. So, once again, if your dreams are dashed, or you are bending the cover of this book in rage, put it down and I hope you saved your receipt, because this is only going to get worse. I heard they just dropped the price of Disney +.

Now, before we go any further, I must tell you about this storm a few nights ago. The house shook in the wind and the rain sounded like the tropical storms I've heard described by Vietnam vets. If there is anything that the whole Coronavirus situation has taught me, it's that global warming is real and people are a lot dumber than I thought. Not that either were newsflashes, but it illustrated both points in spades.

Back in September of 2017, the first half of the *IT* remake was released into theaters. That is something I will never forget. Not because I watched the shit (because I didn't), but for how the world felt when it was happening. The southern portion of the United States was being pummeled by back to back category four and five hurricanes, that destroyed large sections of Puerto Rico and the Dominican Republic. People feared Katrina: Act II. All major Florida theme parks braced for impact and whole families were abandoning their homes overnight to flee north. The last in a string of five mass shootings that year occurred less than a month after the film's release, when Stephen Paddock checked into a Las Vegas hotel with an action film's amount of semi-automatic weapons and opened fire on a music festival across the street, killing and/or maiming over 800 people.

None of this fear, the bone-deep sense of impending destruction and doom, could hold a single Balsam & Cedar scented candle to the caffeine fueled sixty-cycle hum of nerves and anticipation for the release of *IT*. Those who lived through it know (unless you were blissfully unware of all news and media at the time, in which case I envy you) there was no shaking or avoiding hearing about this god damn movie for the better part of two months. People that didn't read were buying multiple copies of the book for family and friends. People who hated horror movies were standing in line to see it. People actively escaping an impending *category five hurri-*

cane, were taking time out of their busy schedules of *running for their lives* to drop into theaters to see it. To those who did not live through it, I am not exaggerating. To those unaware of it happening, I can assure you, it did. I am by no means a tough or well-traveled person. I've never seen combat. But I have seen some shit. And I'm telling you, nothing, and I mean *nothing*, I've experienced in my life compares to the overall sense of anxiety and paranoia created by the release of that fucking movie. Up to and including the pandemic that is/was COVID-19.

That now historical event, ran around in my head for a while the other night while I felt the house shake and listened to the bedlam just outside my bedroom walls. I remembered a similar night back in September of 2017, where I was lying in bed and sat down my copy of *The Crying of Lot 49* to listen to the spilt milk of a south Atlantic nightmare outside. That was when I knew, beyond the shadow of a doubt, that the whole world was fucked. Now, to walk you through, step-by-step, my math as to how I arrived at this conclusion would require a sleepless night and fear of impending death. But I should note, at a certain point I just rolled over and drifted off, mumbling what I knew could have been my final words, "If we go, we go." The thought that in a climate of political unrest, jack-in-the-box mass shootings, and life-threatening meteorological events within eyeshot just off the shoreline, that people's primary concern and top priority was sitting through a shitty two-hour movie about a CGI killer clown, in the parlance of our times, did not restore any of my faith in humanity. Ever since then, I have regarded the world with a great sense of suspicion and general disdain. So, a few months ago, after the national order of Shelter in Place, when a man that looked like a bum started hurling wine bottles at people in a Seattle grocery store, I laughed. When people show obvious signs of fear and distress over anything as ambiguous as a news article or third-hand reports of "danger at the edge of town", as Jim Morrison once put it, I shrug. Where the fuck were these people during the Ebola outbreak, or when, seemingly, the whole country loaded up with automatic weapons and went on a six-year killing spree? When "Be careful at the store, don't get shot" became a regular joke between the most benevolent of Americans.

Now, I'm not the saying the entire population of the country is responsible for anything I just described or mentioned. But I can say, just now is the first time I've heard any of those events mentioned in recent memory. And it was *me* that brought it up.

As I write this, the country is being thrown into another bout of social upheaval. In many ways it is a mirror of the LA riots of '92, only spread nationwide. News feeds went from being choked with "everything you need to know today about Corona" to "the entire fucking country is on fire". This, of course, being an exaggeration, but things aren't looking too good. And while a lot of people are nervous and upset, I know it won't last forever. Because right alongside the news bulletins are stories about "this summer's hot new trends" and "what not to get caught in at this beach season". It's like that scene in *Signs* where the guy is counting the pop commercials run between newscasts. The ship's going down, but we will be looking relaxed and beachy with a refreshing soft drink clutched in our hand.

It is with this attitude and perspective, that I wrote the following stories. As someone who has very little time for bullshit and even less time for handwringing. Call me what you will, but if I have to hear panic in someone's voice about a current life-threatening event, and the mouth it's coming out of doesn't belong to a) a first responder, b) a victim or c) a relative/victim's relative, I'm not even going to acknowledge that you're speaking. As far as I'm concerned, you had your chance. And you chose a digital fucking clown.

As antagonistic as I may seem to those still reading, I'm really a fairly laid-back kind of guy. Constantly paranoid, maybe. Simmering rage, for certain. But I do my best to not let those things spill over onto other people. I wrote these stories, because very little entertainment grabs my attention these days. Most everything out there seems to be aimed at kids and families (ahem) and anything that is labeled "adult", and isn't pornography, has had its teeth pulled. As Tom Waits once said, "The world is a hellish place and bad writing is ruining the quality of our suffering." I don't want to live in that reality. And I when I sat down to write these stories, I didn't want to perpetuate it for anyone else. I knew this could potentially limit my audience and exposure, but I would sooner go down as the writer of a book that was banned from libraries, that parents issued warnings about to their children, then crank out some tripe that will be forgotten in the annals (or anus) of bullshit fiction. This is hardboiled for the angry and disenfranchised. Cold soup for the paranoid heart. Murder ballads for the grief-stricken and world-weary. I know there are others out there who understand. If not, let this serve as my tombstone.

But, if you've gotten this far, this means *you*. And I'm glad you stuck around.

I have a few stories to rock you with, if you'd like to hear them. Some stories I heard through the grapevine about some people you may have heard about, in a place not too far from here. So, let's get down to brass tacks; throw on your shoes real quick. I want you to meet me down at the corner by the post office, near the neighborhood watch sign. We've got some walking to do.

Raistlin Skelley
(Wednesday June 3, 2020, 11:08 a.m.)

Pass a Hat

The brakes were questionable, but the ice didn't help. I nearly banged a hole in the floor as I slid over the hill from the Steak and Shake drive-thru to the Ikea parking lot. My roll finally came to stop when I clipped a decorative tree, then tapped a light pole. Luckily, the airbag didn't deploy. I couldn't hear the sirens yet, but I knew it wouldn't be long. I kicked open the door and took off through the snow for the liquor store parking lot almost two-hundred yards away.

The job had not gone down as planned. We were cocky that it would and hadn't come up with a plan B. I was thinking on my feet. Which had no traction in the powdered-sugar snow and were sliding all over the place. I heard a chirp. Then a long siren scream. No lights yet. But I didn't have much time.

I didn't know if we pissed someone off or tipped someone off, but the cops knew we were coming. Even if the people we robbed weren't pissed before, they would have been come morning after a mil and a half of chips had walked out the door in the night. It was a joint gang/cop outfit in the Oakmont Business Park. A rock climbing equipment business called Arete. They kept all their cash, in the form of poker chips from a West Virginia casino, in a basement vault. The plan was to tap it, bag the chips, rendezvous, then split the chips and cash them separately and be on our merry ways. But now all the crew was either dead or stuffed in a cruiser. The chips, left to collect snow in the middle of the street and be roped off as evidence.

I didn't have many options at that point. Get caught, do a dime to twenty, then get out, pass a hat and work minimum wage as an ex-con the rest of my life.

Or make a break for it. There was one plan I kept in my back pocket. I just had to boost a car with the least amount of problems to get me there.

I came to a sliding stop next to a CRV. Checked the door for the lock. I love arrogance. My feet hung out the door, facing the road as I worked the wires and listened to the sirens get louder. Less than a minute later, some shitty country music filled the car and the heat kicked on as the engine buzzed to life. All I had to do was drive slow and I'd be home free.

I could see lights over the hill behind where I ditched the car. There was no one else on the road, so I took it easy. The key is, don't steal one car and take it as far as you can. You steal several, ditch them in populated areas and hope the cops get lost in the shuffle.

I made it from Robinson to Moon with no problem and

ditched the mom-mobile in the Walmart parking lot. The place was busier than I had expected, but that played to my advantage. I took the long walk from the front of the store to the back of the parking lot. My footsteps stomped black patches into the scriffin of snow and gave me away. I took the hill up out of the parking lot at a run.

There were no cars. There were no people. Just me and some pissed off dog somewhere that had been thrown out of the house for a party. I heard the light change at the intersection of Broadhead and Beer School and crossed the street toward the Stardust Lounge. *Sweet Caroline* was thumping out of the building. There wasn't a chance in hell I would risk hiding out in there, not being a regular. Might as well be a sign on all western PA bars that reads:

WALK-INS NOT WELCOME, FIRST-TIMERS NEED NOT APPLY

I hid out in the car wash next to the Stardust. The wind was vicious. All I needed was the snow to cover my tracks and the cops to pass me by. I heard sirens up on Beer School, but nothing ever came my way. A quick time check on the phone told me it was 12:11 and my fingers were numb.

Happy New Year.

At 12:20 I left the car wash and crossed the dealership satellite lot to the Giant Eagle. All I needed was a few minutes to thaw out and straighten my head. I took what I knew would be my last walk around the store and tried my best not to think about growing up there. The intercom system was playing that Matchbox Twenty song about a raincoat. My body had warmed up, but I was starting to get cold feet about the whole situation. I lifted a few protein bars to snap myself out of it and went out to the parking lot to pick a car.

A Hyundai Elantra did the trick. I took the back roads at average speeds and made my way to the rendezvous. A white two-story converted schoolhouse in some backwoods town by the Ohio River, about a mile from the state line. It was around 1:30 in the morning when I got there. Late enough that all the small town looky-loos should have been in bed. And no one from the crew who was still alive had blabbed to the cops about the house. Yet. I shut the car off and left the keys in the ignition. It wasn't arrogance this time; it was confidence.

I flipped my keyring to the copy I had made in secret. Not that there was more to it than three minutes and a trip to Lowe's, but all the better that Ben didn't know. His parents had left him the house five years ago when they retired to Florida. The trouble started shortly after. I had been working with him for about eight months. Figured I could get a bigger score as part of a crew than I could by myself and walk away for good.

But I was wrong.

The only thing I had left was Ben's paranoia. All his money either came from or funded some sort of illegal activity. Because of that, he didn't trust banks. He talked once about a trust fund his parents set up for him on his thirteenth birthday. Said his parents knew about what he did and had alerted the FBI and the FDIC and that they would catch him in a sting operation if he ever touched the money. If the trust fund even existed. Did I mention that Ben really likes drugs?

He never told anyone where he kept his money, but we were all certain it was in the house. My guess was somewhere on the second floor. Near his bed, if not in it. I walked to the toolbox in the kitchen for a hammer and crowbar. Very much aware of how loud my footsteps were in the empty house. Every other time I had been there, it sounded like a frat party. Or at least a small gettogether. I walked into the living room at the front of the house and flipped the remote for a minute. Finally, I dropped it and went upstairs. It was good to be nervous. And even more important to be quiet.

The first thing I went for was the mattress. I ripped off the sheets and began slicing it open with my knife. A few minutes later, all I had was a sliced mattress. I pushed it off the bedframe and checked the box springs. No go.

I elbowed the clothes jam packed into the walk-in closet out of the way enough to touch the back wall. The lightbulb swung on its chain in the small room and reminded me of that scene into *Psycho*. Seemed appropriate. I knocked on the wall looking for hollow spaces or anything that sounded off. Nothing. My shoe kicked something big on the floor. I reached down and felt a footlocker.

It scraped paint off the floorboards and chipped wood as I dragged it into the bedroom. I was never really good at math, but I knew I didn't have all night to dick around with lock combinations. It took a good eight to ten hits before the lock gave up and dropped to the floor like a dead bird. My muscles burned, and I could feel my clothes stick to me. I ripped off my coat, threw it towards the stairs and pressed on.

The footlocker smelled like must and was full of bullshit. Knick-knacks, toys, Polaroids and an Altoids can full of shit that rattled. About half way down, I realized that, unless there was a false bottom, the likelihood of finding the cash was slim. I took my chances with an olive-green canvas bag tucked in the upper right-hand corner. Not big enough for the amount Ben claimed to have, but maybe for a one-way ticket to Adios. No luck. Pages ripped out of a teen mag with pictures of underage girls in bikinis and most of an ounce of weed. The paper looked old and the weed was dust. More than likely, they had both been there for a while. But with Ben, there was no telling. I threw it all across the room and turned back to the footlocker.

The musty smell got stronger the deeper I dug. When I got there, I found a sawed-off double barrel shotgun with a pistol grip wrapped in duct tape and most of a box of shells. Ben had talked about it before. But he never was straight about where he got it. Rumor had it that it was used in a homicide out near Falling Water a few years back. I didn't really care. At least now I had something that could go *bang*.

The drywall was a lot easier than the padlock. I used the crowbar to knock football sized holes in the stucco. No Bueno. Every creaky floorboard had its day in court. Ditto. I slammed the footlocker shut and sat on the lid, sweating like a racehorse. I could see my breath in the cool air of the house. If I couldn't find the cash upstairs, I was gonna have to search the rest of the house. I didn't have that kind of time. I needed the fuck out of Dodge.

On my way down, the top step creaked. I hadn't noticed it on my way up. Upon closer inspection, the top riser had chipped paint at the edges. The stair beneath it was scratched and faded. I stood on the top stair with my legs spread and held the hammer over my head. One tap knocked the riser back easy. It fell about thirty degrees, then stopped. In the dead space between the floor to the bedroom and the ceiling to the dining room was about eight pounds of illegal substances wrapped in cellophane. I pushed the bricks out of the way and found the big brother of the green canvas bag in the footlocker. The struggle it put up as I yanked it out of the staircase told me Ben wasn't lying about how much he had stashed. But I didn't have time to count it. I stuffed the sawed-off and its little red friends in with the cash and clipped down the stairs.

A train blared by on the other side of the river. A barge on the Ohio honked back in kind. I scanned the backwoods suburbia for anything that was awake and could operate a phone.

I eyed the gas can on the front porch and tossed around the idea of skipping town with a 904 in my wake.

I kicked the Elantra in the ass before I had too much time to think about it. With a nine-year old sized bag of cash in the trunk, I had better things to think about. I made the West Virginia line at about three in the morning with the *Sealab-2020* theme on my lips.

The Blue Witch of Hell's Kitchen

Madeline O'Toole was born in Trenton, New Jersey in 1924. Born to a father, whose identity remains unknown, and her mother, Darcy Bough, a laundress. Darcy was an Irish immigrant who moved to America as a child in the late 1800's. Little is known about Madeline's early years in New Jersey and even less about Darcy's, but it was rumored that Bough spent several summers working as a fortune teller on the Atlantic City boardwalk, before moving herself and her daughter to Hell's Kitchen. There, "Madge", as she was called, grew up and worked as a housekeeper, along with her mother, until Darcy died of tuberculosis in 1940.

Madge continued to work as housekeeper and laundress until 1942 when, at the age of 18, she applied to work as a secretary at the Midtown Police Precinct North on West 54th Street. Her application noted a proficiency in typing, despite her experience, (historians have theorized she took correspondence courses on rare days off and holidays, in her sleeping quarters provided by various employers) and she was hired on part time over the summer. Within a year, due to a shortage of man-power during the war, she became a uniformed officer working from West 43rd to 46th.

That was when the trouble began.

"Madge the Badge", as she came to be called, set the highest rookie arrest record in her first three months at the department. She was known to be harsh and unsympathetic in her treatment of perps and suspects, in a time where criminal rights were, at best, a joke. Madge did not discriminate ethnicities, gender or age, except in the case of very young children. She was, however, particularly cruel to Russians. (It is believed that her mother had contracted tuberculosis while working as a housekeeper for relatives of a Russian diplomat who was being treated for the disease at home.) In the early spring of 1945, a small chapter of the Odessa mafia attempted to purchase and move in to a West 44th Street five and dime. Less than twenty-four hours after their names had been signed to the deed for the building, the three alleged Ukrainian mafiosos were found dead after having been beaten, shot, burned and hung upside down from meat hooks in the rear of the building. A note was found taped to the front door of the establishment, "Snowballs don't stand a chance in Hell's Kitchen."

Historians believe it was known within the police force and the community who was responsible for the "March 4th Thaw", but no-one fessed to it. It was better to have a woman like Madge O'Toole working with you, than against you.

Though with time, Madge's toe began to slip over the line. Pay for inner-city police officers was not the best, coupled with being a woman; Madge was earning less than what she had as a housekeeper and laundress. Notoriously resistant to extracurricular police activities known to be fiscally rewarding, in 1946 O'Toole jumped in with both feet. She began accepting payoffs from sidewalk craps games and known criminals committing crimes against other known criminals. Near the end of '47, O'Toole was finally issued a radio car, and Madge the Badge's web spun wider.

It was in the period between '47 and '52 that O'Toole was given the moniker The Blue Witch of Hell's Kitchen. Less for her ruthlessness and more for what people referred to as "bell, book and candle". O'Toole graduated from taking drops from bookies, to being one. She never shorted anyone and no one dared to ever short her. Madeline had a knack for falsifying property damage and is suspected to be responsible for several large warehouse and business fires in lower Manhattan and Long Island throughout the 1950's. She had an on again, off again relationship with the Irish mob working as security and lookout. The day she retired from the force, Hughie Mulligan and Mickey J. Spillane gave her a gold appointed, mother of pearl bell the size of a small pumpkin. O'Toole laughed and hugged them both.

In 1953, we find the first report of Madge being seen with a sawed-off shotgun, near the Pine Barrens in Whitesbog, New Jersey. Patrolling officers attempted to arrest her for possessing an illegal firearm, until she told them she was a New

York City cop and showed them her badge. The officers agreed to let her go in exchange for the firearm, but it is unclear in their report as to why they let her leave with it. The report does, however, contain a brief description of the firearm: "...a shamrock etched into the right side of the barrel and something in Latin written around it..."

The mid-fifties marked a change in O'Toole's behavior. The rise in drug use on the streets of New York led to higher crime rates, most notably, a surge in robbery and homicide. Madge, known for her harsh treatment of pushers, was several times pulled from suspects at the scene and ordered to leave the premises. During one particular case in July of 1955, Madeline beat a dope pusher with a length of copper pipe, breaking his nose, jaw, three teeth, crushing his larynx, and destroying the orbit of his left eye, leaving him half blind. She was suspended from duty for three weeks in which time five known street level dealers were murdered, two of whom burned to death in an Airstream Liner that was set ablaze on 46th and 8th. Madge returned to her beat in mid-August of '55.

As the decade came to a close, Madeline became less and less covert in her actions. Her arrest record took a dip from 1956 to '57 while her shooting and physical suppression reports skyrocketed. She also began working more and more outside of Hell's Kitchen. A New York *Times* story from February of '56 describes an unnamed woman, that strongly resembled O'Toole, walking into a Bronx bar, shooting the bartender, Peter Oblonsky, point blank in the face with a sawed-off shotgun, then leaving. The bartender, it was revealed, was a key member of an underground child pornography ring and frequenter of a traveling child brothel. The alleged operator of the brothel worked vice at a precinct in the South Bronx. Three days later, another fire was started in an abandoned building in Throg's Neck. Neither the shooter, nor the arsonist were ever identified.

In December of '59, O'Toole was attacked outside of her home in Hell's Kitchen. Two unknown assailants tackled her to the ground and began beating her with bats and chains. One, smashed a beer bottle and sliced O'Toole from the left corner of her mouth to the center of her bottom lip. Madeline managed to pull her sidearm and fire four shots, fatally injuring one assailant, who was found face down in the snow with a bullet wound in the neck, yards away from O'Toole's front door. The attacker was later revealed to be Roman Oblonsky, brother of the murdered Bronx bartender.

Due to outcries from the community and within the precinct about O'Toole's crimes and behavior, she was forced to retire from the department in July of 1960, after only eighteen years of service. Madeline spent the summer antsy and kept busy working security details for Spillane. She applied for a private investigator's license in August and by October, had opened her own agency on 49th and 10th (the building has since been razed). This seemed to quell the residents of Hell's Kitchen, who over time had become dubious and antagonistic toward her exploits as a uniformed officer. The Blue Witch once again was welcome in Hell's Kitchen.

Throughout her career as an officer and a private detective, Madeline never married nor had any children, though she was known to have had many affairs with men on both sides of the law. It was rumored that she and Spillane had eloped in Cuba a month before her retirement from the force, to ensure her protection by and loyalty to the Irish mob. These rumors, however, were never substantiated. The most widely reported and documented of her affairs, was with Fergus "Noon" Noonan, a Korean War veteran, ex-junkie and prolific thief and bank robber. Historians believe it was one of Noonan's pushers that O'Toole beat half blind in the summer of '55, causing her three-week suspension from the department. The two lived together in Madeline's 44th Street apartment from August of '55 to late November of '58, at which point Fergus dropped off the map completely. He was spotted again, with O'Toole, in mid-February of '62. Noonan was known to be occasionally hired as a consultant by Madeline's private investigation firm for the next ten years.

On the evening of Sunday July 2nd, 1972, Madeline was walking from her car parked in an alley behind her business when she was attacked by three youths with guns and knives. One held a blade to her throat, the other a gun to her head, while the third dug through her pockets for money. Madeline was able to free her hands and knock the blade away from her throat, creating a small surface laceration. She then kicked the left kneecap of the gunman, knocking him to the ground. He in turn, aimed his .22 automatic at O'Toole and fired five times. A single bullet pierced her left lung and lodged into her heart. The three youths then fled the scene. Madeline struggled to her feet, and managed to stumble down the sidewalk to the front door of her agency, unlock it, and dial the police before collapsing to the floor behind her desk. Medics declared her dead-on-arrival. The Blue Witch of Hell's Kitchen was forty-eight years old.

The three youths were later identified as Curtis Young (14), Jeremy Ram (15) and Leonard Spinoza (17). Young and Ram received six years incarceration and Spinoza, the gunman, received eighteen. Only Spinoza served his full sentence.

Madeline O'Toole was interred on July 5th, 1972 at Riverview cemetery in Trenton, New Jersey, in a plot she had purchased next to her mother. She received an officer's funeral.

Follow the Leader

Keith Neptune was sitting on the couch with his feet propped up on the duffel bag in front of him. He was eating a bowl of cereal and flipping through tv he didn't normally get to see. There were weird things on at three in the morning. His parents would be up in about an hour, and he figured even if he fell asleep before then, at least they wouldn't have any complaints because he'd be ready to go. He was changing the channels in a daze and wishing there were more marshmallows in a box when he saw a flash of Willie the Pimp. The image disappeared as fast as it had come and he had to click back several channels before he found it again. It was a special report done by GraphiteTV for the anniversary of the Rats' Nest. It was something he only knew a bit about, but he was learning more and more each day as he chewed through the copy of *Beyond the Valley of the Rats* he had stuffed in his duffel bag.

The report tried to spice up ancient overplayed news footage with slick editing. Keith chewed bored, a bit disappointed that the show didn't seem to be promising anything new. Before it cut to commercial, the narrator reminded that they would have a clip of never-before-seen footage after the break. Keith picked up the remote and found *King of the Hill* to watch for a while as he waited. About three minutes later, he flipped back. The show was already in progress.

"---has agreed to sit with us and give her take on the footage."

Intense *Law & Order* type music whined over the image of an aging hippie in clothes raided from Stevie Nicks and Juice Newton as she walked to a chair in the middle of a dark empty room. Hanging limply to the right of the screen was a plain white bedsheet suspended on thin wire. The camera cut to a close up of the woman as she brushed her grey streaked black hair away from her glasses. She looked up at the screen and shook her head to keep her hair in place.

Keith stopped chewing and dropped his spoon.

"This footage was originally shot by a freelance camera-man in August of 1970 after Duane Leifland's arrest. The film sat developed and unsold in a warehouse for forty years. It will be shown for the first time on this program."

The bedsheet in the empty room with the hippie flashed to life with the dark scratchy image of a man. Leifland was sitting on the floor of a dimly lit cell. He was pulled back a few feet from the bars, twiddling his fingers like Groucho Marx with a cigar. There was a wide smile under his red beard, but his eyes were hidden by the shadow of long dark hair.

"The little blue ants and the big black flies think they stole the cheese from the mice, but they didn't," his voice rang through the empty jail cell in 1970 and echoed tinny into Keith's living room in 2010. "The mice are gonna come. You can't keep mice from cheese. Even the farmer's cat can't keep all the mice from the cheese."

The woman in the room with the bedsheet sat stone faced, staring at the footage. A distorted mirror of Duane Leifland reflected in her glasses. Quick as lightning, a small smile shot across her face then dropped.

"They're in your fish bowl and under your bed," Duane smiled back, "They smell with their minds and can find the little blue ants in their cradle. They like cheese. The ants can't drag it into their anthill, it's too big. Tiny little flies get caught in big black spider webs. Mice eat spiders too."

The reel ran out in a quick series of hand written numbers and the bedsheet was once again white. Lights came up in the studio and the woman adjusted her hair before turning to someone off camera. A man's voice was too far off mic to be heard and had to be deciphered in subtitles.

"Can you tell us what he was saying? Like, what he meant by that?"

The hippie woman smirked and started to speak, her eyes upturned to the ceiling.

"Are you already up?"

Keith instinctively shut off the tv with the remote and turned around to look at his mother. "Yeah, I was, uh...I just had some breakfast."

"Jesus, I thought I was gonna have to kick you out of bed," she shuffled yawning into the kitchen in a long t-shirt.

"I figured," Keith fumbled to pick up his bowl and follow her into the kitchen, "I might as well try to make things as easy as possible. And make the last time you see me at least a semi-positive experience, instead of riding my ass to get out the door."

"That's kind of you," Jeanene yawned sarcastically. She reached into a cupboard and sat a mug down on the counter. "Are you sure you're gonna be alright? I mean, it's not too late to cancel."

"It would be ridiculous to cancel everything this late in the game," Keith stood at the sink washing his bowl, "And I'll be fine. It's not like I'm going to the moon." He had a flash of the woman on the news and did his best not to blurt it out.

"Yeah, but it's your last summer before college," his mother had a sad look in her eyes as she ran an open palm down his face.

Keith turned to her and wiped his hands on a dish rag by

the sink, "And I guarantee you, it will be as thrilling as the last seventeen summers you've spent with me. Besides dad would be pissed." The hippie was going to say something about the footage of Leifland just before he turned off the tv.

Jeanene fought tears as she looked from the duffel bag in the living room, to her son standing in front of her. She wasn't so hot on the plan of spending three months cruising and sailing around Europe. Especially, once she knew her husband had no intention of taking their son with them. It was going to be their "getting out of jail" prize as Neal had put it, which implied they were sending Keith to one, or at the very least, leaving him in one. Jeanene pulled him into a hug and squeezed tight.

"Try not to grow up too much, ok?" Her voice was on the brink of tears, "I still want to see a boy resembling my son when I get back."

"I'll try, mom," he spoke loud enough to be heard over his mouth buried in her shoulder.

They got to the house a little after seven. The sun had already started to creep up behind the horizon. Keith's dad pulled the car stuffed full of his family and their luggage, into the uphill driveway. The asphalt job was done eight years ago, but still looked fresh and was flanked on either side at the entrance by four-foot tall brick pillars topped with decorative stone lions, fake lanterns hanging from their mouths lit with electric candles. The dark ranch home was about forty yards from the road, twelve feet up a hill. The sun was still behind the house in the east, but small shimmers of light were already visible on the wall of glass in the front of the house.

"Alright, tuck and roll," Neal brought the car to a stop in front of the attached garage.

"Stop it," his mother chastised.

Keith creaked out of the car to stretch before reaching in the backseat to pull out his duffel bag. His mom and dad stepped out to do the same. Jeanene looked over the roof at her husband.

"Is she up yet?" she said low.

"I don't know," Neal broke his stretch and started for the front door.

Keith still had his back turned to the house when he heard the sounds of a warm welcome.

"Hey, I thought I heard a car."

"Hey, mom."

Keith could hear his father go in for a hug. Just as he turned around he saw his father pull away to reveal the hippie he saw on tv.

"Keith! My god, you're growing like a weed!" Her smile was wide and honest. She always seemed younger than her age, even though Kevin never knew it. He looked at her bare feet and tried to not think of her smiling at the footage of Duane Leifland.

"Hey, grandma," he said low.

Jeanene intercepted the hug. Keith was thankful for it.

"Are you sure you're going to be ok having him here all summer?" she sounded truly concerned. "I mean, it's not gonna be too much?"

"Oh, not at all," the hippie smiled, "It will be like having Neal back in the house. Just without his father." She let out a warm laugh that cut through the cool morning air.

Neal rolled his eyes and dragged Keith's duffel a few feet closer to the door, "Won't that be a relief?"

Jeanene and Neal said their good-byes and be-goods. Keith watched them get in the car and waved as they disappeared down the road. The first few seconds they were out of sight, he tried to come to terms with who he was standing next to, and how the hell he was going to get through the summer. Part of him was hoping there was something to be learned, the other was terrified of broaching the subject at all, and wondering how he was going to hide this information for the rest of his life. He gripped the strap of his duffel tight and wished he could crawl in it.

"Would you like some breakfast?" His grandmother turned to him with a smile. "I have eggs. I can make French toast."

"No, thanks," he forced a smile and met her eyes for the first time, "I uh...ate before we came."

"Well, you can watch me eat and be jealous, then," she said playfully and walked in the house, holding the door for him.

The house Keith had grown up visiting looked different to him. Like everything was a lie. He knew it wasn't, he couldn't have been lied to about his childhood. But he did approach every step and piece of furniture with caution.

"I made up the spare room for you," her voice had disappeared into the house. "There's clean sheets and everything."

"Thanks," Keith pitched his voice just enough to be heard.

He kicked off his shoes and turned from the front door, down a hall and dropped his bag on a bed made with clean sheets. A bird chirped outside and his stack of books slid off the pile of clothes in his duffel and hit the bed inside the canvas of his bag. Keith wasn't sure what to do. He wasn't big on confrontation of any type and he certainly didn't want to make things awkward, but he couldn't think of any way to make it not. She had gone on tv, though. And Graphite wasn't exactly local. There was probably a corresponding article for it online, so it wasn't any secret. He just couldn't figure out why she wouldn't have told anyone. Unless, she was banking on her family seeing her on tv as her coming out party. Or maybe she was banking on them never watching it at all. He spent an inordinate amount of time in the room trying to figure out his play. When he smelled breakfast drifting down the hall, he decided to tackle it head on and grabbed the book out of his bag before heading out to the kitchen.

His grandmother was standing at the stove, toasting bread in a pan, swaying and bobbing to *Madge Session #1* on the kitchen CD player. The pink sun was cutting through the blue morning light and creeping up the walls. The air was cool enough that Keith knew it was going to be a hot day. And it would take a lot more than eighty-some degrees for his grand-mother to turn on the a/c. She believed in open windows and fresh air. He sat on a stool at the kitchen bar and laid the book down next to a plate that had been set out for him.

His grandmother glanced over her shoulder and turned back to the pan. "I thought you fell asleep," she chuckled. She spun from the stove, turning off the burner and looked over at Keith, licking something off her thumb. Keith watched her, without really watching, as she walked out of the kitchen and into the den. She came back in clicking something in her hand. Very calmly, she strode up to the kitchen side of the bar, stood in front of Keith and spun the book around to face her. She clicked again, then opened to the dedication page and signed it.

"I take it you saw my special?" she said cordially.

"Just uh…this morning, as a matter of fact," Keith didn't feel like he was talking to his grandmother. He felt like he was talking to the woman his grandmother had been.

"Pretty much figured you had," she looked up at him from under her eyelashes and finished her signature with a *xoxo*. "You were too standoffish at the door, even for a teenager." She flipped through the book and found his book mark about a third of the way through the eight hundred pages.

"Does…does dad know?" Keith was leaning on the bar with his arms folded.

"No." she said plainly and closed the book, sliding it back to him. "When he was growing up, I tried to protect him from it. Those people from the news contacted me for the special and I couldn't think of any reason to hide from it anymore. He's grown enough to handle the news now. When he was a boy it would have been too much. And I was afraid of him getting teased about it in school. You're going to college and that's ancient history now. I didn't think that you would even care." She shrugged and smirked before returning to the French toast and plating it.

"I uh…," Keith ran his hand through his hair and looked

out the window. The world felt all at once surreal and normal. Addressing things straight off had been a good choice. But now he had to sit with everyone knowing it. "I've always had a bit of interest in it. It being somewhat local. But, uh...I didn't start reading it until about two months ago. They had it out on display at the bookstore for the fortieth anniversary---"

"My god," his grandmother tossed her head back and groaned with a laugh. "It hasn't been forty years."

Keith laughed, reminded of the times with his grandmother as a kid. She brought over the powdered sugar and jar of strawberry preserves and pulled her plate over to eat standing across from him.

"This is....," he laughed, "This is going to sound like a really weird question---"

His grandmother waved him off with a mouthful of French toast. They both waited for her to chew before she spoke, "No. No weird questions. If you have a question, feel free. Just...just keep in mind I may not know somethings. I wasn't aware of everything. And it's been a couple days since everything happened."

"Well..." Keith picked up his knife and fork before looking up at his grandmother. "Who *are* you?"

His grandmother looked at him with wide eyes, trying to keep in a laugh before she turned away and choked. They both laughed for a minute. The house dropping its cold austere gaze and replacing it with the air of a summer at grandma's house.

She spoke, finally, after several drinks of water, "Who am I?" she said sarcastically. "Mm. You mean, like, my nickname?"

"Well, come to think of it," he chuckled, "I don't know your real name either."

"My name is Jo-Ann Leigh Byrne," she spoke in the same tone she used when she read aloud to tuck him in. She flipped open the book to the pages of black and white photos in the center. "Byrne was my name before I married your grandfather. When I was in the Rat's Nest..." she trailed off, scanning the photos, "they called me Ginger Bee."

Jo-Ann held her finger to a picture and spun the book around so Keith could see. It was a group of girls and boys, only a few years older than him, sitting, standing and leaning on the open bed of a pick-up truck on a dirt road in the woods. His grandmother was pressing her finger to the chest of a girl about nineteen, with collar length hair, holding onto the pole of an American flag attached to the rail of the truck. She was dressed in a man's tank top and jeans cut off above the knee, barefoot as always. Her mouth was slightly open, as if she wasn't ready for the picture to be taken. There was enough about her that looked similar to his grandmother, that it was more than easy to be believed. She also looked like the dark-haired twin of his girlfriend.

Jo-Ann was surrounded by people in the photo Keith *did* recognize: Blitz Templeton was leaned on the truck near Jo-Ann's feet, in an old-style football jersey, his legs crossed and looking off camera as he fidgeted with something in his hands. Dinky was sitting on the dropped tailgate of the truck with her shoulders hunched, hands under her thighs and squinting in the sun. Cletus Flagg was leaned shirtless and barefoot, his back against the opposite side of the truck from Blitz, his arm smeared in space as he threw something off into the woods. The other people in the photo, Keith had to read the caption to know.

"Also," Jo-Ann added as she chewed, "keep in mind...I've never read it." She held her wrist to her mouth and looked over her hand at Keith. "I flipped through it in the store a couple times when it came out. And I've heard about a few things that are in it. Some of it is true, but a lot of it I think was just jive the author put in there to spice it up."

"Well," Keith picked up the book and flipped to a section he had already read, "there's one thing that they never really cleared up...and it doesn't make any sense..."

"Ok," Jo-Ann said thoughtfully, cutting a piece of toast with her knife.

"He said, the author, the cops gave Leifland the nickname

Willie the Pimp after they caught him for running girls out of a motel in Kammerer."

Jo-Ann laughed and looked up at Keith, "No. *We* gave him that name. I'm sure it was a little bit of ribbing from some people because of how many times he had been busted for pimping, but it was mostly because he went around whistling it and singing it all the time. At least as much as I knew. Duane didn't really start talking about Hot Rats until a while after that And I don't think any of the cops that busted him had any clue who Zappa was."

Keith and the woman he now knew as Jo-Ann talked a little bit more over breakfast, then settled into the routines they had whenever he stayed over. Keith would read or watch tv, and Jo-Ann would work with her house plants or her whittling and painting, meeting up in the middle for random talks and meals. There wasn't much talk about Leifland for a few days or anything to do with the Rats' Nest. Though, occasionally, Jo-Ann would walk by Keith as he was reading and ask, "How am I doing?" with a smile.

About a week into his three month stay, a visitor came that he wasn't expecting so soon. There was a knock at the door around eleven in the morning that Jo-Ann answered. It was a seventeen-year old girl, dressed like she was ready for volleyball practice, her blonde hair pulled back and skin peeling from her sunburned cheeks.

"Hey, Mrs. Neptune," she smiled, "is Keith in?"

"Sam?" Jo-Ann was surprised, "Oh my god, what are you doing here?"

"Oh? Didn't Keith tell you?" she furrowed her brow and pointed down the road to the west. "My parents rented a house for the summer just down the road. He invited me to come over and visit."

"Well, I can tell you Keith is definitely his father's son, because he didn't tell me anything about it," Jo-Ann slouched against the door and rolled her eyes, "Boys. Would you like to come in---"

"Sam?" Keith called out from somewhere inside the house. Footsteps thumped down a hallway and Keith slid into frame of the front door, almost immediately putting on his shoes.

"Thanks for telling me Sam was going to be showing up," Jo-Ann teased, "I could have started making lunch."

"Sorry about that," Keith said rushed, "I forgot about it. She just said there's something she needed me to help her with real quick. We'll be right back."

"I did?" Sam pulled her eyebrows together.

"When?" Jo-Ann mimicked Sam.

"The other night when I was on the phone." He finished tying his last shoe and stood impatiently in the door.

"So *that's* who you've been talking to all the time?" Jo-Ann was not in the same rush as her grandson. "Ohh-kay. Here I thought you were talking to your parents."

"Sorry," Keith jumped out the door and grabbed Sam by her elbow.

"Hey!"

The couple stopped a few feet away from the door and turned back to face it. "You know I'm not your parents, and I keep you on a pretty long leash, but you still have to tell me things, Keith."

"I'm sorry," Keith looked from Sam, to his grandmother, to the ground.

"I was a kid too, once. And you're learning about some of the things I did," she nodded in his direction, "so I'm no prude. But I'm also no fool."

Sam's look of confusion had not left her face since it first arrived. She looked back and forth between Keith and Jo-Ann, not knowing what to say.

"I won't tell your parents anything you don't. Run naked through the woods and make love on beds of moss---"

"Grandma!"

Sam turned her head away and blushed.

Jo-Ann continued with a smile, "Do it all. Play. Be young. Have fun. Just play safe. Miss Hoffman?"

"Yeah?" Sam turned back to the hippie, covering her mouth with the palm of her hand, doing her best to look natural.

"It was very nice to see you again. And I hope once you two get caught up, you'll come back for lunch and a visit." She smiled pleasantly and drummed her fingers on the door.

"Sure thing," tears of nervous embarrassment were held back by a well-timed smile. She added, "It was nice seeing you again," with a wave as Keith pulled her around the corner of the house. "What was that all about?"

"It's why I called you," Keith spoke low as he dragged her along.

"Is there something going on?" Sam gave him a dubious look.

"It's sort of a long story," Keith pressed her against a tree just inside the wood line on the edge of Jo-Ann's property.

"But first," he kissed her and played with a lock of her hair, "I missed you."

Sam and Keith moved deeper into the woods and stayed there for about forty-five minutes. Until it became too hot and humid to do anything more than lay next to each other. He gave her a brief history of Leifland and the story of the Rats' Nest, before recounting what he saw on tv and his grandmother had told him his first morning there. Sam was concerned and scared at first until Keith assured her Jo-Ann hadn't been part of any of the crimes. She was just in the group for a time. She hadn't even gone to the court house during the trial. After that, Sam settled into it and was a bit excited by the whole thing.

"That's kinda cool, actually," she laid on her back, her arms folded under her head and legs crossed at the ankles, looking up at the summer sky through the leaves, "I mean, I don't think anyone in my family has done anything. I think my great-grandfather was in World War II or something? But I think he deserted or wasn't eligible to join or something," She propped herself up on her elbows and looked down at Keith as he petted the bare patch of skin between her shirt and her shorts, "I mean, you have someone in your family who is kinda famous. And she didn't have to kill anyone to do it."

"Well, she was kinda involved," he looked up at her, "in a round-about way."

The next few weeks of the summer went better than Keith

had hoped. Sam frequently came over for visits, sometimes staying over in his room, and his grandmother was more than happy to share stories about her youth and time in the Rats' Nest. Often cutting herself off to ask Sam and Keith about where and how they'd been. The only hurdle in their lives was Sam sneaking around her parents, but their commitment to alcohol in all its forms and flavors often did the job for them.

But one morning in early July, Keith woke up to an empty house. Sam had not spent the night and his grandmother was nowhere to be found. He walked around the house for a few minutes calling out, until he found a note on the bar:

Keith,
　　　Had to go out for a bit. Hopefully, be back before supper. If not I will pick some up or we can order **PIZZA!** Had to borrow your book, don't be upset. I'll bring it back.
　　　Love,
　　　　　Ginger Bee

There was a quick sketch of a winking face flanked by *xoxo*.

Keith thought about it all morning but couldn't figure it out. His grandmother taking off suddenly wasn't normal, but he was past the age where that sort of thing would matter. She was a free-wheelin' hippie of the Love Generation. The likelihood that she would be doing anything more insidious than bathing naked in a waterfall would be slim to none. He dwelled on that thought for a moment, switching his mental picture to Sam, then a younger Jo-Ann. Finally, he shrugged it off and spent the rest of the day bumming around the house, watching tv, texting Sam, and reading a copy of *Ronin* he had packed for when he finished *Beyond the Valley of the Rats*. He didn't start tapping his foot until around eight o'clock. About eight-thirty he decided to just call for the pizza and have some left over when she got back. Then she did.

"I'm back!" Jo-Ann called from the front door, over the sound of shuffling. She kicked off her cardboard thin sandals and walked into the living room with a big smile and an armful of stuff. "Have you ate yet?"

Keith muted *Scream* on the tv and hung up the phone from where he had started dialing. "No, I was uh...just getting ready to call."

"Oh, good," Jo-Ann had a huge smile and mischievous twinkle in her eye. She let out a deep sigh, as if she had just finished a hundred-meter dash, "How was your day?"

Keith shrugged and gestured to the living room. "Not a whole lot goin' on."

"Good," she nodded again, not listening. "I have something for you." She walked into the kitchen and laid her armful of things out on the bar. "I talked to some people...and got some things...that might help open up your reading a little bit."

Keith got off the couch and slowly made his way toward

the kitchen. There were several manila envelopes laid out on the counter, alongside his book. "What is it?" He didn't know how to process the sudden flurry of activity in his otherwise numb day.

"Well, first off," Jo-Ann picked up the book and held it out to him, right hand on top, left hand supporting the bottom. "I need to give this back."

Keith took it cautiously and sat down on a high bar chair. "Thanks."

Jo-Ann smiled at him then bobbed up and down on her heels. "Open it!"

He didn't take his eyes off her as he slowly opened the front cover. The title looked just as it had the last time he saw it. Lifted the title page and turned to the dedication page. He caught a flash of red ink. His heartrate quickened but he didn't know why. Until he read closely. The page was covered in six signatures, including his grandmother's. Blitz. Dinky. Steve Clean. Sunshine. And Duane Leifland.

His jaw dropped. The world felt cold and alien for a moment. Every signature was addressed directly to him. A few had short messages included. The ink was fresh. The back of the dedication page was polka-dotted with red, blue and black ink from where the book had been closed while it was still wet. He looked up from his newly acquired murderer signature collection to his grandmother's smiling face.

"Where did...how?"

"I went a few places," she responded slyly. "You're not the only one who has been making phone calls."

"But..."

"We were all *friends*, Keith," Jo-Ann nodded her head as she spoke. "It's not like I'm some psycho-killer groupie. I just made a few phone calls, then went to visit a few friends."

"But...Blitz and Dinky and...Duane...are all in prison."

"Prisons have visiting hours." She gave Keith a chance to speak then continued, "I told you, you could ask me anything, but there would be some gaps in my knowledge. So, I reached out to some people who remembered more than me. And these here," she pulled over the manila office envelopes, stacked them and unstacked them as she read off, "are from Jerry, Billie, Duane, Steve....and Jessica."

Even though she used their real names, Keith knew who they were. Jo-Ann opened the envelope from Jessica "Dinky" Ambrose, and pulled out a stack of handwritten pages on ruled legal paper, bound with a paperclip. She flipped through the pages with a smile, then handed it to Keith. He quickly scanned over the papers. It was the account of the fall of 1969 through the summer of 1970 from Dinky's perspective. Keith looked up at his grandmother with a loss for words. She gave him a wink, then gripped his hand and ordered pizza.

Over the next few days, Keith read through the accounts his grandmother had delivered him from prison inmates. It filled in a lot of gaps, and presented a different perspective on the events than the book. Duane's in particular was rather lengthy and detailed, and surprisingly coherent. But he was still confused about many things; chiefly, his grandmother. Her sudden verve and gusto regarding his education seemed to be motivated by something he couldn't quite understand. Or possibly didn't want to. He told Sam about it, and she said not to worry about it.

"She said herself that she's never talked about any of this to anyone," she said over the phone, late one night, "and now she's getting a chance to get all of this off of her chest. And to her own grandson no less. How often are grandkids actually interested in what their grandparents did when they were younger? And now here you are reading a book about it! It's really quite sweet what she's done. I think it's pretty awesome."

Keith tried to approach it from that angle. He thought over the story and his summer so far and it all did seem like one extended confession. Finally copping to a life changing event you partook in in your youth. He hadn't really asked many questions up to that point. One because he didn't have many, two, because his grandmother was so frank and open with information, there wasn't much left to ask about. One morning when they were eating breakfast on the back patio, he asked one.

"What is 'going dutch'?"

"Hm?" Jo-Ann wiped her mouth with her napkin.

"In the book," Keith motioned toward the house, "Capaldi talks about something you guys did called 'going dutch'. Duane, Sunshine and Dinky talked about it, too, in their letters. Dinky even said she did it to you once."

Jo-Ann smiled and stared off into space as she returned her napkin to her lap. "Ah," she looked back up at Keith, "he really didn't get into that? Capaldi?"

Keith shook his head.

"Going dutch was the name Duane gave to the initiation ritual for the Rats' Nest. Have you ever seen that old black and white movie Freaks?"

Keith shook his head again.

"Well...that's sort of where he, like, got the idea. They have this part where they..." Jo-Ann thought for a moment, "Well, you can't really compare the two." She sucked a back tooth with her tongue, then dropped her napkin on the glass patio table and stood up "It would make more sense if I just showed you. Wait here."

Less than a minute later, she walked through the sliding

glass doors to the patio, with a sawed-off double barrel shotgun tucked under her arm, counting through a box of shells.

"Jesus Christ," Keith's eyes widened and he gripped the arms of his chair instinctively.

"Oh, hush," she said playfully.

"Where did you get that?" he asked, almost out of breath.

"Oh, *years* ago," she palmed four shells and set the box on the table. "I dated this guy a few years ago. Used to be in a van gang."

"A van gang?"

"Yeah, it was, like, bikers but they drove vans instead?" Jo-Ann snapped the barrels shut and dropped the shotgun to her side. "I don't know. He was out of it by the time I met him. But he used to carry this when he was in it, then he lost it and got it back. It was a whole story. Come with me."

Jo-Ann took off, barefoot, for the woods. Keith sat dazed at the table for a minute, his mind trying its damnedest to absorb new information. Seconds later, he got up and trailed behind. His grandmother stopped a few feet from the tree line. Crickets echoed out of the cool dark forest into the early Pennsylvania morning. She looked at the shells in her hand and tucked them in the pocket of her hippie skirt as Keith approached.

"What we would do," she started before he caught up to her, "was we would take a shotgun, like this....this isn't the one. It's probably in states evidence now, but...one of the members would take a pup, that's what we called uninitiated members, out into the woods and we would do this."

Jo-Ann lifted her skirt to the thigh and gripped the shotgun between her knees to free her hands. She gently took Keith by his and looked into his eyes. Once again, he didn't see his grandmother. He saw the nineteen-year old flower child of 1970. Except this time, it spread past her eyes. Her entire body changed, her posture straighter and movements more fluid. Keith wished Sam had black hair.

"Keith Thomas Neptune, do you believe in the power of the weak and mal-aligned forces of this great and mighty planet Mother Earth?"

Keith stared at her and said nothing.

"Just say yes," she whispered.

"Yes." He said it louder than he intended.

"Do you believe that it is the few but mighty powers of the forests, deserts, and seas that truly control the destiny of the world?"

"Yes." He was starting to catch on.

"Do you feel you are part of that number?…This part you say *no* to."

"No," he said loud again.

"Do you wish to become part of that number?"

"Yes."

"Do you believe in the power of Sunshine, Blitz, Moloch, Hubba, Moon Child, Sea Breeze, Lamby, Cletus, Terry the Pirate, Dinky, Ginger Bee, and Steve Clean?"

"Yes."

"Do you accept them with love into your heart and count them as your family?"

"Yes."

"Do you believe in the strength and power of Duane Leifland, Willie the Pimp, and his vision for a brighter world owned by the legion of the Rats' Nest?"

"Yes."

"Do you wish to be welcomed into the warm fold of our family?"

"Yes."

"Do you place whole-hearted trust into your initiate, I, Ginger Bee?"

"Yes."

In one motion, Jo-Ann dropped Keith's hands, took several steps back, pulled the shotgun from between her knees and fired into the woods with both barrels. Keith flinched but did not move. His grandmother kicked open the barrels and took out the spent shells. She looked up from the smoking fire arm at her grandson.

"Do you trust me?" She asked seriously.

"Yes."

She pulled the shotgun shells from her pocket and began loading the weapon. "Then close your eyes."

Keith closed his eyes and began breathing heavy. He heard the sound of the shotgun closing and flinched again, a small sound escaping his throat. The air changed as his grandmother stepped up to him. She covered his eyes with her hand and he watched the pink light of the world through his eyelids fade to black.

"If you trust me," Keith heard the voice of a young woman, "and you have fully committed your heart to the legion of the Rats' Nest," he felt the cold steel of the double shotgun barrels pressed under his chin, "then nothing in this world can hurt you." There was a pause before, "Do you trust me?"

"Yes," he shivered in the eighty-two degree morning.

"Promise?" her voice was still the voice of a young woman.

Keith dreamed about Sam. "Yes."

There was no sound over the sound of his heartbeat. There was a slight tap under his chin and the sound of a hollow metallic *click*. The world became brighter. He could see the pink filtered sunlight again. Slowly, he opened his eyes and saw the old hippie that was his grandmother standing in front of him with a smile.

"Welcome, Spaceman, to the Rats' Nest."

"Space---Spaceman?" Keith stuttered.

"Everyone in the group had a nickname" she said relaxed, raising an eyebrow.

"Yeah?...yeah!" Keith tried to relax, too, but could feel himself still shaking on a bowel level.

"Yours will be Spaceman," she smiled. Her eyes twinkled as she searched Keith's for a sense of recognition. Finally, she pulled him into a big hug. "Welcome to my family." Her voice was buried into his shoulder.

The rest of that day, Keith felt like he was in a dream. He wanted to call Sam, tell her everything that had happened, but it felt like a bridge too far. There was no rational way he could conceive of telling or hearing that story. A part of him was nervous and leery, the other part was proud. That was the biggest obstacle, he felt, in trying to explain what happened. That he was grateful for it. That he felt, in both a fraternal and familial way, that he was now part of something larger than himself.

He didn't talk much to Sam after that and eventually fell into radio silence. Any call or text she made to him was not returned. Any visit she made to the house was ignored. There also never appeared to be anyone home. After a few days of no answers, she broke down and called his parents. They hadn't heard from Keith or Jo-Ann either. The last message they had received was from Jo-Ann, saying she was taking Keith on a trip to Cook Forest State Park. That was days before she called. Sam accepted the news, but was hurt that Keith never told her he was leaving. She tried to ride out the rest of the summer alone, but endless days of being locked in a house with her drunk parents had never been her idea of a good time. The only reason she agreed to go with them, was she knew she would be within walking distance of Keith.

Sam made the trip, every day, down the road to Jo-Ann's house. It became something of a ritual. Before she even snuck into the kitchen for a quick breakfast before her parents rolled out of their hangovers, she would walk the mile and half down the road, up and down paved hills to the little dark ranch house on the hill. There was never anyone there.

Summer was coming to a close. Sam was going on daily rollercoasters of emotions regarding Keith. She hated him, she missed him, she never wanted to see him, she wanted to hold him again. Even if it was the last time. Then one day, near the middle of August, she saw smoke in the distance near Jo-Ann's house, looking out the kitchen window. She took her normally hour long round trip in cut time. Jogging up and down hills until she reached the house. The column of smoke had become thicker, and streamed up from the back yard. About seventy-five yards from the house, she saw something laying in the middle of the road. She took off at a run. Her lungs burned and the sunburns on her face stung in the wind. As she got closer, she could tell it was a body, laying at the base of the driveway in a battlefield of cracked bricks. One of the lion-topped brick pillars had been smashed, removing a large section of brick from the steel column inside. Laying headfirst down the driveway, clothes torn, hands cuffed, a deep slash on his face, was Keith Neptune. Sam couldn't help screaming when she saw him. For a few seconds, she couldn't tell if he was breathing due to her fear. Finally, she could tell he was, but it was shallow. Sam screamed for help, slapping Keith's face, trying to wake him up. She looked around for help, but there was no help to be seen.

Her phone had no signal. She ran into the trashed empty house and called the police on the landline. The living room had been dismantled and reorganized to accommodate what looked like a meditation circle of throw pillows around a small city of melted candles. The ambulance arrived after almost twenty minutes, shortly accompanied by the cops. Sam stayed down with Keith on the edge of the road. His breathing was shallow and he didn't seem to comprehend anything that was going on. In the ambulance, the EMTs cut off his shirt and revealed symbols carved into his skin, wrapping around his torso like a belt. Sam cried. Keith stayed delirious.

Sam wasn't allowed in the hospital room. She called his parents and gave them a brief rundown of what had happened. They said they wouldn't be able to get back to Pennsylvania for about three days, but they were leaving immediately. Sam sat out in the waiting room, kneading her hands and unconsciously rocking. She didn't realize there was blood on her clothes until another person in the waiting room so kindly pointed it out. The constant hammering of medication advertisements in between the morning news didn't do anything to quell her nerves. *The Late Morning News* droned on for a while before something about it caught her attention.

"---from several maximum-security prisons early last night."

Sam's eyes immediately shot to the television and her ears tuned in.

"All escapees were previous members of the infamous cult family the Rats' Nest, responsible for multiple crimes during the summer of 1970, specifically, the ritualistic murder of famous Billboard artist Becky Overstreet and her music producer fiancé Gerald Braun. The most infamous member of the group, Duane Leifland, is believed to be the first one who escaped, dressed in costume as his teenage granddaughter who was found in his cell late last night."

The screen showed a grainy, black and white digital photo captured from a prison security camera. It was obviously an old man, dressed in the clothes of a preteen girl, his face covered by an unnatural looking full head mask of a woman, complete with hair and make-up. Sam shivered and felt like she was going to throw up.

"Other members of the so-called family that escaped last night were Jerry 'Blitz' Templeton and Jessica 'Dinky' Ambrose. A massive armed police search party has been raised, but all whereabouts are still unknown."

The Omelette Heist

All three bank robberies had gone off without a hitch. Three men in City National, three in Premier, and three more in Northwood Trust. Each team consisted of only a bag man, one for crowd control, and a getaway driver. The theory was, with three banks robbed simultaneously, the cops would be caught with their pants down and all nine men could make a clean getaway in the confusion. So far, it had worked.

A '76 Chrysler Cordoba, '77 Plymouth Volare, and a '72 Plymouth Duster peeled out of Lewisburg, West Virginia on the evening of May 9th, 1979, each flying in different directions. The sirens abandoned two of the cars and focused on the Cordoba, being driven by Dwight Gareth, 27, of Somerset, West Virginia. He was the getaway driver for perpetrators of the Northwood Trust robbery, Jason Rodgers, 24, and Paul Rodgers, 25. They lost the cops after only a few miles of pursuit and laced through dirt roads to their rendezvous in the woods along Seneca Trail, just outside of Organ Cave. When they arrived, the other six men were waiting in their cars: Bart Dandridge (31), Macon Ambrose (19), Lester Flynn (29), Peter Guile (25), Mitch Kerns (25), Matt Pugh (23).

By flash and lantern light, the nine men unloaded the cash from their vehicles and loaded it into the back of an ambulance that had been stashed in the woods under cargo nets and deadfall. The ambulance had been bought at auction eleven months earlier by Gareth. Once all the cash had been pooled into one vehicle, Dwight Gareth and the Rodgers Brothers opened fire on the other six men with M-14s they had hidden in the trunk of the Cordoba. They hid the bodies under the same cargo net and dead fall, then left the scene in the ambulance.

The ambulance was heading south on 219 towards the state line when it had a head on collision with a pick-up truck. The driver, Reginald Faire, 52, had just finished working a double shift as a janitor at St. Afra Medical Center in Union and fell asleep at the wheel. Both drivers and all passengers died on impact.

Bud Moon, 38, and James Young, 24, were the EMTs on duty, just off Sweet Spring Valley Rd when they received a call to respond to a car crash involving a pick-up truck and another ambulance, north of Union, near Walnut Grove Lane. The medics were confused when they received the call from dispatch and proceeded with caution toward the crash.

When they arrived on the scene, the entire front end, half way through the cab of the '64 Ford pickup had been crushed, crumpling the unibody, almost bending it in half. An oak tree had slammed into the tailgate and sliced through a quarter length of the bed. The front of the ambulance had been crushed, and was sitting half in, half on the front end of Faire's truck and the back doors had been blown open. The headlights of the active ambulance illuminated small gusts of bills like dead leaves blowing through the early summer night. Moon and Young inspected the rear of the vehicle and found the duffel bags of cash. In a snap decision, the two men looked at each other and began the task of collecting and moving the cash from one bus to the next.

A call had gone out over the scanner. Police caught wind of an unidentified and unmarked ambulance driving at top speeds south from Organ Cave. A few people later reported hearing automatic weapons fire that night, but believed it to be a man, a Korean war veteran, who often camped out in a cabin near Morgan Cemetery. Bruce Weiman, 42, of Midway, Maryland, heard the call over a scanner sitting at home with his Shetland Sheepdog, Clyde, in Ballard, West Virginia. An ex-Marine and retired police officer, Weiman loaded his hunting rifle and set out to intercept the speeding ambulance.

Bruce Weiman never made it to the scene of the accident. He took the back way from Ballard to Assurance and followed Cooks Run Road past James Monroe High School, hoping the catch the thieves on 219 before Lindside. Whispering Pines Drive intersects with 219 after a blind curve. Weiman parked his truck even with the tree line at the edge of the road and waited. He listened to the scanner for any new developments. An ambulance had been sent to assist at the scene of a car accident with another emergency response vehicle. But there hadn't been any further developments in the one connected to the Lewisburg robberies. Sirens rose in the distance. Clyde noticed the lights through the trees first. He indicated to Bruce, who rolled down his window and leaned out with his rifle, the barrel resting on the side mirror. Bruce timed the shot. When the nose of the ambulance became even with his right headlight, he fired. The shot came through the open driver's side window and glanced off the brow ridge of Bud Moon's skull cracking the windshield. The ambulance made a 270 degree turn in the road before tipping over on its side and coming to rest sixty-five yards from Bruce's truck.

When Bruce approached the vehicle, he knew he had ambushed his own plan. Both the driver and man riding shotgun were wearing uniforms for St. Afra Medical Center. Clyde jumped out of the truck, ran over to the wreckage and began lapping the blood pooling near the driver's side window. Bruce walked around to the back of the bus, looking to see if whoever they were hauling was still alive. Instead, he found the cash. Tempted by the sight of the money and terrified of jail time and execution for the double murder he did the only thing he knew to do. He set up road flares to divert traffic from the north, and began loading the cash into the bed of his truck.

Bruce made Pearlsburg, Virginia in less than an hour. He pulled into the driveway of his cousin, Ron Sullivan, a little a before two. Ron Sullivan, 32, had served eight years in Moundsville for armed robbery and grand theft auto. It was the only person Bruce new to turn to. He woke Ron and his girlfriend, Amanda Tiffin, (25, of Knoxville, Tennessee) and explained to them his predicament. The police weren't after him, he had listened to the scanner the whole way down. They had only recently found his roadblock. Bruce offered to split the money fifty/fifty if Ron would lend him the use of his truck to make it to North Carolina. Ron's truck had a cap on the bed. Sullivan thought it over briefly and agreed. Citing blood being thicker than water. Amanda chased Clyde out of the house and began cleaning bloody paw prints out of the carpet.

Weiman crashed at Sullivan's place that night. At seven o'clock, he and Sullivan dragged the money into the house and began counting it in the basement; they came out with $27,000 apiece. Ron stashed his half behind the water heater and Bruce dropped his in the bed of Ron's capped truck. As he walked back into the house, Sullivan shot him in the chest twice with a silenced .9mm Beretta. Amanda did her best to clean the blood off the concrete front step before it dried. Ron shot Clyde once in the head and the couple dumped the bodies, along with the Welcome mat, in the woods behind the house. After adding their cash to Bruce's in the truck, they took off for Winston-Salem.

Just north of Mt. Airy, Sullivan and Tiffin were caught in a routine traffic stop. The police were checking all vehicles for valid driver's licenses. Ron began to itch. He pulled a pump action Mossberg off the gun rack in the cab of the truck and held it in his lap until he stopped. Officer Matt Delby, 26, tapped on his window and asked for his license and registration. Sullivan lifted the shotgun and fired once in his face. The blast, put Amanda Tiffin deaf in her left ear. Police converged on the truck and demanded Sullivan to drop the weapon and step out of the vehicle. Amanda dove out of the passenger side door and was drug away by two uniformed officers. Sullivan stepped out of the truck and immediately began firing at the police. Two officers caught buckshot to the face, hands and arms, but none were fatally wounded. Ron Sullivan was shot nine times and reported dead on arrival.

Amanda Tiffin was sentenced to fifteen years at Swannanoa Correctional Facility for Women for accepting stolen goods and assisted manslaughter. She was released after four for good behavior.

The Rake

I'm a gambler, which sounds a lot more romantic than it really is. People tend to have different reactions to me and it depends on who you are as to what you'll do. Girls with a thing for bad boys go all googly-eyed, others give you the stink eye and bolt. Some guys get antsy and throw down a pair of dice. Most other guys get pissed and try to jump you. And if they can't get you on their own, they get a bunch of other cats to help. It's crazy how many cats want to clean your clock just because you don't have a "real job". But being a gambler is more than a job; it's a career.

Consider this, clock-punchers, no matter how much they hate their jobs, they know they will have work in the morning. Even contract plumbers will have to fix a bathtub or something stupid like that. To be a successful gambler, you need more than crooked cards and light feet. You need a schedule.

Start the week, Monday morning at Pat O'Brien's. Stretch your legs by raking out-of-towners on their last legs over the coals on a pick-up card game that started Friday night. Tuesday from 3-5 am, do the same to fishermen out back over a game of craps. Wednesday, black jack with locals at the

Carousel. Thursday night, camp out at the Sazerac and hustle the businessmen checking in to the Grand Roosevelt. Friday morning, gin rummy with the cooks behind the Bucket of Blood; afternoon, scope out which bars are filling up fastest, run catch the early shift of rubes at O'Brien's, then swing back to the Quarter looking for cats with itchy palms and big eyes. Keep an ear out Saturday and Sunday, catching pick-up games and hitting bars that haven't been raided by the cops. Stay cool and quick and try not to choke on your nut. Come Sunday, pawn all jewelry too cumbersome and conspicuous to carry. Zonk out on your stack of hard earned cash, so you can be fresh and ready to start again.

That's just your structured week. There is a lot of dead air in between, so you always have to be on the lookout for any game or hustle you can find. At any given point on the clock, there is always *some* rube *somewhere* just *waiting* to lose his money. And I am always there to perform that service.

But it takes time to learn a routine like that. I had been in town for about a year before I had mine down pat. Then after eighteen months, I started to get bored with it. I couldn't give it up, I liked the money and it was too easy to get, at times just falling out of the air, but I was starting to feel the grind. The sour attitude my old man had working at the mill. I was smart for my age, but I was getting bitter before my time, and that's just something I couldn't risk. So, one cold January night, I took a walk into Storyville.

I had heard a lot of cats talk about it. Most of the rubes I shook down had either come from or were going there, right after I stole their shirt. But I had never gone there myself. It wasn't far from where I worked, but it was far enough outside that I couldn't risk stopping by, or else I'd miss a game. I had enough coin by now that I could afford to take a night off and maybe share it with the right smile.

What took me by surprise was most of the place was gone. To hear cats talk about it over cards, you'd a thought there were a thousand houses up there, filled with millions of women. In reality there were only four: Lulu White's Saloon (run by a man named Bert Dickering, pretty cool cat, despite his name), Joe Victor's Saloon (run by his son Joe Victor Jr., a real winner), and Terry Musa's (never got to know him, but I don't think the cat was Terry, anyway). The last place was the one that really caught my eye. Old Creole class, so smooth it felt like a warm feather bed just standing in the street. It was a joint called Maison du Soleil Levant, run by a half-colored lady by the name Esmeralda Le Bon (that really was her name).

When you stepped inside it smelled like a woman, which made sense because the place was filled with them. The floor was plush red carpet and expensive looking rugs. Velvet ropes and tassels hung off of everything and there was nothing but classy looking paintings on the walls, which were draped in red fabric, stitched in gold and purple trim. A big mural of a sunrise was painted on the wall in the sitting room. And vases upon vases of fresh cut flowers everywhere and not a dower temperament to be seen.

My first memory of stepping inside the Mansion was women laughing. There was a poker table in the back of the parlor, with a mixed bag of men and women sitting around it. One woman sitting with her back to the wall, was sporting cat's eye glasses and laughing to beat the band, a stack of chips the size of a small house sitting in front of her. The cats sitting around her didn't seem to mind. They were red-faced and crying, while their shoulders jumped up and down, laughter coming out in wheezes and short bursts. A girl with a silk scarf walked past me and let it brush against my belt. She shot a glance at me over her shoulder and walked past the gold-leaf staircase into the next room with a knowing smirk. She thought she'd eyed her mark, but I had already eyed mine.

"What are you ladies playing?" I took out my own deck and shuffled it between my hands as I spoke.

The dark-haired woman in the cat's eyes was raking in more chips when she looked up at me and stopped laughing. The rest of the table did the same. For a moment, I wasn't sure how, but I thought I blew it. There were a few other houses on the street to choose from, but this place looked like paradise wrapped in crushed velvet.

"Bridge," cat's eyes said, with one of those sarcastic looks.

The whole table burst out laughing again. It was just then that I realized, the rest of the house never noticed a thing. Neither did these two lovebirds at the nine o'clock position. They had been necking the whole time and it seemed, somewhere in the silence, the girl had convinced her human chair that going someplace quieter was a better idea. The two stood up as one person with four legs and made their way to the staircase. I pulled up their chair and sat down.

"No hats at the table," one of the younger girls said, shuffling the deck, "and we play with our own cards."

"I can guarantee you, there's nothing my wearing a hat is gonna change in the outcome of the game."

"Then, take it off," the girl said snidely. She might have been decent looking, if she hadn't started to get on my nerves.

I leaned back and rocked the chair up on two legs, then dropped it again. The dealer and I locked eyes and not with tender feelings. I realized, I had brought too much of my street gambler personality in with me. But I also couldn't figure out how to put it down, I was afraid to.

"Screw it," the woman in the cat's eyes said quickly. She dropped a small stack of chips from her pile in front of me, "I'll win it and he won't have any choice then." She was a bit older than the rest of the girls, maybe in her very early thirties. All the other girls looked to be somewhere between sixteen and twenty-three. Still kids, even by my standards.

"I'd like to see you try," I rocked back in my chair and smiled.

"I promise you, honey, there are many other things you'd like to see me try. But this one I'll let you see for free."

The laughter had returned to the table. This time at my expense. I can't say that I was too upset by it. I always enjoyed a bit of lip before a game. It showed who was serious and who was in it to get played. As it turned out, that person was me. The woman I came to know as Alice robbed my hat on the first hand, forcing me to sit at the table with messy hair while she sat under my lid, mocking me every chance she got. I had no shortage of fond feelings for her after that. And my first night at the Mansion, was one I carried with me for the rest of my life.

I started going back to the Mansion every weekend then. Soon, a couple times a week. Time didn't slow down there, it just didn't exist. Until, the peanut vendors walked shouting up the street from the French Quarter. I would stumble out of someone's bed, most times Alice's, get dressed and go back to work. The hardest part was knowing, as soon as I opened my eyes, it was the farthest I would be from getting back there again. To the laughs, music and good times.

Alice and I became friends, of a type, and we learned a lot about each other. Turns out she was married with two children, but that never shook me at all. I never met her husband, but it never bothered me when she talked about him. After all, there was no way he spent more time with her than me. And she never took off her ring.

I started spending so much time at the Mansion, I got to know all the girls on a first name basis. And there wasn't a bed in the house I hadn't slept in. Except for Esmerelda's. One night, she joked that she'd have to start putting me on the payroll. And for the first time, having something that resembled a straight job didn't seem that bad. Instead, she had me work with Alice and a few other girls (chiefly Crystal, the other card shark of the house) to set up and rook guys at the table. One night, old Jimbo, the house security, had a heart attack dragging trash out to the curb. It was a few hours before anyone noticed he was gone. Some john started getting rough with Jeanie in the den and I had to run and pull him off her. When I chucked him out the front door, he landed on top of Jimbo. Some of the girls were upset. Esmerelda appointed me head of house security.

Spring had finally rolled around and was dipping its toe into summer. The windows of the Mansion were open almost all the time and when you stood on the sidewalk outside, the world smelled like perfume. I had gotten to the point where I didn't even roll with the girls most of the time, though I did every once in a while, I just enjoyed the ambience. At first, the Mansion seemed like a dream in the middle of the real world. After a time, it felt like the Mansion was the real world and everything else was the dream. It made trolling the streets for rubes and eyeing up marks from the other side of the table much easier, but all I could ever think about was getting back. Then something happened one night, that made me never want to leave.

I was standing at the small bar by the stairs, when I heard screams from the second floor. Instantly, I knew it was Alice. I took the steps two at a time, girls diving out of my way as I slid on my brass knuckles. When I ripped open the door to Alice's room, there was a man standing over top of her in nothing but a shirt, his hands gripped around her throat. I grabbed him by the shoulder and punched him once but good in the mouth. He practically bounced when he hit the floor and came up with a punch from somewhere around Yucatan. That hit knocked me off my feet and into Alice's vanity. I heard something glass *crack* and it gave me a second wind. Three more blows knocked him to the floor and I stood on his chest for three more. Alice was screaming something, but I couldn't hear what it was. Finally, I picked him up by his hair, grabbed his duds off the floor and frog marched him down the stairs and out the front door. He was pretty punch drunk after the beating I gave him, but his head bouncing off the sidewalk woke him up a bit. He looked up at me with two black eyes and a split lip as I dug through his jeans and pulled out his wallet. I tossed him his clothes and started counting money.

"What am I supposed to tell my wife and kids?" The cat sounded genuinely afraid for a man who had just tried to strangle a woman to death.

"The same thing you're gonna tell the cops," I said as I tucked about two hundred dollars in my pocket, "You lost all your cash to a gambler at a whorehouse." I held his wallet up between my hands and aimed it at him like a slingshot. It flipped through the air and caught him in the face. "Kite."

The john stood up and shot daggers at me while he tucked his family jewels back in his jeans. And by the looks of it, his family wouldn't be inheriting much when he passed. I made sure he was down the street and around the block before I turned back inside. Everyone in the house, johns and all, clapped. I gave a few quick smiles, but waved them off and went back to my post at the bar. A needle dropped on a record in the next room, and the Mansion was back to its regular party self. Alice slowly came down the stairs, dressed in a pink slip, a blanket wrapped around her shoulders. When she stepped up to the bar, I slipped the cash into her hand.

"What's this?" she held it up and looked at it.

"His nut." I could feel my jaw beginning to swell.

"If I wanted that, I wouldn't have screamed."

Normally, I loved when Alice was sarcastic. It was one of my favorite attributes about her. But right then, I couldn't shake seeing that bum's hands around her throat and was just glad she wasn't hurt. I spun around and put my back to the bar, looking across the foyer, into the sitting room.

Alice walked up close to me and spoke low, "What do I owe you?"

"A glass of ice and a submarine of your peach cobbler." It was all I truly wanted at the time.

"Is that all?" Alice raised an eyebrow and stepped behind the bar, filling a glass with ice.

I knew what she was getting at, but it felt wrong to ask for it as payment. I spun around to face her and leaned in, intentionally changing the way I spoke to seem more lighthearted, "When did you start shaving?"

"How would you like to wear a full beard all summer?" Alice handed me the tumbler of ice.

"Point taken," I held the glass to my jaw and felt the cool sink in, "Pencil me in for November, huh?"

Alice pulled the glass away from my jaw and yanked me across the bar by my tie. The swelling stung as she kissed it, but I could feel her breath on my cheek. She lingered there for a moment and I caught a flash in her eyes. Then as quickly as it started, she let go and stepped out from behind the bar to make her way upstairs.

"I'll mark my calendar."

I listened to her footsteps climb the stairs and disappear behind her bedroom door as it closed. The ice was cool on my jaw and I could still smell Alice on my cheek when I felt someone standing next to me. I opened my eyes and turned to my right to see a girl about my age that looked like she got lost on her way to a church picnic. She leaned on her elbow against the bar and started sliding off a pair of white lace gloves.

"What's got you blue?"

I pulled the glass away from my face and showed her my swollen purple jaw.

The girl smirked at me and twinkled her eyes. "Good Samaritan."

"Bad Samaritan," I said and plucked a cube of ice from the tumbler and popped it in my mouth. "Half decent muscle."

"Really?" she sounded genuinely interested, then switched gears, "What's the color for?"

I was getting sick of taking my relief away, but pulled the ice from my face long enough to wipe my bruise with my open hand. My fingers came away smeared with Alice's lipstick. "Thank you note." I put the tumbler back to my face with a clack.

"I think I can do better than that."

Her voice was pure honey. Not the corn syrup even Crystal would lay on me when business was slow. I didn't have the first clue who this girl was, but I knew for certain that I had never met anyone like her in my life. For the first time, I turned to get a really good look at her. She had long brown hair pulled back in a ponytail and the deepest brown eyes I had ever seen. Her smile was the genuine article and she carried herself like she knew where she was going in life.

"Oh good, you're in." Esmeralda stomped in from the parlor, straight up to the girl. "It's about time you got in. You were supposed to be here at three."

The girl turned toward Esmerelda and wrapped her arms around her in a big hug. "Izzy!"

Esmeralda fought to get free, slapping the girl's hands away. "Alright, that's enough! You're messin' up my things, now."

The confidence the girl had shown me moments before took the backseat to the excitement of a little girl meeting her aunt after a long period away. "I'm sorry I'm late. The dumb train got stalled outside of Lafayette."

"Don't make a habit of it," Esmeralda said curtly, "Where's your case?"

"By the door," the girl turned back to me and smiled, still holding Esmerelda by the hands, "I was going to see if this nice man would help me carry it upstairs."

"I don't think he'll have any objections to that," Esmerelda was all business, "Jesse here is our new Jimbo."

The girl listened intently to Esmeralda then turned back to me, raising an eyebrow, "So you *are* a good Samaritan."

I had nothing to say. I couldn't even feel the sting in my jaw anymore.

"Oh, sweet Jesus," Esmerelda rolled her eyes, "now you've gone and broke him."

The girl turned to her and giggled, "What?"

"Normally, you couldn't get this boy to shut his yap for all the dice in the Vieux Carre." Esmeralda snapped her fingers in front of my face and yelled, "Campbell!"

I pulled my focus away from the girl in her Sunday best and turned toward Esmerelda.

"Help Betty take her things upstairs to Bobbie's old room," she turned back to the girl and spoke sternly, "And if you're gonna roll 'im, make it fast. He's still on the clock." She started walking away in a huff before she added, "Lord knows you're the only girl in this house he *hasn't* tried."

We both watched her walk away before turning to face each other. The girl with a pleasant smile and me, I'm sure, with a dumb look. She held out her hand for a shake.

"I'm Beverly Dulaine."

I returned her shake and introduced myself before picking up her suitcase and following her to the third floor. Bobbie had moved out not a week before, but her room felt as if no one had lived in it for a year. Beverly sat down on the bed and bounced on it. She kicked her feet, knocking her shoes off on the floor.

"I always preferred this room," Beverly looked around the room thoughtfully, as if there was something she was looking for that was written on the ceiling. "It can get damn hot in the summer, but the breeze is cool coming through the windows. And the air smells better than down there on the street."

I sat down her suitcases and took off my hat to fan myself before walking over to the windows behind the bed. "Speaking of which," they stuck for a moment at the bottom, then almost got away from me when they broke free. The sounds of late spring came in from outside, "You're libel to cook to death if those aren't open."

"Is that something Bobbie taught you?" Beverly smirked.

"No, ma'am." I held my hat to my chest, which I never did.

"Do you call all the girls ma'am? Jesse?"

"No, ma'am."

Beverly bounced up off the bed and covered the distance

between us in the blink of an eye. "Well, you don't have to treat me any differently." She wrapped one arm around the back of my neck and pressed into me. There was something about her that was different from all the other girls. And it wasn't even because I didn't know her body like the back of my hand. There was this pull I felt in my chest, and I knew if I took my hat away, I wouldn't be able to fight it. She let out a deep sigh and held her mouth to my forehead. I didn't even know I had turned my face away from her until then, but I knew I couldn't look her in the eye.

"Are you afraid of me?" she said no louder than a whisper.

"No, ma'am. Beverly. Ma'am." I tried not to think about her arm around my neck or the toes of her stockinged feet touching my shoes. I knew I had to get out of the room. But I also knew I didn't want to.

"I'm not going to hurt you," Beverly ducked her head and tried to lift my chin with her eyes.

The only thing I could do was grip my fist as tightly as I could. I had fought off men twice my size and outrun entire radio cars full of cops. I had spent a whole night bleeding in a dumpster down in the Eleventh Ward after a gang of business-men had accused me of cheating. I had handled tougher cases than a girl in her Sunday's best. But she was getting the better of me. I held my hat firmly in place and stared at the frame of the bed.

A jazz trio came to life down on the street. The same up-beat number they used to kick off every night. Beverly turned quickly toward the window and I could see out the corner of my eye as a small smile came to visit her face. "God, how I've missed it here." She turned back to me with a smile as fresh and clean as the Furtile Crescent. "Do you like to dance?" her voice still at a whisper.

"Afraid I'm not much of a dancer, Miss Beverly." I knew this was my out. I could feel in my gut I was ready to make my way for the door.

"It's not as difficult as folks make it out to be." She pulled my hat from my hand and tossed it on the dresser behind me, before wrapping her fingers through mine and pressing in close, shortening the distance between us to nothing.

Instinctively, I moved my right hand to the small of her back and lifted her left hand in the air. It wasn't right for the music, but the box step was all that I knew. Beverly laughed and looked down at our feet, then back up to me. After a few times around the square, she dropped her head on my shoul-der and we squeaked across the floorboards until the song was over.

But that wasn't the last time I danced with Beverly Du-laine. Not by a longshot. Every game I played was a race against the clock to get back to the Mansion. I would goof around in her room, just talking, laughing, until I would have to leave for a few minutes, sometimes an hour and then we would pick up talking as if nothing happened. I tried not to get jealous, but some nights it was hard. As demure as she was, Beverly had her loud moments. Something the rest of the girls in the house would tease me about often.

One day in early May, I took her out to eat at a restaurant in the French Quarter. It was the first time I had seen any of the girls outside the Mansion. She told me about growing up in Fall River, Massachusetts and running away from home at sixteen. She hadn't been back since. Just bumming around, making her way down south, doing odd jobs: waitress, cook, day laborer. That was the most surprising part. I never knew of any construction outfit to hire girls, but she said if you find a small enough town, they'll let girls do most anything if they need the help. I asked her how long she had been at the Mansion. She said this would be her second year. The previous year she had fallen down the staircase and broken her leg. The doc in town set her splint wrong and her leg started healing funny, so she had to go up to a doctor Esmerelda knew in Lyon, Mississippi, just outside Clarksdale. She'd been gone since a few weeks before Christmas and was just now getting back. I told her I was sorry she was injured, but she laughed it off, happy that she could still dance.

Our afternoon was not long, but being out of the Mansion somehow brought us closer together. Like there had been some sort of question floating in the air if we would still like each other when we stepped outside the walls of the house. The Mansion's glamour had no effect on Beverly. She had a beauty all her own.

Alice, on the other hand, started giving me the cold shoulder. I wasn't sure why. We were still friends, in my eyes, and had had some good times together, but I couldn't understand what got her so bent out of shape. She started ignoring me when we passed on the stairs and freezing me out of the rube-rooking poker games in the parlor. I wrote her a few notes and tacked them to her door, but I never got a letter back. Not even word passed through the other girls.

One night in late June, I was taking the stairs up out of the foyer to the second floor when I met Alice at the top. Her face was stone hard and just as cold. I said Hi but she never even acknowledged me. I grabbed her by the shoulder and she pulled away faster than a timber rattler.

"*Don't...touch* me." Her eyes never met mine. She just turned toward the stairs and walked down to the main floor.

When I got to Beverly's room, things weren't any better. Her door was cracked open and I could hear her sobbing over the street noise outside. I came in without knocking, and tried to comfort her, but she would only turn away. Every time I asked her what was wrong, she would stare deeper into the floor and cry, her brown eyes glazed in tears.

"I have to go away again," she said finally.

"Wha-...what do you mean go away? Go away where?"

"You have to go away, too" she turned to me, her face serious and sad.

"We can go away together, then," I tried to smile.

"No. You can't go with me," Beverly stood up from the bed and began to pace the floor. "No one can go with me. And I can't go with you. You never should have been here. I never should have let you into my room."

"Beverly, what is going on?" I didn't know what to do but watch and listen.

"You! That's the problem!" Beverly looked at me with an expression I had never seen her look at me with before. Anger. "You always want so much of me, but I can't give it! I can't be with you. We never should have been together. Why wouldn't you just go?" She collapsed to floor like someone cut her strings. Every time she sobbed I felt my heart crack like Fall River ice.

"Bev," I knelt down next to her and gently held her shoulders to comfort, "if you just tell me what's wrong---"

"Why won't you listen?" Her brown eyes were bloodshot now. They screamed at me along with her words, "Just *get out*!"

I didn't have a choice. There was nothing else I could do and sticking around would have just made things worse. I closed the door as softly as I could behind me and made the long walk down the stairs to the foyer. The world down there was unchanged. People laughed and carried on. And for the first time, it made me sick to my stomach. I stepped out onto the sidewalk and looked up at Beverly's window for a long time. I could see the light from her lamp on the ceiling. I felt as helpless as she had looked. If there was something I could have done, I would have done it in a heartbeat. But there wasn't. Finally, I put my back to the Mansion and walked back towards the Quarter to find a game.

I didn't go back to the house for a few days. I figured it was better to give everyone in the house, not just Beverly, a break from me for a while. Even my job as house security, there was always some cat in the sitting room or the parlor that was willing to hop to if some other john got rowdy. I knew I wouldn't be missed. What I wasn't ready for was no one to want me back. Or for Beverly to split.

"What do you mean she's not here?" I stood on the front steps of the Mansion, Esmerelda blocking my way.

"She said she went back up to Fall River," Esmerelda now taking a tone with me I'd never heard her use. "Told me to give you her best."

I looked around the street, unsure of where to go or what to do. "But...I don't understand."

"There's nothing to understand, boy. She's gone."

"What abo---"

"Alice doesn't want to talk to you either," Esmerelda leaned in the doorway, smoking one of her hand rolled cigarettes through a filter.

I had lost big pots in my day. I had had strings of bad luck. But none of them ever hit this hard or fast. I didn't know what to say. Just looked around for some answer, any answer, someone may have dropped on the ground.

"Go back to the Quarter, kid," Esmerelda spoke to me in the cold business tone she used on drunks. "Go get yourself some money, spend it on some other girl. Preferably, one that doesn't see twelve other guys a night. Take her back home and settle down."

I kneaded the brim of my hat in my hands and stared up at Esmerelda. "I want to see Alice. And I want to know where Beverly is."

"Well, Alice doesn't want to see you, kid," she said with no small amount of sass. "And Beverly's gone where the cold wind blows." Esmerelda turned her back on me and stepped back inside the house. Before she shut the door she said, "And you're officially barred from the Mansion."

I stood on the front stoop of the building that once housed all of my happiness, defeated. The one place I had felt at home since I left mine. I could feel tears, but choked them down, clearing my throat. My fists clenched around my hat. I looked up and down the street with a quick tough guy sniff and positioned my brim before taking off for the Quarter at a run. I could not get away from the Mansion fast enough. Or out of the city soon enough. I needed a big pot to skip town.

There was a serious poker game going on when I reached Pat O'Brien's. I waited out a hand, then convinced a guy to give up his chair. Didn't even have to get the brass knuckles wet. Just gave them a flash when I itched my chin. The cat running the game was a spud I had run into before named Rod Henmen, usually during the craps games with the fishermen on Tuesdays. The guy couldn't shoot craps for shit. I gave him fifty-fifty odds on knowing the difference between a flush and a straight. He stared daggers at me when I sat down. I got it. After almost two years of someone winning money off you hand over fist, you tend to harbor bad feelings about a person. He was working at a disadvantage that night, though. Other times, I was just out for money. This time I was out for blood. Anything to make someone hurt worse than I did.

Five hands in and people were starting to get pissy. The mood I had brought to the table wasn't lifting anyone's spirits. But watching everyone get ticked off and mean lifted mine. Several guys folded before they lost their nut and the table was down to four including me. I'd had to have been blind to have not seen the other two guys with Rod were his cronies. He had a conversation with his eyes with his three o'clock crony and the dealer stood up and left the table.

"Let's take a breather," Rod's teeth were green. It always made me sick when he smiled. "You've been running us pretty hot there, doughboy."

"It's called a winning streak," I said flatly, "You should try catching one sometime."

Rod laughed but I could tell he wanted to punch my lights out. There were about two minutes of hot air between us, before his dealer crony came back with a tray of drinks and something hanging heavy in his back right pocket. Rod pulled it out and dropped it in his lap when the dealer stood next to him to dole out drinks. Once the libations were dispensed, the dealer sat down and waited for the word from Rod.

I knew something was coming, but I didn't know what. In the meantime, I just kept my feet angled toward the door. On the third hand, Rod made his play and dropped a .45 in the kitty. There was a small four-leaf clover and words stenciled on the side above the grip. My instinct was to fold. But there was enough cash on the table underneath of it, I couldn't turn away.

"You bettin' toys now, Henman?"

"No toy," Rod gave his green smile. "It's fully functional. Just bought it this afternoon."

"Then why are you betting it?"

"Forgot I was on parole. If I get got with a piece, I'm back in the slammer for twenty years."

"Wouldn't that be a god damn shame?" I muttered and made my bet.

"You'd have one less person to take over a barrel on a weekly basis. And less money to pour into those cheap whores you visit every night."

I wanted to kill him. Right then and there. No one would be sorry that he was dead. And I knew I was fast enough I could outrun the cops before they were even called. It would give me reason to never come back again, either. I chose a more modest approach.

"Eat shit, cake-eater," I dropped a dead man's hand on the table.

The nine o'clock crony seemed hurt. Rod and his three o'clock smiled. He began clapping slowly, the dealer joining off beat. "Bravo, doughboy. You got me."

I took off my hat and began raking the cash and jewelry into it, leaving the piece for last.
"What's the story with this thing anyway?" I glanced at the piece.

"No story," Rod shook his head. "Honest injun" he held up his hand in a Tonto salute.

I felt a pulling in my chest again as I stared at the gun. I never liked guns. Never had much use for them either. They were heavy and loud and slowed you down. There hadn't ever been a fight I got into I couldn't punch my way out of. And after I won the knucks, there were few I didn't win. I picked up the piece and looked at it. It looked like it worked and it didn't feel like a toy. As best I could tell, there were three bullets missing.

"Come to think of it, though," Rod rocked back in his chair and stretched his hands behind his head. I felt my stomach sink. "I think I did use a gun very similar to that one, on a police officer in Gentilly this afternoon. Pretty sure he didn't make it."

Until that moment, I thought I had reached bottom. Turns out there were only a few inches to go. I couldn't think of anything to say. But there were a million things I wanted to do.

Rod looked up at me with his green teeth and waved at me like you would a child or a small dog. Just then I heard the sirens and saw the lights come through the window. Rod was either stupider than he looked or dumber than I thought, but he forgot entirely about the back door. I took a run for it through the bar and cut through the rear courtyard and in the back door of a neighboring dress shop. I made a big square, hoping to lose the cops in a tight area and ran down Royal, to Toulouse, to St Peter, to Cabildo Alley, slamming against the wall of St. Louis Cathedral at the crossroads with Pirates Alley.

I took a breather for a minute, then realized I was still clutching the gun. Just then I felt a burning pain in my groin, like my bladder had caught fire and exploded. I listened to the distant sound of police and commotion and scrambled to undo my pants and relieve myself against the wall near a set of French doors. After a few minutes of pain and sweat, I began to piss blood. I didn't know if I was dying, but it sure felt like I was. The weight of the evening finally came down on me and I couldn't fight throwing up. I was scared. I was angry. And now I was wanted for a murder I didn't commit.

I picked up what few things I had left at the hotel where I stayed off and on. Mostly for quick naps during the day, when the Mansion had been too far of a walk. Then I took off for the train station. I didn't know where I was going, all I knew was to get as far out of the city as possible. I bought a ticket for Meridian, Mississippi and figured that was far enough I could lay low for a while.

I kept pissing blood the whole train ride up. Finally, I decided to stop drinking, even though it only got hotter the farther north I traveled. When I landed at the train station in Meridian, I felt like a dried-out dish rag. I checked into a room at the McTier Hotel and collapsed on the bed, not knowing what to do. My head spun, thinking about Beverly and Alice and the Mansion. I finally caved, went down to the bar in the hotel and ordered a meal with four glasses of ice water.

I held up at the McTier for a few days, wondering how far I was from Lyon. When I asked an old man on the street, he told me he wouldn't advise walking it. It was hard for me to believe that Beverly would go back to Fall River, especially after the hell she had been through to leave it. The only town I knew for certain she had stayed in was Lyon, even then it was just to visit a doctor. A telephone operator connected me to the only doctor in town, a Huddie Johnson. I asked him if he remembered a girl coming in with a broken leg back near Christmas, trying to not speak too loudly over the phone in the hotel lobby. He said he hadn't seen a broken leg in four, five years. After dancing around the subject for a few minutes, I finally asked him point blank.

"Do you remember treating a girl by the name of Beverly Dulaine?"

He was slow to reply, and when he did, he wasn't exactly to the point. "Yes, I do. Treated her back around Christmas. She had a...she was in trouble. A little bit of trouble. Asked me to take care of it for her."

"What kind of trouble?"

"Well, she had inherited something, you know, that had, uh... put her in the female way. You understand."

Everything made sense and I somehow wished I hadn't asked. "Yeah. Yeah, I think I do understand."

"Now, what's all this about a broken le---"

I hung up on him and stood at the phone for a minute. My bladder burned, and I felt sick. The Fall River ice in my chest cracked again. I picked up the phone to dial a different number, but the clerk chimed in behind me.

"That's a dime for a call, sir."

"What?" I asked barely turning my head.

"Another call. That's gonna be another dime, sir."

I stomped over to the front desk and slammed down a five-dollar bill. "Leave me alone."

The clerk twitched his pencil thin mustache and looked at me as if I had slapped him in the face. Which I had, in a way, but at least he got paid for it. I picked up the handset and dialed a number I knew by heart.

"Hello?" Crystal must have been the closest to the phone.

"Hey, please don't hang up." I felt the fire rise inside of me. I had to grit my teeth to talk.

"Who is this?"

"It's Jesse."

Crystal immediately slid into her sweet tone. Business must have been slow. "Hey, Jesse. I haven't seen you in a few days."

"I know," I gasped, "That's because I've been banned."

"You what?" I could the see the face she made when she said it.

"Please, I need to speak with Esmerelda. Or Alice. Either one, please. Just if it's Alice, don't tell her it's me."

"Uh...She's right here. I'll hand her the phone."

"Alice, please don't hang up."

"Campbell?"

"Esmerelda? Thank god it's you."

"I thought I told you, you were banned."

"You did, but, please..." The pain flared again and I clenched my teeth for a few moments, waiting for it to die down. "Please, I need to ask you something and I'll be out of your life forever."

"If you're calling about Beverly, she's dead."

Nothing mattered anymore. Not even my pain. "She...what?"

"Beverly died this morning. They found her body in the hotel where she was staying."

"Wait. No. No, Esmerelda, Beverly can't be dead. Listen, I need to talk to her."

"Campbell," Esmerelda spoke to me the way a mother would to a stubborn child, "I need you to listen to me. Beverly. Is. Dead. And she's not coming back. Not to this house, not to you, not to anyone. Now, I know you two were close. Christ, I told her countless times to shake you loose, but believe me when I tell you, Beverly Dulaine has passed away."

I don't know how long I didn't say anything. But she held the line the whole time. "What...what happened?"

"She caught a dose," Esmerelda said it so callously I wanted to hit her through the phone. "I don't know when, I don't know from whom, but she didn't do anything about it and it killed her. To be honest, she may have not known till it was too late. After her operation, I'm sure it was hard for her to know which way was up down there, if you catch my meaning."

"I don't think it works like that." It was everything in me not to scream.

"Yeah, well," she blew smoke, "it doesn't matter now. Funeral service is tomorrow. I will allow you back in the house one last time if you want to pay your respects."

Our conversation didn't go on much longer after that. I spent the rest of the day in a fog. Just packed up my things and took off down the road for the train station. I sweated out the night like a bum in the New Orleans train station. Sooner have someone take me for a vagrant, then arrest me for murder. Early the next morning, I took a walk to the Mansion. All the girls were lined up in their best dresses outside the front door. Esmerelda saw me, gave a slight nod and started the rainbow march of colorful dresses down the center of the street in Storyville. Alice was the last in line, with me bringing up the rear about a half a block back.

The Mansion ladies couldn't afford a church service. They met a priest and cemetery groundskeeper near the gates of St. Louis Cemetery No. 2. I watched from a far, straining to hear the service. Occasionally, one of the girls would glance over, most of them just ignored me. I guess nobody knows you when you're down and out. When the service was over, I didn't move from my spot near the gate. The girls marched passed me one by one, giving me the same treatment as they had minutes prior. I didn't care if they saw me. I just wasn't leaving without time alone.

Alice stopped as she walked by. She waited for the rest of the group to march away, then turned to me with the cold intense stare of an owl. "So, that's the way you're gonna go too, huh?" She looked away then turned back. "To be honest, Campbell, I thought you were smarter than that."

My voice was so hoarse, all I could manage was a croak, "It's all I've got left of her."

Alice's eyes flashed with an anger I hadn't seen since Beverly. She lifted her right hand and slapped me through the face. Then came back with the back of her hand and did it again. I didn't do anything. I just stood there and took it. Alice stared at me for a moment, she looked as if there was something she was going to say, she just didn't know how to put it into words. "I can't believe you made me fall in love with you."

"Alice, believe me when I say---"

"Shut up," she turned to face me square. Her voice trembled as she spoke and tears streaked her face, but she never moved. "I told you I was married. I told you I had children and you just kept pushing. And you know what," she fought a laugh, "None of it was even true. I had a husband, but he died in the war. And I have been pregnant. Twice. But they never made it to term. But you never asked about any of it. You never asked about my husband. You never asked about my children. And you know why? Because you're selfish. And you don't care. I would have told you the truth. I was only doing it to protect myself and keep distance from all the johns and bums I roll with every night. But I would have come clean about *everything* to *you*. Because, for some reason I thought you cared. But you were just like everyone else. And I let myself get too involved and you stomped all over my heart, just like you stomped all over her heart," Alice pointed to Beverly's coffin where the priest and groundskeeper were craning to see us, "And now I get to watch you die too. What, because of her? You know she didn't love you?"

"Don't say that, Alice."

"I know she didn't. She told me. Girls talk, Jesse."

"Be careful, Alice."

"Or what? You'll hit me? Is that why you pulled those guys off me, so you could hit me yourself?"

"Alice, I know you are upset, but please---"

"Take your feelings into consideration?" Alice laughed again. "That's rich, Campbell. That's real rich." And with that she turned and walked away, but not before adding, "Have fun with your corpse."

I took a few minutes to compose myself before walking over to Beverly's coffin. The priest and groundskeeper didn't know what to say, especially after that episode, and just bowed their heads in silence. Standing over her coffin, I realized, for the first time, that I loved her. And as long as we had talked, I had never said it to her face. I'd hit rock bottom, been kicked in the ribs, and then began making my way down past the sea floor. After what felt like hours, I nodded to the priest and groundskeeper and left the cemetery.

I wandered around New Orleans for a while. Not going anywhere in particular, just drifting. The hustler magnets in my feet brought me back to the French Quarter and before I knew it, I was stumbling past my old work places. I heard dice rattling in an alley, but didn't feel any sort of way about it. I adjusted my grip on the drawstring bag over my shoulder and kept walking.

I had turned on Decatur Street in front of Jackson Square when I heard a familiar green toothed voice in front of me. It was Rod and his dealer crony throwing bottle caps against the curb. He snapped one at the ground then stood up on the sidewalk to face me.

"I thought you had left town for a few days." Even from a few feet away, I could still smell his breath.

I dropped the drawstring sack on the ground in front of me and pulled out the .45 where I had left it on top. Rod didn't stop smiling when he saw it, but he should have.

"Yeah, I did. Just came back to return something." I pulled the hammer back and fired once into Rod's chest. The force of the shot threw my arm back and I struggled to aim it again.

The dealer crony had started off down the street, but his chubby little legs couldn't carry him so fast. I fired again and had time enough to see him drop, before I felt something punch me in the back and I dropped to the ground myself.

The girls barely had changed out of their funeral best before they had to go back to St. Louis No. 2 for me. There were more tears this time. From Alice in particular. She had the groundskeeper take the lid off my coffin and slid her wedding ring onto my finger. The rest of the girls cried and tossed flowers on top of me from the vases in the foyer and parlor. Esmerelda used the cash they found on me to pay for my funeral. She put a pair of dice in one of my shoes and my deck of cards in the other. She kept the rest of my money and my hat. I didn't mind, though. They hung it on the hat rack in the foyer alongside Beverly's lace gloves until the Mansion shuttered for good.

At least they finally let us back inside.

Shock Theater

Gary Clark was born in Casper, Wyoming on September 15, 1951. His mother, Denise Clark née Thompson, was a school teacher and his father, Russell, was a traveling salesman. Upon graduating high school in 1969, Gary joined the Navy and served for eighteen months in a communications office in San Diego, until he received an honorable discharge in April of 1971. He moved back home and attended the University of Wyoming on the G.I. Bill, majoring in broadcasting and communications. After graduation, he shortly landed a job at KSMB in Phoenix, Arizona.

Gary worked in production at the station for a year as a programmer and editor of the morning and evening news. In February of 1976, KSMB station owner and president, Marky Symcox, signed off on the purchase of the Shock Theater and Son of Shock film packages, rolling out the stations Friday night Monster Mayhem block. Clark was appointed as host with only four days notice of the first live episode. After seeing the already half built haunted saloon set, Gary created the character of Marshal Boneyard, The Phantom Creep of Calabasas.

The show was slow and rocky to start. Recordings of early episodes show Clark in dismal skeleton make-up and cowboy regalia, fumbling through monologues and jokes about ghosts. Cardboard cut-outs of undead cowboys randomly popped up around the set, triggering Clark to fire at them with a cap gun. Clark's performance and the show's writing and production failed, but ratings continued to grow gradually throughout the spring and early summer.

By August of '76, it was a brand-new show. Small changes to the set eventually led to major upgrades, transforming Boneyard's rickety saloon into a full stop sheriff's office, complete with weather machine and a skeletal dog puppet named Snap. Clark also became more comfortable in his role as host and head writer, and began writing smoother, wittier monologues and changing to a more acerbic, tongue-in-cheek brand of humor. Gary Clark and Marshal Boneyard had put Phoenix on the horror host map.

In late January of '77, a new character was introduced to Monster Mayhem. Laurie Laudanum, played by Gary's real-life girlfriend Annie Towne, was a ghostly saloon girl that operated as Boneyard's sidekick and regular scene partner for jokes and sketches. Towne was the cousin of Stephanie Rubel, the script supervisor of the morning and evening news and Monster Mayhem. Clark was introduced to Towne at KSMB's annual Christmas party and the two hit it off instantly. Annie, who had been visiting down from San Francisco, quickly moved in with Clark and within weeks was brought onto the show as a regular character.

After moving into Gary's apartment, Annie introduced him to New Age medicine and philosophy. She claimed to be a shaman and possess "strong knowledge of magic and crystals". The two began taking day, then weekend long trips into the desert, with little more than food and water. Clark, an occasional social drinker, began showing up to his regular job at the station stoned and taking long lunches by himself in his car.

In early August of '77, Clark took a week long unannounced leave of absence from KSMB with Towne. The station along with friends and family all tried to contact the missing couple to no avail. In the end, Clark's mother and Towne's cousin filed missing persons cases and the station was forced to re-run a previously aired episode of Monster Mayhem. Clark returned the following Friday, just in time for air, disheveled and obviously paranoid. Towne was nowhere to be found.

Over the following weeks, Gary began weaving short monologues into the show about the government, the FBI and Area 51. As the summer drew to a close, Gary became more and more erratic on air, sometimes appearing in only half of his costume, poorly applied make-up and missing his hat. The character of Laurie Laudanum no longer appeared after Clark and Towne's disappearance. On the show, Marshal Boneyard made references to Laurie "going away" and being taken from town by "truth-hiders". Gary became insistent on showing only the sci-fi and spy thrillers from the Shock and

Son of Shock packages: *Dr. Death*, *Enemy Agent*, *The Invisible Ray* and *Behind the Mask*. During the show, Boneyard's witty dialogue was replaced with espousing the works of Erich Von Däniken and Zecharia Sitchen, along with readings of long passages from *The 12ᵗʰ Planet* and *Chariots of the Gods?*. Annie's missing persons report remained open.

Finally, on October 11th, 1978, after receiving notice of being fired from KSMB, Clark locked himself into the studio and began broadcasting Monster Mayhem all day. In costume as Boneyard, he brandished a real revolver and fired several times at the set to prove it was loaded. He filmed himself live, with no commercial breaks, playing only *The Beast of Yucca Flats* on an endless loop (he had previously purchased a copy of the film to air on the show). Clark took phone calls from the police on camera as they tried to negotiate and played the incoming calls through the studio's PA system. When asked by the police what he wanted, he screamed, "I want people to listen!"

During his marathon hijacking, Gary spoke of the *reptilians* that inhabited the planet before humans and how they lived at the core of the Earth. Staring into the camera, he spoke for minutes on end about the occurrence at Roswell and what really happened was not a landing, but an explosion. That Area 51 was a station built by the government to prevent humans from passing through a doorway and entering the underground world of the *inhuman reptiles*. The *terrestrials* had wormed their way into high levels of the government and were suppressing the truth about their existence. He claimed they were the ones that had "stolen Annie" in the New Mexico desert and left him to die. Six hours into his broadcast, Clark broke down sobbing, saying, "All I want to do is get the real truth out there. The public is asleep and they need to wake up. They need to know the truth."

After eight tense hours, the police finally stormed the studio. Gary threatened officers with his revolver, but never fired. Footage shows, Clark leaving frame with his arm extended, holding the gun, the makeup smeared and streaking off his face. His words with police were mostly garbled and indecipherable, until, finally, he moved back into frame, shaking the pistol in his fist at the off-camera police, screaming, "You can't hide the truth anymore! You can't hide them from the truth!" As abruptly as the entire ordeal began, Gary Clark turned toward the camera and said, "You can't hide the truth." Police screamed for Clark to drop his weapon as he put the barrel in his mouth and pulled the trigger.

The state of Arizona has not had a late-night horror host since.

Annie Towne's whereabouts are still unknown.

Oddball

It had been a long week. And Natalie was over it. The only thing on her side was her forethought the night before and putting her laundry bag in the car before going to the hospital. Standing in the Kwik-n-Klean parking lot, she hefted thirty pounds of dirty laundry out of the trunk, trying to beat the rain. The first light drops had already started to speck her scrubs.

Natalie was inside for a few minutes before the sky opened up. Right around the same time she remembered she'd left her book and charger on the passenger seat. The tv selection was minimal. Kid shows and the strange, bordering on dull, saga of Casey Kasem's body. By a stroke of luck, she found re-runs of *That 70's Show* and pocketed the remote. The only other person in the laundromat was a man asleep in a chair, but Natalie didn't feel like risking it. She filled up two industrial sized washing machines and turned bills into change.

Natalie's own washer had gone out early Monday morning. She woke up at five AM to her kitchen linoleum trying to absorb almost an inch of water. Her car was in the shop sucking up all the money she didn't have, getting new brakes and switching out winter tires to summer. She had spent most of the week getting Rydes to work, home and the grocery store. Her student loan payments were coming up. Rent was due. And somewhere in the middle there had been a double-shift. But at this point she couldn't really remember or care. All she wanted was two days off in clean clothes.

The humidity from the rain mixed with the heat from the dryers, turning the air thick with lint into an almost tangible paste. Natalie sat down on a chair in front of her machines and dropped her head in her hands with a sigh. She was hoping for a break in the rain and soon. The last Maytag repairman in the world was supposed to call her at six with a status update on the washer, and her phone was at 59% battery. She tried to shut everything out and take a few minutes to breathe.

Then her phone rang.

"Hello?" she attempted to sound professional, but it just came out tired.

There was no answer on the other end. Only the sound of shuffling.

"*Hello?*"

The shuffling continued for a moment, then was replaced by a soft low moan.

"Who is this?" Natalie pulled the phone away from her ear

and checked the number on the screen. It was an unknown caller with an out of state number. "Hello?"

The moan turned to a whimper and the sound of heavy breathing. Then the scared whisper of a child came over the line, "Help me. You have to help me, please, hel---"

Then nothing.

Natalie instantly became cold and broke out in a sweat. She wiped her phone screen on her scrubs and checked the call history for the number, 573 area code. A quick internet search determined the call came from a town called Oddball in Missouri. Natalie redialed the number and pressed the phone firmly to her head, chewing her thumb.

The phone rang five times before it was picked up by the same whimpering voice. "Hello?"

"Hello," Natalie bobbed her right knee up and down and began gnawing the quick of her thumb. "I believe you just called me."

"Is that you?" the voice sounded excited, but still spoke at a whisper.

"Is this a joke?"

"Please," the voice begged, "You need to help me. I don't know when he will be back."

"When *who* will be back?" Natalie's eyes had zeroed in on a bend in the arm of a chair next to her. The exhaustion made her stare all the more surreal.

"The *man*," the voice sounded matter of fact, but terrified. This pushed Natalie over the edge.

"Who is this man? Did he hurt you?" Natalie instinctively pulled her legs up to her chest and wrapped her left arm around them.

"He's going to hurt me when he gets back...if he finds me," the voice trailed off.

"I won't let him hurt you, just tell me where you are." Natalie knew that she had made a promise she couldn't back up, but it was all she knew to say.

"I don't know," the voice became more frightened, "It's dark...and it's cold...and I'm scared and all alone."

"Are you in a house? Are you...*outside*? Can you see anything?" Natalie began moving her left hand as she spoke, trying to coax a voice on the phone to speak.

"It's a house...I think." There was another round of shuffling and the sound of a child breathing into the phone, then nothing.

"No, no, no, no," Natalie rocked up on her heels and sat on the back of the chair, "Stay with me! Stay with me. What is your name, hun? Can you tell me your name?"

The child breaths continued, then gave way to the dragged-out humming of deep thought. "Nikki," the voice said at last, "Nikki Navarro."

"Hi, Nikki," Natalie couldn't help but to smile, "My name's Natalie. I'm going to try to get you some help, ok? Just stay on the phone."

"Ok, Natalie," Nikki's voice was soft and trusting, "What's your last name?"

"Breen," Natalie spoke into the speaker phone and prepared to make a separate call. "Natalie Breen. Hold on, sweetheart, don't go away, ok? I'll be right back."

"Don't go!" Nikki said, scared.

"I'm not leaving," Natalie assured, "I'm still going to be here, I'll just be back in one minute, ok?"

"Natalie?"

"Yes, Nikki?" Natalie's thumb waited to press *call* for 911.

"What's your favorite color?"

"Pink," Natalie smiled again, "What's yours?"

"Purple," Nikki's sounded more content and confident. "What's your favorite animal?"

"Oh, wow," Natalie pressed the heel of her hand into her forehead then dragged it back through her hair. "There are so many to choose from. I tell you what, give me a minute to think about it and I will be right back to tell you. How's that sound?"

"Ok," Nikki sounded a bit sad, but she seemed to understand.

"Ok? I'll be right back." Natalie barely finished her sentence before she pressed go and dialed the police. The phone picked up after only one ring.

"911, what is your emergency?" the dispatcher was an older woman, with a thick Chicago accent.

"Yes," Natalie sat hunched with her toes pressed into the seat of the chair, her free hand cradling the back of her neck, "My name is Natalie Breen, I didn't know who to call, but I have a situation with a little girl on the other line, she says that there is some man that is going to hurt her. It sounds like she's been kidnapped."

"Do you know the child's name?" the dispatcher went through the motions.

"Nikki Navarro," Natalie spoke slowly and clearly, "My phone says she is in Oddball, Missouri."

"The child is on the phone with you now?"

"Yes, she's on the other line. I said I would be back to her in a minute. I can merge the calls if you would like."

"That's not necessary," the dispatcher responded quickly, "I'm going to connect you to Captain Strauss of the St. Louis Police Department. He will be able to further assist you."

"Don't you need to...trace the call or something?" Natalie said, frustrated.

"Missouri is out of our jurisdiction ma'am. We also don't have the permission or ability to trace calls we don't receive. Captain Strauss will help you from here."

"Ok, but..." Natalie rubbed her eyes and felt like crying, "I need to get back on the other line. I said I would only be gone a minute. I'm really scared and I'm really scared for her."

"I understand ma'am," the dispatcher's voice was entirely devoid of emotion. "Just wait for Captain Strauss, then you can go back over."

The background noise of the 911 call center cut out with a

pop and was replaced with the stern Missouri accent of a middle-aged man. "Is this Ms. Breen?"

"Yes, I'm Natalie Breen," she chewed her lip between words and couldn't help from moving her legs, "Hold on one minute I have to check on her."

Whatever Strauss was about to say was cut off as Natalie pulled the phone from her ear and tapped the little girl's call.

"Nikki?"

"Natalie?" Nikki sounded excited to hear her again.

"How are you doin', hun?"

"I'm cold," Nikki whined softly, "*and* hungry."

"I'm talking to some people who are going to help you, o---"

"Natalie"

"Yes, Nikki?"

"Did you think of your favorite animal?"

Natalie rubbed her bottom lip, frantically thinking. "Umm...zebras. I've always really liked zebras."

"Zebras are nice," Nikki sounded happy to hear the answer. "Did you get a zebra for your birthday?"

"No, I didn't, sweetie. But there is always next year."

"When is your birthday, Natalie? Mine is April 3rd."

"January 29th." Natalie suddenly became very aware, that she couldn't hold conversations with two different people at this speed. But she couldn't leave Nikki alone again.

"Happy birthday, Natalie!" Nikki suddenly sounded very excited.

"It's a little late," Natalie laughed, "but thank you. Happy birthday to you, too."

"I turned five on my birthday this year." The pride in Nikki's voice was palpable. "How many did you turn?"

"Not five," Natalie laughed again, embarrassed, "I can tell you that much."

"How many?" The child that was a mere voice on the phone, suddenly became so vivid in Natalie's mind's eye, she could almost see her bouncing at her feet in the laundromat.

"Thirty-two," Natalie said softly, and ran her fingers through her hair again. "I need you to hold on for me again, ok? I still have to talk to the people that can help you."

"Ok, Natalie," Nikki's voice was no longer soft or scared. This eased Natalie somewhat.

"I'll be right back," Natalie switched calls and returned the phone to her ear, "Captain Strauss."

"I was starting to think this was some sort of prank," Strauss said, gruffly.

"I'm sorry. I'm trying to keep her on the line, but it's very difficult---"

"The dispatcher there in Decatur told me this child called you from a town called Oddball?"

"Yes, but I don't know where she is at *exactly*. She says that she thinks she's in a house maybe? I don't know, she didn't seem sure."

"Whatever sort of structure it is, I'd sure love to see how they built it on the cloud its floating on." Strauss's voice became more relaxed, albeit, condescending.

Natalie's leg stopped shaking. She shook her head, instead, to clear it. "What?"

"Oddball, Missouri, is not a town that you'll find on any map, Ms. Breen, because it does not exist."

"I looked it up online, sir," Natalie became irritated and stood up from her chair, pacing, "I searched the phone number and it says right here, that this number came from this town."

"There is no town, city, municipality, township or borough anywhere in the great state of Missouri named Oddball, Ms. Breen. That is just plain facts. I would think I should know my own home state."

Natalie had her dying phone on speaker once again, pinching and twisting through a street view of Oddball. "I'm looking at it on the god damn map!"

"Where did you find this map, Ms. Breen?" Strauss spoke with a calmer and even tone. "Candyland? Wonderland? Neverland? Cause I can assure you, as sure as you are steamed at me right now, that this Oddball does not exist."

Natalie took her phone off speaker, pressed it to her ear and began pacing furiously up and down in front of her machines. "Captain Strauss, I am, right now, on the other line, talking to a little girl who is being held *captive* by a man who she fears intends to do her harm. Now, I don't think that you are taking this situation very seriously."

"A little girl?" Strauss repeated, bored, "Mm-hmm. In a town that doesn't exist. How do you know this little girl exists?"

Natalie ran her fingers tightly through her hair, ripping out her hair tie in the process, leaving strands to fall into her face. "Captain Strauss! I am *not* insane! I---"

"How do you know it's a little girl at all?" His words were as bored and plain as Natalie had ever heard. And he didn't say anything further.

Natalie stood in the center of the laundromat, her legs pressed tight together, and her left arm stretched out to its full wingspan. Her phone arm had become tense and froze with her elbow pointing up and out away from her body at some strange Dali-esque angle. Her tired eyes, searched the blue and white checkered tiles for the math to solve Strauss' riddle. Finally, all the pieces fell into place and her stomach dropped along with them.

Her last name. Her favorite color. Her favorite animal. Her birthday.

Over the last few weeks, Natalie had received a series of phone calls from random upstate and out of state numbers, demanding payment on her student loans. Finally, after a screaming match over the phone with a man that claimed to be both a police officer and college admissions officer, she had managed to get her name removed from their list. Things had been quiet, until today.

"Mr. Strauss," she said calmly, after an extended silence, "Will you hold for just a moment?"

"Tell you what, if I'm wrong, call me back." With no more words, he hung up.

Natalie switched back to the call with the alleged Nikki. This time, with a decidedly different attitude. "Is there anything else you need from me?"

"What?" Nikki sounded confused and hurt.

"Social security? Routing and checking account number? My mother's maiden name?"

"What's a maiden name?" Nikki giggled.

"Uh-huh? How many sites did you manage to get logged into?"

"...I don't know what you are talking about, Ms. Breen."

Another thing occurred to Natalie as she stood at the window, watching the storm pass and the rain die as it fell on her car. The voicemails. The one's from the overly chipper office bunny that, *every time,* gave her the same case and reference number for re-evaluations of her student loan payments. The ones from Nikki Navarro.

"You might want to try using a different name the next time you pull this off," she said coldly.

There was a long pause. What Natalie had once been sure were small quick child breaths, now sounded like the nose whistle of the man she had screamed at weeks prior. For the first time, she heard clicking in the background. And a sound like a mouth brushing against the microphone of a gaming headset. Or something equally as ludicrous.

"Yeah, but I almost got you, didn't I?" The voice distortion program that was "Nikki" now sounded like a child from hell. There was a both annoying and unsettling laugh that went on for far too long.

"Take me off your list, asshole." Natalie pulled her phone away from her ear and hung up.

Her phone felt like a slab of lava. The opening theme to *That 70's Show* played on the tv behind her. Natalie looked out the window again. The rain had slowed enough that she could go to her car. The man in the chair jerked awake as the door slammed behind her.

Green Bananas

It's a cliché, but Howie Reagan was a quiet man. Husband and father of two grown children, he kept himself to himself and his wife in their Royalton home along the bank of the Susquehanna River. He worked at a hardware store in Middletown, fixed lawnmowers in his garage for beer and taught neighborhood kids how to repair their bikes on their own. Howie wasn't the brightest of men, but he would give the shirt off his back for a stranger in need. Several people had witnessed as much over the years, once for a mother and her baby during a Fourth of July parade after she collapsed with heat stroke.

In April of 1980, Howie's wife of twenty-nine years, Margret Reagan née Huth, died of thyroid cancer. Howie spent several weeks isolated in his home, before putting his house on the market and relocating to Harrisburg. He dumped his life savings and a twenty-thousand dollar bank loan into a three story red brick building on Derry Street in Allison Hill and quickly converted it into a bed and breakfast.

"It was always Margie's dream to own a bed and breakfast," he told local reporters when they interviewed him a few months after opening. "It was our plan to open one in our retirement. It's not much, but it's the best way I know to honor her memory."

Hendrie and Sons Bed and Breakfast ("Hendrie was Margie's middle name, she was named after her father") opened for business in early July 1980. Howie lived in a small servant's quarters in the rear of the top floor, leaving the rest of the building open for rooms. The store front on the bottom level, he converted into the kitchen and dining room, eventually serving walk-ins for lunch and dinner. He ran the bed and breakfast himself. He did the laundry, made the beds and acted as groundskeeper and handyman for the entire property. Customers were often surprised, but charmed, when the man washing the windows or fixing an air conditioner followed them inside to give them the keys to their room. In time, and after strong suggestions from his financial advisor, he hired a local retired tax preparer to work the front desk and keep the books in order.

Howie also worked in the kitchen. He insisted on preparing breakfast for his guests, his specialty being bananas foster, and even on occasion picked up a lunch shift when a prominent or important public figure would stop by. Harrisburg being a regular stop for touring and out of town politicians, Howie Reagan prepared meals for New York lawyer and representative Joseph Patrick Abbaddo, Max J. Pincus of the Wayne State Michigan board of governors and even President of United Steel Workers and delegate to the Democratic National Convention, Iorwith Wilbur "I.W." Abel. Several celebrity guests were also frequent visitors, including Charlotte Rae of *Facts of Life* and Buddy Ebson of *Barnaby Jones*. Howie cooked using fruits and vegetables he grew himself on the roof in a homemade greenhouse. He also often sold his produce during the Memorial Day street fair and several times won prizes for biggest tomatoes, peppers and bananas.

"Both my wife and my mother were real green thumbs. I'm not nearly as gifted as them, but I learned a few things being around them."

In late 1985, Howie's restaurant and kitchen came under scrutiny after several people reported violent illness and vomiting after visiting his dining room. The health inspector did not initially notice anything wrong in the kitchen, except for a rather pale and sickly-looking Reagan, who would pull away from the stove every few minutes to cough blood into a handkerchief. Knowing about Howie's rooftop greenhouse, the health inspector asked to see it and was refused. Returning less than an hour later with two uniformed Harrisburg police officers, the three broke the lock to the rooftop access door and entered Howie's greenhouse. The wave of heat that poured out upon opening the door turned the cold November morning into mid-August. The younger of the two police officer's ran to the edge of the roof and vomited before passing out in shock and had to be dragged back away from the ledge. The health inspector recoiled in fear and immediately called the CDC. In the base of every planter was a metal rod approximately two feet long and an inch in diameter. Stocks struggled to support warped and distorted tomatoes the size of soccer balls and distended bananas the size of cocker spaniels. A small, yellow, dirt encrusted book resting on one of the tables gave the answer; *Atomic Gardening for the Laymen* by Muriel Howorth.

Howie Reagan was arrested and the bed and breakfast shut down. CDC officials ordered an immediate evacuation of all buildings within a two-block radius. That night in jail, Howie Reagan stopped breathing in his cell and was admitted to the hospital wing of the Harrisburg Community Corrections center, where he was attended to by doctors and nurses in paper suits. Court proceedings were delayed for several months as the judge waited for him to be well enough to attend his trial. In March of 1986, doctors advised if they waited any longer, there would be no trial and no Howie.

The City of Harrisburg v Howard Reagan began on March 30th, 1986. To the side of the court room, flanked by his lawyer, Mitch Young, and a nurse, Ruth Oblonsky, both dressed in paper suits, Howie listened silently to the proceedings from a hospital gurney. When asked any question, he would only respond *guilty*. On April 14th, the prosecution cited the recent death of a member of the New York House of Representatives and frequent visitor of the Hendrie and Sons Bed and Breakfast, Joseph Abbaddo, as the result of kidney cancer a "direct victim of Mr. Reagan's plot to poison and assassinate his patrons." Howie Reagan laughed. Softly at first and was corrected by his lawyer. Within minutes, his laughter grew so loud it interrupted the proceedings. Judge Harold

Kerns II demanded a reason for Reagan's outburst. Howie's laughter turned to tears before he exploded.

"Is it cause for alarm now, Hendrie! Is it cause for alarm now, you bastard! You killed my wife!"

A bailiff, in no suit, quickly wheeled Howie out of the court room. Kerns called for a twenty-minute recess, then adjourned the court until the following day. Young, with the assistance of a local reporter uncovered the meaning behind Howie's ravings. Margret Reagan had worked at Three Mile Island Nuclear Generating Station for six years until the meltdown of the TMI-2 reactor on March 28, 1979. In the immediate wake of the disaster, Nuclear Regulatory Commission chairman Joseph Hendrie stated that the meltdown was "a cause for concern but not alarm." A little over a year later, Margret Reagan was dead.

Within a month of his courtroom outburst, so was Howie Reagan.

The Las Vegas Story

Alright! Alright. Fine. Three years ago, I got out of the joint and headed for Vegas on a tip I got from John Schlosser. Alright, less of a tip, more of a...I don't know, we were fucking partners, alright? Benny got diagnosed with HIV and died in prison and John told me Paul got ventilated just outside Provo. That took it down to two shares. He told me he buried it somewhere outside of Vegas, but it was split up in sections, so if someone found it they wouldn't find all of it. So everyone could get their shares and not screw it for the other guy. The deal was we all get caught, we all go to the clink, we get out, we nab our cash and we never see each other again. I knew where my share was. I didn't know where the other three were. John flew me a kite on my last day and gave me a map to his. I was supposed to find the rest, split it in half, then send him a get-well card and a hundred dollars cash in good faith.

Only it didn't work out like that.

I get out of Folsom mid-March '97. I set up shop in Sacramento, got a straight job unloading boxes at K-Mart and got this thing going with this cute little redhead that worked the snack bar. Mid-June, I tell my P.O. that I'm going to Salt Lake

City for my uncle's funeral and book Sacramento for Vegas. I checked into the Stardust Motel out on Paradise overnight then the next morning went into town to the Magic Carpet. Schlosser's brother worked as bartender in the Forty Thieves Lounge and he was supposed to give me the coordinates to the other two spots disguised as escort service phone numbers.

I'm chain-smoking at the bar, waiting for his brother to show up, when lo and behold, who sits down catty-corner to me but fucking Tatum Kincaid. I haven't seen her since before I got locked up. Almost six years ago. She's lost the engagement ring, but past that she looks like she was frozen in fucking time.

"Hiya, Clayton," she flipped her red hair out of her face and leaned her head to the side as she lit a cigarette, flashing the tattoo she got of my zodiac sign on her neck. Her brown eyes shined under the overhead lighting and burned straight into the back of my fucking head. "Fancy meeting you here."

I choked on my smoke and stumbled away from the bar. She just gave me that mirthless champion grin and licked her eyetooth.

"What the fuck are you doing here?" I says.

"I think the real question is, what the fuck are *you* doing here?" she pointed her cigarette hand at me. "Aren't we supposed to be on probation?"

"As a matter of fact, I am," stubbed out my cigarette and lit another one. "A former-model prisoner and newly reformed civilian, so get off my ass."

"Oh," she pouted sarcastically, "I thought you would be happy to see me."

I leaned in to her to keep our conversation quiet, "I thought I would have too, until you actually showed up here. Now, I'm wondering what the fuck you're doing."

"Just spending some of my hard-earned cash at America's playground," she looked away from me and tapped the bar twice to bring over the wall-eyed dago on duty.

"You fucking *hate* Vegas," the angrier I got, the lower I spoke.

"I've learned to love it," she smiled at me. I couldn't ever tell when she was playing me or being serious. "Lots has changed since you've been gone. Welcome back, by the way."

"I noticed you're sporting less hardware nowadays," I got back on my stool and seethed.

Tatum glanced down at her left ring finger then looked back up at me and shrugged. I focused on the tattoos that crawled down her freckled arms onto her pale hands. Remembered seeing her wince in the chair as she got them. Remembered seeing them in bed next to me for two years.

Remembered seeing them wrapped around that asshole's neck as she stood on her toes to kiss him. We went out for two years. She married him while I was inside. She was engaged before we even met.

"Things change," she smiled at the bartender as he set down her drink and turned back to me, taking a sip.

"No shit." I didn't want to talk anymore.

After all the fucking time I had spent inside thinking about her, dreaming about her, knowing it would never fucking happen. Knowing she was off somewhere with that fucking shit-kicker and his blown-out Camaro. The first three years inside, all I could do was think about her. The last two, I tried to forget her. Now I just wanted to push her head first into the San Joaquin.

"That's some attitude to have when you're about to get hitched yourself," Tatum pulled my ashtray over to her and put out her cigarette. She started digging through her pockets for another one.

"Tatum," I rubbed my eyes, doing a rain dance in my head to make Schlosser's brother get on shift, "I don't know what *the fuck* you're talking about, but I also really don't care. You want me to say it was nice seeing you? Fine, it was nice seeing you. *Past tense.* Leave me the fuck alone and forget we ever met. Maybe if we both try hard enough, it will come true."

"What's her name?" She was looking past me, over my shoulder to the other side of the bar. Not listening to a thing I said. Suddenly I was sitting at the breakfast table in our Portland apartment. I stared at her, grinding my teeth.

"You always denied it, but I knew you had a type," she was still searching her pockets. "God damn, Clayton, she could be my kid."

I took the bait and turned around. Across the bar, in the private room, was a bunch of girls surrounded by gift bags and wearing tiaras. They were giggling like teenagers, standing in a circle around this cute little redhead, strapping her into a wedding veil.

"What the fuck?" my mouth spoke without my permission.

"What's her name?" I could hear her smile without turning around.

I turned back to the bar, stubbing out my cigarette and making a serious effort to not look her in the face. "Ursula," my mouth mumbled again without permission.

"Ursula?", Tatum leaned her head back and laughed. It was this borderline witch cackle that I used to love when she used it on other people. Now she was using it on me. "I thought that was only a name for fat Italian chicks with mustaches and huge tits," Tatum's eyes zeroed in on me like a shark. There was no pupil left.

"Who the fuck said that?" I turned back to her, truly confused.

"You did," she gave a sarcastic nod as she spoke. Her face lost all its spite and returned to its cool, smooth, normal expression. "You got a smoke?"

I wanted to hit her. I wanted teeth and blood and tears. I reached into my jacket, pulled out a cigarette with one hand and held it up to her lips. She leaned in close and took it with her mouth.

"Wanna hear a riddle?" I asked with no emotion whatsoever.

"Sure," she looked up at me under thin red eyebrows and slurred around the cigarette.

"What's red," I flipped open the Zippo I had palmed in the same hand and struck a flame, "and white and green all over?"

She drew on the cigarette and answered through her teeth, "An alligator at clown school?"

"A jealous red head," I flipped the Zippo closed and pocketed it. "Go fuck yourself."

She pulled the cigarette out of her mouth and blew smoke, "I'll let you watch." She gave me her all-knowing smirk.

I pointed my finger in her face right between her eyes. "Die." I held it there for a moment before I walked away.

When I turned she was smiling. I pushed her out of my mind and walked over the private room full of bridesmaids and my girlfriend. She didn't see me at first. I had to knock on the glass a few times. When she saw me she smiled and jumped up and down, hopped up on estrogen and bridal shower ya-yas.

"Oh my god, Clay," she threw her arms around my neck and kissed me on the cheek a few times. "What are you doing here?"

"Fuck *me*," I pushed her away and held her by the shoulders, "What the fuck are *you* doing here?"

Her big brown eyes pouted up at me and she tried to slink away from my hands. "It's Rebecca's bridal shower. I told you it was this weekend."

"No, you didn't," I shook my head. "But if it's Rebecca's shower, what the fuck are you doing in the god damn veil?"

"It was just a joke," she smiled and patted my chest. "Everyone was trying it on. We started talking about who was going to get married next." She looked down then looked back up at me with that glint in her eye.

"*We're* not," I says. "So Rebecca can keep her veil to her damn self. Isn't she the one you told me had lice, anyway?"

A look of panic came over her face and she patted the top of her head as she pulled away. "No. That was Julia."

"Did Julia where the veil?" I says.

She looked back at the group and then up at me. "Just for a little," she was doing that thing she did when she got upset and said everything in a whisper.

I looked her in the face and could see the waterworks pre-show building up on the corners of her eyes. I grabbed her by the wrist and pulled her into my chest and squeezed her tight. "It's alright. Alright? It's just...I'm out here on business and you caught me by surprise being here. I'm happy to see you, I just don't want you getting lice."

"I'm happy to see you, too," her mouth was muffled by my arm and she pulled her face away to talk clearer, "But what are you doing here? I thought you were going to your uncle's funeral in Salt Lake."

"I am," I had to talk quick so she didn't think I was lying. "I am. I'm going up there. But I had to pass through here to do some business first, I told you that."

"No, you didn't," she whimpered.

"Yeah, I did," I petted her head and looked down at her. "I did tell you, you must have just forgot."

She looked up at me with that small calm smile of hers, "Ok," she stood on her toes and kissed me then did that thing where she tried to hug me as tight as she could. "Let me know when you get back to Sacramento, ok?"

"You too, alright?" I gave her a hug, kissed her on the head and patted her away, back to the *Real World* crowd.

"I love you," she threw it over her shoulder as she ran away. I gave her a wave then walked back to the bar.

Tatum was still there, nursing her drink and looking way too amused. "Clayton and Ursula sitting in a tree," she chanted softly into her glass.

"Jealous?" I raised my eyebrow and cocked my head towards her.

"Me?" she leaned back, acting incredulous. "I'm as free as a jailbird."

I snapped my head toward her and locked my jaw.

"Sorry," she grinned. "Freudian slip."

"Go fuck yourself."

I took an empty spot at the other end of the bar and waited for Schlosser's brother to come on duty. He got there a half hour late. Tatum finally left before he gave me the numbers. I thanked him, slipped him a twenty and started to make my way back to the front door.

I could almost taste the fucking desert when I felt something grab my jacket and pull me towards the wall behind some potted plant. Suddenly there was just someone all over me, but I couldn't fight them off. It took a few seconds for it to click in, it was fucking Tatum. She was kissing my fucking face and running her arms up and down my back under my jacket. I felt my one hand grab a fistful of her hair and rip her away from me, but nothing else fought back. She looked up at me with those brown eyes and gave me that evil fucking redhead grin.

"Elevator," she said low. I could feel her hand slapping the wall behind me. "Now."

A few seconds later, I heard a ding and I fell backwards with her on top of me. She started climbing the wall with her feet and kicking buttons until the doors closed. I could smell her deodorant and remembered our road trip to New Mexico. Her sleeping on the leather seat in the car next to me. Bruised jaw, blood on my knuckles and bullet holes in the rear windshield.

She grabbed ahold of my sides with her knees and squeezed tight. I reached for the button on her jeans and she slapped my hand away.

"What would *Ursula* think?" she spoke in between panting.

"Fuck Ursula," I grabbed her arm and pulled her down on top of me. I heard the elevator door ding again, followed by some old lady swearing in Spanish. I kicked the buttons like Tatum had.

"No thanks," she whispered in my ear, her hair covering my face. "I'll leave that to you."

Then as fast as she was on me, she was off. I watched her run her tattooed hand down the buttons to every level, then shoot those brown eyes over her shoulder as she ran away. The old Mexican couple in the hallway looked at me like a I was a pile of shit. I gave them the finger as the door closed.

When the elevator hit the next floor, I got off and took the stairs back down to the lobby. People walking out of the casino were looking at me like a I was a fucking leper. I caught my reflection in the mirrored wall and realized they weren't far off. Tatum's lipstick was all the fuck over me, from my neck to my forehead. I'm standing there, looking at my reflection on the mirror-wall, trying to wipe it off, with assholes saying shit as they walked by, then I see another redhead standing behind me. Only this one's wearing a tiara and got her arms folded. Backed up by like five other girls in tiaras standing the same way.

"Here on business, huh?"

I quick turned around to Ursula giving me the evil eye. She was biting her lip and her chin was crinkled up.

"Hey, baby!" I tried to act like there was nothing wrong.

"Don't 'hey, baby' me," she did that imitation she always did of me when she was pissed off. "What the fuck, Clayton?"

"Look," I stepped towards her and grabbed her shoulders, "this isn't what it looks like."

"Bullshit, this isn't what it looks like!" She pulled away from me and started waving her arms around. "What the fuck are you doing? Who is she?"

"She's nothing!" I says. "What the fuck do you want me to do? She tackled me!"

"Oh, and what? You couldn't fight her off?" She was making a scene. A crowd of fat flyover tourists were standing around like we were some fucking magic show on the strip. The rest of the bridal party had showed up too.

"You don't think I'm here on business? Fine!" I reached

into my pocket for the slip with the coordinates. "I was going to keep this a surprise but...fuck it!" I checked my other pocket. "I just got a list of phone numbers," I checked my pants pockets, "of guys who are going to set us up with a chance at some big fucking money!" I checked deeper in my pants pockets. "*Big* fucking money! Guaranteed!" I started checking my jacket pockets again.

Ursula was giving me that no nonsense redhead look that means *it's fucking over*. "Don't try to bullshit me, Clayton. You're not that good at it. You never have been."

"I had it!" I ripped off my jacket and started going through it that way. "I *fucking* had it! It was right here."

The crowd started oohing and laughing. I told them to shut the fuck up. One of the girls in the bridal party tapped Ursula on the shoulder but she brushed her off.

"I saw you talking to that slut at the bar, Clayton." There wasn't anything remotely resembling humor in her voice.

I snapped my head toward the crowd and zoned out. I could see Tatum's evil fucking smile as she ran out of the elevator.

"I'm not stupid. If you wanted to break it off you should have just told me. I knew I was nothing more than a fetish to you anyway."

"That fucking bitch," I said it more under my breath than anything else.

"Yeah. I'm a bitch, Clayton," Ursula walked up to me with her arms still folded. "But you're an asshole." She slapped me as hard as she could through the face. Then she came back around with the other hand and did it again. "*Fuck* you."

The slaps did good to snap me out of my trance. I came to with her and her bunch of queen bees walking toward the elevator. Regaining composure, I slid on my jacket and hollered after her. "I'll call you."

The chick in the veil turned around long enough to yell, "Get *fucked*, asshole!" then kept walking.

I ran back to the Forty Thieves Lounge and pushed my way toward the bar. The afternoon alchies had started to clock in for the day. I told Schlosser's brother I needed the phone numbers again. He told me he didn't have them. He wrote them down as they were told to him over the phone.

And see, this is the key thing here. I called him. I *did* fucking call him. I went to the payphone in the lobby and actually called Folsom, but I couldn't get ahold of him. They said he was in with his shrink or something, I can't fucking remember, but I did call him. After that, I had no recourse. I just started driving to where my stash was.

I still had the map to John's site in my wallet. And I had

packed the car with shovels and shit before I left Sacramento. My only hope was that Tatum couldn't figure out the code with the phone numbers. I couldn't figure out how the fuck she knew about any of it. How did she know I was out? How did she know I was in Vegas? How did she know what the fuck I was doing there and where to find me? She knew about the job we pulled six years ago, but I didn't remember telling her. Maybe I had, I don't know. That was still before everything went south with her and the shit-kicker. I was a lot dumber then. She hadn't given me any reason to not trust her yet. That got me thinking. John was about to have half a million reasons not to trust me. Unless I could beat her to it.

My stash site was north of Vegas, three hundred and fifty yards past a firing range walking into the desert. The sound of distant gunfire did a lot to bring back memories, but it was nice knowing that it wasn't coming up on me. It took about 15 minutes to hit the duffel bag. Then it was a quick brush off and hit the road toward John's stash site further west near Garnet. His cash was buried about a half mile past a power station, down the Great Basin Highway, two hundred yards west of the road.

That was when things went South. Again.

Tatum was already there. Smoking, sitting on the trunk of her car staring out toward the road. Her pale skin had started to turn red in the sun. She knew I was coming.

"Clayton," her voice was even and calm. "After all these

years, who would have thunk we would run into each other twice in one day?"

"What the fuck are you doing here, Tatum?" I says.

"Actually," she held her cigarette between her lips and pulled this scrap of paper out from under her leg. "I was wondering if you could help me with something."

She held the paper with the phone number coordinates up to my face. I reached out to grab it from her but she pulled it away. "Ah, ah, ah," She pulled out her cigarette and blew smoke downwind. "That's not playing nice."

"You're one to talk," I says. "What the fuck are you doing following me around and stealing my shit?"

She gave me that fucking witch cackle. "Your shit? Is that why you went to prison? For stealing and burying *your shit* out in the middle of the desert?"

"How many fucking times are you going to do this to me?" I got right in her face and screamed it. "Just waltz right into my life and take fucking everything! Leave me a shell of a fucking human being and then drive off into the fucking sunset?"

"What about Ursula?" she was still mocking me. I hadn't scared her at all.

"Oh, that girl that could be your kid?" I says. "Yeah, you ruined that too. Thanks a fucking lot."

"I may have been exaggerating with the kid part," she tapped her ash into the breeze. "But she is old enough to be my cousin." Tatum tapped the trunk of the car three times. The rear driver's side door opened and fucking Ursula stepped out pointing a sawed-off shotgun at me. My sawed-off shotgun.

It was triple digits outside, but everything inside me went cold. Tatum and Ursula gave me that fucking evil redhead grin in tandem. Ursula aimed the shotgun at my face.

"Where's the rest of it?"

Tatum raised both of her eyebrows at me real fast then dropped them, taking a drag.

"Oh, fuck me." I realized I had my hands raised. "What the fuck, guys? How long have you two been planning this?"

"Since around the time you two started shacking up." Tatum smiled at me.

"What are the phone numbers for?" Ursula looked more serious than I had ever seen her before. I felt like everything I knew was a lie.

"Ursula told me about this guy she was dating at work and

how he was bragging about just getting out of prison." She let that sit there before adding, "And has a serious thing for red-heads."

"Neither of us are as stupid as you thought we were." Ursula was talking through her teeth.

My mind went into overdrive. I didn't know what to do. I wanted to get the fuck out of there, but I needed the money. I thought maybe trying to barter with them.

"Alright, look," I was desperately trying to get my mouth wet again, "I don't know how you found out about this or know why I'm here, but I'm telling you right now when the people you're stealing from find out where you are---"

Tatum pulled a Polaroid from under her leg, where she had the phone numbers, and showed it to me. It was a picture of the map from my wallet. The kite Schlosser sent me with his map to the cash.

"Didn't take much digging after that," Ursula said.

"Sacramento is a pretty small town," Tatum sounded way to happy with herself. "And we don't exactly run in different circles. We still know a lot of the same people." She drew out *a lot* in the condescending tone I used to love to hear her take with other people.

There was nothing for a few seconds. I could hear the wind

whistle through my own ears. Tatum quietly smoked and Ursula held the sawed-off inches from my face. Then I had this vision. One of those crystal-clear visions you get maybe twice in a lifetime.

I grabbed the barrel of the shotgun and pushed it away from my head. Tatum jumped off the car and punched me in the face as Ursula screamed and grabbed her shoulder. I stumbled for a second then stood up long enough to catch the pistol grip across the bridge of my nose and I hit the ground. I blacked out for a second and woke up choking on dust and breathing my own blood. Ursula was holding her right arm. She walked up to me and screamed something before kicking me in the crotch. I might have been looking at the sun or something, I don't know, but everything went white and my ears started to ring. I felt the barrel of the shotgun pressed to my head and Tatum's voice come over the ringing.

"Who are the phone numbers for?"

I tried to talk but just choked on dust. "What the fuck, Tatum?"

"Don't you fucking same my name, you prick," she pressed the barrel harder into my temple. I saw my vision go blurry. "Who are the phone numbers for?"

In my mind I could see my cell in Folsom. The underside of the bunk above me. The living room of Schlosser's apartment when we planned the job. Tatum's eyes when I woke up that morning. Ursula standing out back of the store my first day on the job. I was being fucked over. I knew I was. But I still couldn't hurt them. That didn't mean I had to make it easy for them either.

"Not...," the blood had mixed with the dust in my mouth and I choked on the mud it made. "...not who. What?"

I looked up at Tatum out of one eye. Her hair was backlit by the sun and looked even more red than normal.

"And that's all I'm gonna tell you," that was easy to choke out. "Bitch." That one was even easier.

Tatum stood up from where I was laying on the ground and looked around at the desert then turned over to Ursula. "What the fuck does that mean?" She looked back down at me and crouched down a little bit toward me. "What is that supposed to mean?" For the first time, all day, Tatum Kincaid was upset. Because she knew I wasn't going to give her every-thing she wanted. And give it to her *her way*.

She turned toward Ursula, "What the fuck is that sup-posed to mean?"

I couldn't help but laugh. Ursula walked over to the two of us. Holding the scrap of paper with her hurt wing. Her cute little face all scrunched up like the little girl her and her sister/cousin were.

Tatum took the shotgun away from my head and stepped away from me. I managed to sit up and lean against the car. I spit a big wad of blood into the sand and looked up at the two, just watching.

"You're not as smart as you think," I gave them *my* evil grin. "And you need me more than you want to admit."

Tatum ran a few steps before she kicked me in the face. I got the double hit of her foot to the face and my head bouncing off the car. It hurt, to be sure, but all I could do was laugh. I knew she was pissed.

Ursula clicked her tongue like a valley girl and sighed. She rolled her eyes at me then looked to her sister/cousin. "They're not phone numbers. They're coordinates."

Tatum stepped up next to her and looked over her shoulder.

"See, take the first digit off. They're coordinates."

The two stood there for a moment. I watched Tatum's mouth move as she read them off. As she finished she stared nodding. She turned to Ursula and continued to nod, then they both turned to me.

Ursula held up the scrap of paper to me so I could read it. If I would have been able to read. My vision was still fucked.

"We figured it out, asshole, they're coordinates!"

"Bravo," I could feel myself try to grin and clap, but I know I must have looked stupid.

Tatum tightened her lips and nodded. I watched her smile grow across her face. The first real smile she had given me all day. "Well played, Clayton. Well played."

I didn't see her move. But I felt the hit. My head bounced off the ground this time. I don't know how long I was laying there, but I know I couldn't see for a long time. I could hear a little, though. Enough to hear them talk for a few minutes then drive away. Before they peeled off, I heard Tatum whisper in my ear: "Thanks a bunch, Clayton. Call me if you find me."

And that was it. I was left unconscious and bleeding in the desert by the only two women I've ever loved in my life. Out a total of a million dollars. Served five years in prison for no reason and wondering how long it would be before you came knocking at my door.

I fucked up. I know I did. But there really wasn't anything I could do. So, if you're gonna kill someone, kill me. Leave them out of it. I've had this coming for a long time.

If not, will you put the fucking guns down and get out of my house, please?

Longshot

Donald Whalen fueled up at the Conoco before heading out of town. He was excited to try out his new metal detector and wanted to get out to Madison Buffalo Jump early. His doctor had prescribed more walking and movement to deal with the arthritis in his knees. As much as he could, no less than three times weekly. Donald started walking the parks his father took him and his brother to as kids. He hadn't walked them in years, and when he started re-visiting them he remembered why. His father had died in '62, when Donald was only fifteen, of lung cancer; years before asbestos was deemed hazardous. His mother died in '74 of heart failure, and his brother was hit by a drunk driver ten years later. Donald was the last member of his family left alive. The only extended family he had was his niece, Millie, but she spent her time split between college and caring for her mother. And Donald didn't want to be a burden.

Two years prior, a few days before his birthday, Donald got a package in the mail from his niece. It was bigger than a breadbox and heavier than a phonebook. It was a rather spiffy looking metal detector, enclosed with a card introducing him to his new walking companion and wishing him a happy birthday. Donald shed a tear and immediately called Millie.

The parks became easier then. Donald would walk the old familiar trails, head down, listening to cassette tapes of Buddy Holly and the Rolling Stones on a Walkman he picked up at a yard sale, waiting for the red light on the stick to blink. Most of what he found was garbage, but a few times he got lucky with a ring, a hunting knife, a pendant and chain, and an Indian head belt buckle. He cleaned up and sent any jewelry he found to Millie and her mother, gave the knife to a blacksmith buddy in town, but kept and used the buckle for himself. He called it his "lucky buckle" and would wear it anytime he went out "treasure hunting". It sounded a lot more romantic and exciting than battling knee pain.

During the winter, he didn't get to use his detector much. If he could stand the cold, he would just take a lap or two around the block, then alternate hot and cold on his joints. There usually wasn't much sleep to be had those nights, though Donald did it as much as he could stand, in the name of health. One of those restless nights as he tossed and turned watching tv, on came an informercial for a new type of metal detector. This one was space aged, more something out of Buck Rogers than his loyal walking companion. It had a readout that showed the penetration of the magnet into the earth and a screen that told you exactly what was underground without digging it up. Sleek flat black with a cushioned grip and adjustable elbow support. Re-chargeable battery, so no more penny pinching and stretching to buy nine volts. A vibration option for when something was detected, so Donald could listen to The Crickets as loud as he wanted. *Anything can be found, by a Longshot.* Just the idea of owning one made him feel like a spaceman.

But he already had a metal detector. And as excited as he was by this new one on tv, the thought of parting with the one Millie had bought for his birthday broke his heart. It would be an insult to her to trade it in on a newer, fancier model. Until Millie brought it up herself. A few days later, Millie called up Donald from college to check in on him. She had seen the commercial on tv at the Hanrahan's where she waitressed and asked him if he was interested. She told him they could sell his old one on eBay and use the money to pay for the Longshot. Donald was excited and agreed. Over Christmas break, Millie stopped by his trailer, picked it up and took it with her back to college. By mid-January, it sold. She got the money and negotiated with Donald over the phone about buying the Longshot. The money they got from selling the old one would only cover half the cost. Donald squeaked by on Ramen for a month and donated a substantial chunk of his social security to the cause. Then, come early March 2005, Donald got another large package in the mail from Millie.

It had been a long Spring, waiting for the weather to be clear enough to go walking again. It wasn't perfect; the wind blew cold and the ground was soggy from rain. But Donald had waited long enough. Today was the day. He grabbed a bag of chips and a bottle of Coke after gassing up and headed off for Madison Buffalo Jump.

The golden Montana sun was washing over the blue early morning as Donald pulled his pick-up into the parking lot. He was feeling good about the day. As he double checked his pockets and made sure he didn't lock the keys in the truck, he decided to walk all the way up to Scrubby Ridge (a nickname he gave to the only spot on the trail with trees and brush, an area usually too steep for him to climb and marked the extreme end of his walks). It was too early to tell, he didn't know if he'd be able to climb it, but he was damn sure going to make it that far down the trail. He queued up *Let It Bleed* on his Walkman and started his first hunt with the Longshot.

At his usual pace, he knew he was looking at about a two to three hour walk for a round trip. Early on, he thought he might even walk it twice. Harsh reality set in a quarter mile in to his walk. But it was still groovy to see all the pop tabs and loose change underground, without having to pull out his spade.

When he got back near the edge of Scrubby Ridge, the Longshot buzzed and whirred in his hand. There was a setting he had read about in the manual, that the metal detector would vibrate harder and more frequently based on its proximity to an object, or the larger an object was. The readout displayed a question mark next to a bar graph that read as near full. Whatever it was, the machine couldn't suss it out, but it was *big*. Donald knelt down with his spade and dug through the wet dirt until he hit metal. At first it looked like a circle, just a dark metal ring in the ground, and he was excited to send Millie another piece of jewelry, spoils of his first trip out with the Longshot. But as he dug deeper, the story changed. It was a pistol, some caliber of revolver, buried grip first in the ground, the barrel aimed at the sky. Donald was cautious digging it out, afraid that it was still loaded and might fire. Time and bugs had eaten away the wooden grips, but the frame was still holding strong. He brushed away the gritty wet soil with his thumbs and looked it over in the morning light. Donald didn't know the make and model, but there was a four-leaf clover inside a semi-circle of gobbledygook etched on the frame, left-hand side behind the cylinder. He thought about going to library to look it up, or maybe taking it to his blacksmith buddy to see if he knew.

Finally, he dropped the firearm in his canvas "spoils sack" and reached for the Longshot. As he wrapped his fingers around it, he realized it was still buzzing. Another wave of excitement shot through him and he leaned down on all fours to read the display. This time, it showed a belt buckle. Donald shuffled over to the side of the trail, not even thinking about his aching knees, and began digging. He hadn't bothered to check the depth readout, and when he got almost a foot down, he wished he had. In a moment of frustration, he chucked the spade to the side and began digging through the earth with his hands. His left index finger caught on something cold and nearly stoved. Donald rolled around onto his stomach and looked down into the hole he had dug. A few quick brushes with his fingers and he found it; a small, almost child sized gold belt buckle. He scrunched up his face, a little annoyed that that's all the more there was after all his hard work, but decided to pull it out anyway. But it wouldn't pull. He excavated around the buckle, thinking maybe there was suction holding it in place. It still wouldn't move. Then he felt something underneath of it. The hole was deep enough, and the sun low enough, that he couldn't make out what it was. More work for the spade. And the mystery grew.

The buckle was laced through with a leather strap, attached to a large brown leather satchel almost two feet across. Donald shifted his body constantly, getting in better positions to dig and pull. He had uncovered enough that he could see what it was, but not enough that he could pull it from the ground, when a couple of joggers happened by. They stood and watched for a few minutes, before asking to help.

"No..." Donald grunted, "I think I....just about....got it."

"What is it?" The girl asked excited.

"I think its..."Donald didn't want to be rude, but it was hard to talk and labor to breathe at the same time, "some sort of....leather...bag or something."

"Oh, yeah," the boy pointed at the metal detector, "is that the new Longshot?" He turned to his girlfriend, "The thing from tv?"

"Just got it," He knew there was more to the story, but it wasn't the best time to get into the details.

All at once, the satchel ripped free from the earth, tearing the leather strap where it connected on one side to the bag. Donald panted for a minute, hugging the bag close to his chest. The couple clapped as much as two people could. Once he had regained his composure, Donald turned around with a smile and thanked them.

"You guys wanna see what's inside?" Donald was excited to share the experience with anyone interested. He had passed people on the trail before, but no one was ever around when he discovered something, not even a bottle cap.

The couple took the few steps closer and leaned over to see inside. Donald undid the leather straps and flipped open the bag. The world was filled with the smell of mold and must. The couple recoiled in disgust, the girlfriend trying not to gag. Donald had no reaction to it but excitement. Inside, were stacks upon stacks of moldered bills. By the looks of them, they were old. As he shuffled around the bag, he heard a jingle. He reached in and pulled out several stacks of money, piling them up off to the side, and found handfuls of gold dollars and fifty cent pieces. Most of the paper money would be useless to all but the most avid of collectors. But the coins could be worth a small fortune. Donald looked up at the couple excited. They had moved back closer to him, but the girl was pinching her nose and the boy was breathing through the collar of his t-shirt.

"Might have been something if it hadn't all molded." The boy shrugged. "Sorry, man."

"No, there's *coins*," Donald insisted. "Look!"

The boy took a half a step closer to stand directly over the bag. "Huh."

The girl let out a blood curdling, ear piercing scream that rocked the full range of the Montana plains. She clutched at her boyfriend's collar and tried to drag him away. Donald looked up at them both, confused and hurt. He glanced back down in the bag then back up at the retreating couple. The boyfriend was walking alongside the girl, begging her to know what's wrong. All she would cop to were indecipherable screams. A chill shot through Donald, starting at his hips and moving up to the top of his forehead. He had the distinct sensation that he was sitting on a hill full of fire ants. When the couple got about fifty yards away, the girl finally said what she saw, prompting the boyfriend to do a double take back to where Donald was sitting. He patted her arm and tried to walk back, but the girlfriend pulled him by the arm back towards the beginning of the trail. Eventually, the boyfriend managed to negotiate leaving the girl where she was, to return to Donald and pass along the information.

"I didn't mean to put the girl off with anything," Donald said slow. "I just thought you might be excited to see."

"Naw, man, it's not that." The boy stepped around Donald and peered over his head down into the hole. Suddenly, he pulled away as if he'd just seen a dead raccoon. "Oh, yeah. We're gonna need to call the cops or something."

Donald slowly turned his head toward the hole and rocked on his hips to see down in. At the edge, still submerged in the earth, was a skeletal hand, reached out to where the satchel had been. There were the vaguest shreds of fabric to indicate there had once been something around its wrist. Donald looked down at the satchel full of money and felt dirty. Dirtier than he in fact was. As if he had done something wrong, like shown pornography to a roomful of the elderly.

"I didn't know," Donald looked up at the boyfriend. "I swear, I didn't know."

Donald brought his things with him, but left the bag in its hole, and followed the couple back to the parking lot. The boyfriend made a call on his cellphone to the cops. After assuring them, it wasn't a freshly dead body, just newly discovered remains, the cops showed up about a half an hour later. Donald led them down the trail, covered in dirt and dried sweat, to where he had dug the hole. By lunchtime, there was a full blown investigation and Madison Buffalo Jump was crawling with police and vehicles. The cops questioned the couple and let them go. They had Donald sit in the back of a police cruiser after they questioned him and a little after one, told him they were going to have to take him back to the station for more questioning. Donald said he'd be happy to help, but wanted to know if he could get his Coke and chips out of his truck. Or maybe take his truck back to his house. The cops told him it would all be taken care of and began the twenty-minute ride back to the Manhattan police station. They placed him in an interrogation room, where he sat for three hours, before two sharply dressed, but slightly overweight detectives appeared.

"Good afternoon, Mr…"

"Whalen."

"Mr. Whalen. I'm Special Agent Martin Slauson," the older one said then indicated to the younger one, "this is my partner, Special Agent Phil Templeton."

"Good afternoon, agents," Donald gave a pained smile. Being that he was in pain and also excited to meet real FBI. "I've never met anyone from the FBI before."

Agent Slauson cleared his throat and adjusted himself in his seat, reading through a thick folder. "Out for a morning walk, I understand? Ran into a bit of trouble?" He looked at Donald from underneath his eyebrows.

"That's right," Donald smiled courteously, "I was trying out the new metal detector my niece got for me."

"You do realize that Madison Buffalo Jump is a state-owned property," Templeton cut in, "and treasure hunting is not allowed?"

Donald wasn't sure if this was something he had known and forgot, or never known previously to forget it. Either way, he didn't have a very good answer. "No. No, I didn't know that."

"How long have you been going to Madison Buffalo Jump?" Slauson had not moved from the last time he spoke.

"Oh," Donald thought, "My whole life, really. My dad took us all there when we were kids."

"Uh-huh." Slauson licked his thumb and flipped a paper inside the folder.

"I really just go out there for the exercise," Donald added quickly, "See, my doctor...I got this inflammation in my knees. Doctor said it's good to walk for the arthritis. My niece got me the metal detector as a birthday gift. She calls it my walking companion," he chuckled, "cause uh...I don't have anyone to walk with. I never really find much of anything, honest. The most I ever found was a necklace, a ring...maybe a few earrings once---"

"A firearm," Templeton glared at him.

"A what?" Donald wasn't ready for the word.

"In your bag, the police found a firearm. I take it this was not something you discovered today."

"No, I did," Donald was trying to stay out in front of the questions. "I did, just before I found the satchel. The bag."

"Then why didn't you mention it?" Templeton gave an antagonistic shrug.

"Well, I uh…" Donald searched for the obvious answer, "With all the excitement…you know…I guess I forgot about it."

"Is there a reason you wanted to take it back to your residence?" Templeton didn't appear to blink.

"Well, like I said," Donald leaned forward on the table and gestured with his hands. "I forgot I had found it. Honestly, until you brought it up, I forgot I had it on me at all. If I would have remembered, I certainly would have told the police."

"Uh-huh," Slauson was still reading. "You said, your father took you out to Buffalo Jump when you were a child?"

"Yes, sir."

"And who was your father, precisely?"

"James Rutherford Whalen."

"This," Slauson slid a mugshot of Donald's father across the table, "James Rutherford Whalen?"

Donald went cold again. He felt like he had back at the park with the girl screaming and fighting to drag her boyfriend away. He hadn't seen a picture of his father in a long time, let alone a picture of him so young. And so mean. His father hadn't been the most tender of men and he had spent most of his youth afraid of him, though he still respected him. All his life, he'd never known of his father having his picture taken outside of his high school graduation, his wedding day, and various IDs.

"Uh...yes, sir. That's..."

"The same James Rutherford Whalen," Slauson tapped the top corner of the photo, "that was wanted for multiple armed robberies and suspected in the murder of his associates, Tom Kunckle and Harry Rapoport?"

"I don't know about all that, Mr. Slauson---"

"You didn't know that your father was wanted for murder and robbery in three states?" Templeton had the look of one of those *loose-cannon* cops on tv, but a baker's body. "That's a little hard to believe, Mr. Whalen."

"You know murder doesn't have a statute of limitations, Mr. Whalen." Slauson's voice was low, his tone ominous.

"Wha---" Donald looked back and forth between the two detectives. "I---"

"What sent you out to Buffalo Jump, Donald?" Slauson leaned back in his chair and folded his hands over his pudgy stomach. "Lotta land in this state. Lotta parks. Plenty of places to go with your little metal detector."

"I---"

"What else have you found on your walks, Mr. Whalen?" Donald couldn't recall the last time he had seen Templeton breathe.

"My father, he…he would take us on these walks," Donald looked down at the grimacing mugshot of his father, back up to Slauson, "we would all go out on the weekends and just go for family walks through the park. I didn't know he killed anyone. Or robbed any banks. Honest. Are you saying that man---"

"We don't know. For sure." Templeton glared.

"But it shouldn't be long before we do," Slauson said casually. "Technology these days. You can find things like that." He snapped quickly then dropped his hand back on his stomach. "Which is part of the reason we're having trouble believing your story."

"We've been to your house." Templeton began tapping his foot.

"Not a big place." Slauson shook his head quickly.

"But someone wouldn't need a lot of room for an operation like you're running."

"Just a metal detector and a few days a week."

"A map would help to."

"Maybe something like this map." Slauson pulled another piece of paper from the folder and slid it across the table next to the mugshot.

This paper was old and yellow, there were dark amber lines forming a grid where it had been folded, and small chunks of paper missing at the intersections. Even without touching the paper, Donald could tell it was soft and fragile. But he also knew he had never seen it before in his life. He tried to make sense of it as Slauson started talking.

"Seems like your dad was out for a little more than fresh air on those family walks."

The paper was a primitive hand drawn map in red and black ink. If you squinted and tilted your head to the side, it looked vaguely like a map of Buffalo Jump. There were circles and X's peppered across it and small notes written in pencil that had faded with time to the point of being near invisible. But Donald could still recognize his father's handwriting.

"Where did you find this?" He asked, fighting tears.

"Same place you left it." Templeton continued his cold stare and tapping foot.

"Footlocker, women's shoe box, bottom left corner." Slauson had the air of a man bragging about his job at a family picnic.

"You..." Donald was afraid to touch anything, "you've been in my house?"

"Trailer. Yes."

"Is there anything you'd like to come clean about now, Donald?" Slauson pulled himself closer to the table with his heel. "Now would be the time."

"I..." Donald looked up from the map and the mugshot of his father to the two Federal agents sitting across from him, his eyes losing the fight against the tears. "I swear, I didn't know anything about any of this."

Slauson sighed, looked down at the floor, sticking out his tongue like a cat coughing up a hairball before quickly pulling it back in and shooting Donald a disappointed look. Templeton stared his nose at his hands and grinded his jaw.

"If I would have known anything about this I would have come to the police first thing. I forgot about the gun. And I never knew my father was a murderer! Or a bank robber! I swear, all I wanted to do was get out of the house and move around some!"

"There's a lot of cash and coin in the bag, Mr. Whalen," Slauson looked at him from under his eyebrows again. "Even at auction you'd be able to fetch a nice chunk of change."

"Might be able to move out of that backwoods *shithole* you live in---"

Slauson held up his hand and cut off Templeton. "What we're saying is we can understand why you would want to go looking for your father's robbery earnings. We can even understand why you wouldn't tell anyone about it. Hell, he's your dad. We get it. But now is the time to come clean. If you were ever going to be honest about this whole deal, it would be right here, right now, to us."

"But, Mr. Slauson," Donald held his hands together and shook them, pleading, "you have to believe me. I didn't know anything. My mother left me that trunk when she died. I never go through it because it hurts too much to remember---"

Slauson began collecting the papers off the table. Templeton stood up and pushed in his chair.

"My niece," Donald's face was streaked with tears, "she bought me the Longshot as a birthday gift. I just wanted to help my knees. I didn't want to hurt anyone or cover up any crime. Please, believe me, Mr. Slauson, I'm telling the truth!"

Templeton was the first one out the door. Slauson closed the door behind them. Donald sat cold and alone, sobbing into his hands in the interrogation room.

The case was dismissed before trial. Agents Slauson and Templeton had started the search of Donald Whalen's home before the search warrant had been signed and approved. Millie was interrogated three days later by the agents and threatened with suppression of evidence and accessory to fencing stolen goods. She presented the receipts for the metal detectors and those charges weren't brought up again for the rest of the interrogation. An hour-long phone call with Donald's sister in-law confirmed his, and the entire family's, ignorance of the crime.

It was nice weather by the time the case was dismissed at the state and Federal level. Slauson and Templeton kept their jobs and were reassigned to a forgery division in Seattle. Donald, with the help of Millie, sold the Longshot and used the proceeds to help him move from Three Forks to Butte, where he now lives, and goes on frequent walks with his dog, Starbuck.

I sat with him for an interview in the fall of 2016. This was the last time he spoke publicly about the case.

The Tragedy Last Summer

The computer lab was empty. Except for one. Rondeletia Campione sat with a pen between her teeth, writing a term paper about the effect of tv dinners on mid-century American families and how it has changed modern spending habits. The paper wasn't due until Christmas, but there was no reason to drag her feet on it. With hardly anyone left on campus, and even less people in the dorms, it was the most peace she would have all year.

The pen, since you asked, had less to do with writing and more to do with Rondeletia grinding her teeth. Her nightguard had broken some months ago, mere months after getting it in the first place, and since she didn't feel like taking a trip back to her dentist to get another, she made due. Dr. Hoffman told her that she was grinding her teeth in her sleep, when deep in thought, and more than likely, due to "the extreme stress of her recent tragedy" whenever she wasn't speaking. Her dentist was more on point than he knew, but Rondeletia didn't feel like explaining it.

A couple of upperclassmen stumbled into the dark computer lab, laughing and swatting at each other's books. They didn't notice her at first and flipped on the lights. The couple stared in shock. Rondeletia kept typing. The boy led the girl to a computer at the extreme end of Rondeletia's row, on the opposite side. Inside a minute, the boy had already peeked over the monitors, his girlfriend slapping and chastising him. Rondeletia put in her earbuds and turned on *Razorblade Suitcase*. She could hear the plastic tube of the Pilot pen creak between her teeth as she worked. After ten minutes she called it. Wrapped up her paragraph, backed up her paper to her thumb drive, cloud and network and packed up. She turned the lights out on the couple as she left.

As she came upstairs out of the computer lab, her phone started dinging and buzzing with all the texts and calls she missed while in the basement. Mostly from her mother, but several sprinkled in from random family and friends. Her friend, Temple, was the only one she hadn't heard from. Everyone else had fallen in line with what Rondeletia feared happening. The first annual round of "just checking in".

She heard her back teeth creak as she walked across campus and slacked her jaw immediately. There wasn't much impetus or reason to go back to her dorm, just as there wasn't much benefit in staying on campus and not going back to Westchester over summer break, except that it wasn't home. After a few minutes of standing with her Ryde app open, she couldn't think of anywhere else to go. It was either The Bent Spoon and get stared at some more, or just wander aimlessly around town when she could have been working.

She didn't pass anyone on her way through the dorm. It was coming up on the time of year that middle-class high school students would go tripping wide-eyed through the halls with their parents. It wasn't something she was chomping at the bit to see, just notable that it wasn't happening. But the emptiness of the dorm made it all the more shocking when her phone rang. It was her mother. She declined the call, walked into her half empty dorm room and threw her bag on her bed. Her roommate had cleared out weeks ago. It somehow made the room a bit cozier.

Her phone rang, again. Her mother, again. She rolled her eyes and sighed. Maybe if she answered it once, her mother would leave her alone for a few days.

"Hey, ma," Rondeletia said, fighting a yawn.

"*Rondeletia, where* have you *been*?" she said it in that old Italian mother way.

"I've been working. I was down in the computer lab. They don't have the best signal down there."

"What are you doing in that nasty computer lab? Did your roommate steal your laptop again? And where is that computer we got for you?" Her mother's questions were fired one after another.

Rondeletia's laptop hadn't ever been stolen. It was a lie she floated once to give herself some room. Hoping to strike gold again, she floated another one.

"They have the power off in the dorms, ma," she said looking out her window at the robin on the sill, "It's a summer thing. For maintenance, remember?"

"I swear to God, there was never so much trouble with electronics and electricity when your father and I were there."

"There weren't as many electronics for you to have trouble *with*," Rondeletia added in her classic sarcastic tone. "Besides, it's summer. It's maintenance season and whatever else. There's not as much reason to keep all this shit on all the time." Whenever she talked with her mother, Rondeletia could always feel herself slipping back into that Long Island accent. The only way she knew to combat it was with profanity, which her mother hated.

"You know I hate it when you do that," her mother clucked.

"Do what?" She had become fully engrossed in the world in the sky outside of her window. Not even the birds, just the air. Blowing around with no other purpose than to be breathed and help things grow.

"You know what," her mother said, coldly. But her tone was not what it had been when Rondeletia was a child, not anymore. The New York claws had been put away and covered up with kid gloves. "Just like you know that you are coming up this weekend. Your father is really looking forward to seeing you."

"Dad never looks forward to seeing me," Rondeletia was more honest in her tone than she intended.

"Rondeletia Sophia Campione, you know that is not true." There was a sadness in her mother's voice that Rondeletia hoped had left a while ago. Her mother held the line a moment before she spoke again. "Now, enough of this silliness! I will have no more of your silliness," That was the word she used to describe any serious emotion her daughter had, "This is a *happy* time! A time for *celebration* and I will not have you bringing it down with your moody millennial *Princeton Blues*, ok? I went to that school, too, and I know how you can get when you're there a long time. Though, I don't think *anyone* has ever stayed there as long as you have. You may have set a school record for most days on campus."

"I can't come up now, ma," Rondeletia hoped sheer exasperation through depression would change her mother's mind and put off the inevitable.

"Oh, yes you can! We're going to have *a party*. Just like we do every year, the whole *family*. And your father, your uncle and I have something *special* planned just for you. We know you are going to love it. And if you stay down there on that smelly old campus you will be denying *us*, your mother and father, your loving parents, the joy of seeing their child happy.

Do you want to do that to your mother and father? Do you want to take their happiness from them?"

"I was thinking all day about how happy they'll be when they see me graduating on my own steam," Rondeletia said lazily, "Completing a four-year degree under my own fucking power, with my own fucking mind---"

"And your father's fucking money." Her mother was no stranger to cutting her off. Nor was she a stranger to cursing, despite how much she hated it, but Rondeletia could tell that she had reached the end of her rope. The next step would be to send someone down to get her.

"Alright," she said low.

"Alright is right. I *swear*," her mother laughed, "even when it means giving you something nice, it's always like pulling teeth getting you to do as your told. You've been like that ever since you were a little girl." Her voice started moseying down memory lane at the end.

"What time is it?" Rondeletia pulled the phone away from her ear and checked the clock. It was eleven minutes after noon. "The train is gonna be about three hours to get up there. I'll probably be up around six."

"Well, would you rather I send someone down to pick you up?" Her mother sounded genuinely concerned.

"No, it's alright. It'll give me some time to work on the train."

"Alright," her Italian mother belabored the point, "but if you want me to call and send someone down, I can do that. You won't have to ride that train."

"It's alright, ma," Rondeletia tried to get off the phone as fast as possible, "I'll let you know when I get on."

"Be safe."

"I will."

"I *love* you."

"I love you too, ma."

Rondeletia dropped her phone to the floor and held her head in her hands with a sigh. Peace, as she knew it, would not be had for the foreseeable future. She took her sweet time getting packed and successfully managed to kill most of an hour. After a round of deep breathing, she put in her earbuds and turned on *The Science of Things* before heading off for the train station.

The streets were pretty much dead. Even a big college town like Princeton doesn't have many people hanging around during the summer months. Most who leave at the end of the semester don't come back until, at best, two days before class.

Rondeletia was thankful for less potential rubberneckers, but angry that they were something she had to worry or think about at all. She was also damn lonely.

A few times earlier that week, she had considered reaching out to what few friends she had. Just send up a flare and see who was willing to throw her a life saver. And while that was the way she genuinely felt, she couldn't risk people knowing it. It would only lead to more pampering, soft-soaping, and all-around claustrophobia that she was more than ready to be over and done with.

Rondeletia thought about these things and cursed to herself under her breath all the way to the station. Not even the breeze and the robins riding on it could snap her mind out of its rut. The walls were closing in and she hadn't even left New Jersey. Once she bought a ticket, she sat down in a chair and began scraping the last chips of polish off her nails. Her grief counselor told her it was a sign of stress. She told him it was something she had been doing since she was twelve. For a guy in his field with that many letters after his last name, he was about as perceptive as roadkill. Her mother told her grief counselor this, after a conversation they had in confidence, and Rondeletia was put on depression medication and assigned to a full time shrink.

Dr. Maurice Ludlow wound up being the only bright spot in her life for the better part of a year. She had no attraction to him outside of him being a genuine person, despite her friends' smirks and ribbing, and from what she could tell, he had no attraction to her. He was just the only person that truly listened to what she had to say. Rondeletia did her best to think it was because he really cared and not because her father was paying him to. She checked the time on her ticket and the time on her phone before shooting him a text.

"Guess who's about to hop a train"

What seemed like an hour later, but was only three minutes, he responded, "Youre not joining the circus r u?"

"Kinda. Going home"

"Do u want 2 talk?"

"Can I call you?"

"Gimme a min"

Almost ten minutes later, Rondeletia's phone cut out of *Disease of the Dancing Cats* for her to answer a Skype call from "dr ludlow". The station didn't have wi-fi, so the signal was a bit choppy, but she could still see him in a Yankees shirt at his desk in his home office. There was a screaming child off mic and Ludlow ran to deal with it before the session started proper. With Maurice's approach, Rondeletia's preference, and number shuffling from her father's accountant, Dr. Ludlow was able to be on call, day and night, to talk. She had been to his office a few times early on, but after several sessions, Ludlow caught on to what was happening and allowed her to do sessions from her dorm.

"So... what's sending the prodigal daughter back to the homestead?" Ludlow finally said, sitting down at his desk.

"Three guesses," Rondeletia tried to sound bored, but her knee bounced up and down like an oil derrick on amphetamines. Thankfully, her leg was out of frame.

"Why don't you tell me instead?" He had the ability to understand Rondeletia's sarcasm and use it back without ever coming across to her as a smartass.

"Ma called. Said she wants me to come back up for my uncle's birthday. She also said that her, my dad and my uncle have something special planned for me. I'm not looking forward to finding out what that is."

"It could be a good thing," Ludlow said, trying to sound optimistic. "From what you have told me, this could be the first year on record that they will have recognized your birthday. Specifically."

"But I know that isn't what this is about. You know those 'check in' texts I told you I was afraid of getting? I started getting them."

"When did that start?"

"Last night. They picked up more today. My mom the biggest offender."

"Has anyone of note *not* messaged you?"

"Just Temple."

"Maybe give him a shot." Ludlow never smiled. Rondeletia told him in an early session that she found smiles condescending and manipulative, especially from authority figures. Instead, he did his best to focus on the positive and underline it whenever it surfaced. "You said he is the one that has been most understanding of what's going on. Who knows, you might be able to commiserate about what you're going through. I'm sure he's going through it, too, in some fashion. You were her cousin, but he was the one that was gonna marry her."

Rondeletia turned away from her phone and stared off at the ticket desk. She held her thumb to her mouth and scraped the polish off her nail with her bottom teeth. The thought had never occurred to her. Temple had always been the levelheaded one of the two of them, ever since they were kids. His fascination with her cousin never made sense to her, but everyone has their foibles. Even in his furtive glances toward Jaimie, he never ignored Rondeletia or changed who he was.

"Is he gonna be at your uncle's party?" Ludlow spoke to kick Rondeletia back into play.

"More than likely," she said with her thumb still in her mouth.

Temple is the son of her father's business associate. Back in the late seventies, her dad and uncle, Marc and Luca Campione started a small business based out of Paramus making a new type of office printer that could fit on a desk. Early in development, they brought on a business partner named Guiseppe Moretti. By the early eighties, the business skyrocketed and the three were a near overnight success. The betrayal came when Moretti claimed the design and ideas to be all his own and cheated Rondeletia's father and uncle out of a business deal. This severed any sort of business relationship the three had, and the Morettis and Campiones became bitter rivals.

Despite the backstabbing, Marc and Luca went on to start their own business, Champion Inc, and created a whole new line of desk printers and fax machines. The Campione legacy was confirmed and their feud with Moretti was set to last for decades on the New York Stock Exchange. This war between the three men, however, did not hold true between their families and extended families. Rumors of affairs, elopement and bastard children between employees, close and distant kin of the Morettis and Campiones stretched back to as early as the mid-eighties.

All this bored Rondeletia no end, and she did her best to distance herself from it and be her own person. But it all came home to roost a little over a year ago at her mother's annual Easter garden party on Long Island.

They didn't live in the Stony Brook house anymore, they hadn't since the late nineties, but every year her mother insisted on holding a party there for Easter. Rondeletia, rolled her eyes and agreed to go, even then not having a desire to leave school. More to avoid time with family than anything else. But while she was there, she found something to take her mind off the stuffy pretense of her mother's Truman-era ideas of fun. A boy she had never seen before wandered into the party with another. The first boy, she came to learn from a conversation that lasted the majority of the afternoon, was named Riley. The other guy with him was his cousin, Benji. He said they were from the neighborhood and decided to crash the party for something to do on a Saturday. Rondeletia felt no small amount of attraction to the boy with the unfortunate, unisex name and the two made out in the bathroom just off her childhood bedroom. She never saw him again after that. Not in person, at least.

Riley had managed to finagle Rondeletia's phone number out of someone at the party. It was short work after that to find her name, Twitter, Facebook and Instagram accounts. She came to find out later that he even tried messaging her long dead MySpace page. He began videoing himself singing songs he wrote about her and sending them to her various accounts. Rondeletia regretted ever even meeting the guy and never returned any of his calls or messages.

Later that summer, Riley snuck into Luca's birthday party in Manhattan to look for Rondeletia. After that night, Riley's messages stopped on a dime. Rondeletia breathed deep and went back to Princeton on her birthday. A few weeks later in mid-August, there was a story on the news about a 1986 Lamborghini Countach that took a header off the 684 northbound bridge near Katonah, New York. Inside the vehicle, stolen from Guiseppe Moretti, was the body of Rondeletia's seventeen-year old cousin, Jaimie, and Riley Moretti, the one and only heir to the Moretti technology empire. Riley had snatched Jaimie from her home in the night, shot two guards and killed another. It was theorized they were escaping to the Moretti summer home in Cape Cod.

The world mourned for about two weeks. Rondeletia wanted to skip the funeral. And not even for fear of mafia-style hits or even good old-fashion old Italian fisticuffs (which never happened, the dual funeral yielded gruff handshakes and some empty promises of future company collaborations). She just didn't care. She was never too impressed with her cousin Jaimie in the first place, not that she wanted her dead, the two just didn't get along. Jaimie was everything Rondeletia wasn't. Blonde haired, blue eyed, a swimmer's body with a peppy attitude and smile that melted and broke hearts with reckless abandon and left the world ready to bow to her every whim, no matter how selfish or nonsensical. Even Temple didn't mourn for that long, but as Dr. Ludlow had recently pointed out, they both were probably going through more than they each realized.

However, the real upset came for Rondeletia just as America's cathartic bawling over the death of young forbidden love was coming to a close. Gossip columnist Melissa Arnold, at the online news outfit *Graphite*, managed to dig up *all* the texts, emails and love songs Riley had sent Rondeletia between April and July of 2011. Something neither her family, nor friends knew anything about. The country now had a place to hang their grief hawk sombrero and a permanent worry stone for lovesickness in the form of Rondeletia Campione.

Journalists and tv crews began following her around campus the remainder of the summer. She was offered countless book, tv and movie deals. When class started up again, Melissa Arnold would barge into lectures and harass Rondeletia on her walks between classes, begging for "her side of the story". Teachers and classmates were paid off by news agencies to bug dorms and offices and get her to open up to them. Rondeletia spoke to and confided in no one. She continued her school work, but as a human being she began to shut down. Her mother, at the suggestion of the school guidance counselor and the heads of the Psychology department (Rondeletia's major), forced her to see a grief therapist. The sessions were relatively few, before she was re-assigned to Dr. Ludlow. But there was a long hard row to hoe before Rondeletia felt comfortable enough talk. Once Ludlow understood that what she was going through was not personal grief bordering on the edge of suicide, but being forced into the role of teddy bear for the *world's* grief, his approach and treatment changed drastically. But while he could understand and sympathize with

Rondeletia's predicament, he couldn't change it. The most he could do was be an ear to chew on, which had worked for about eight or nine months, but she was now being thrown back into, or at the very least being held over, the fire.

Rondeletia zoned out, thinking over Ludlow's suggestion about contacting Temple and the overall Chinese fire drill she was about to head into. Something at the back of her head started tapping, a sort of Morse code reminder to send a text, but she couldn't find it in herself to follow through. An announcement came over the intercom and blew out Ludlow's speakers.

"Are you at the train station now?"

"Yeah," Rondeletia said, distracted.

"What time does your train leave?"

"About fifteen minutes," she continued to drag her thumbnail across her teeth, but there was no polish left to scrape.

"Do you know how long you're gonna be up there?"

"No longer than three days," Rondeletia turned back to her phone and spoke with conviction. "Whatever they plan on doing is gonna take place in that time frame. Luca's birthday is tomorrow and mine is the twenty-seventh. So...there's no real reason to stick around longer than that."

"What if there is?" Ludlow looked around his folded hands where they were propped up by the elbows on his desk.

"Tough," Rondeletia shrugged.

Ludlow leaned back in his chair and crossed his hands behind his head. "I can't tell you what to do, but I would like to *suggest*...that you wait this one out. Take the temperature when you get home. See how things are. Maybe, what they are planning to do is put this whole thing behind them as well. It could be a healing experience for all parties involved."

Rondeletia started to speak, but Ludlow cut her off. Not like her mother. The signal was just that bad.

"And I know that you're going to say that they are the ones that have been healing for the past eleven, twelve months, but I want you to think about it this way for a minute. You're a Psych major, you need to start thinking about things this way, anyway. Would you say that their behavior has fallen in line more with grief..."

"I'd say it's more like obsession," she said bored.

"Bingo," Ludlow shot her a finger pistol and leaned in closer to the camera. "You have been the epicenter, the hub, if you will, of an *en masse* obsession brought on by trauma. Stripping the public aside, you get that, we all get that, that's newspapers. What we are talking about is your family. It is natural, human nature, to be triggered by outside stimuli after experiencing trauma. The main trigger here being the time of year. Your uncle's birthday. Your birthday. And while she may have been detestable to you, Jaimie still was your cousin. Your family is gonna feel a way or two about her death. On top of all the other nuances of the situation surrounding her death. It's a very complex web, you were just that thing left uneaten when the spider died. So to speak." Ludlow paused for a moment then continued, "I'm not saying forgive them, I'm saying, for a few days, cut them a break. Don't forget. Just try to give things a chance to heal, if that is indeed what's happening. Like I said at the top, this could be a good thing."

"And if it isn't?" Rondeletia looked at the camera from the corner of her eye.

"Then none of what I said makes any difference." Ludlow's shrug could have been interpreted as easy going or giving up. Rondeletia wasn't sure which. Neither was Ludlow. "Are you going to drop out of school?"

"No." she was quick to respond.

"Then keep grinding it out till you graduate and write a book about it. You know more than anyone how much people have said your book could sell for. Cut out the middle man. Write it yourself."

Rondeletia bristled at the thought. She got Ludlow's point, she was just irritated that he brought it up. She checked the clock in the station then turned back to the camera. "I've gotta get on the train soon." She said it low and matter-of-factly.

Dr. Ludlow drummed his right fingers on the back of his left hand. Once again, he didn't feel as if he had broken through. Then again, that was how he always felt after all his sessions with Rondeletia. He'd learned to take it in stride. "The line's open if you want to talk. I'll be at the ready. Just do your best to ride it out. It's only a few days."

Rondeletia looked past the camera, down at her shoes as they slid along the tile floor of the station. "Alright." She paused for a moment before she remembered she was the one that had to end the session. "Thanks for talking with me."

"Thanks for listening." Ludlow knocked twice on his wooden desk, then crossed his fingers to the camera. "And sharing how you feel."

With no pretense, Rondeletia ended the call. Music blared back through her headphones. The volume blast didn't shock her. It was a welcome distraction. She restarted the song and paced until the train came.

When she finally got to the house in Thornwood, her mother was at the door to greet her. After a forced family meal of just the two of them (her father was still out of town on business), Rondeletia went up to her adolescent bedroom and hid there for the remainder of the evening. Her mother had "surprised" her with a skin-tight, black sequined evening dress that Rondeletia would have sooner opened her veins than wear in public. She didn't say this out loud, but it did somehow manage to sour the evening even more.

The next day, Rondeletia spent as much time alone and away as possible. She snuck Poptarts from the kitchen and ate them in her room for breakfast. A little bit before noon, disgusted with her high school DVD collection, she tried to work, but couldn't. Around lunchtime her father came tripping through the door and ignored her, despite her mother calling her down to meet him. He was in a rush to prepare for his brother's birthday party that night. Rondeletia took a walk through her old neighborhood to get out of the house. She was confident that no one would notice her and surprised to see that nothing had changed. Both brought her depression to new lows.

She walked down Columbus Ave to the Carvel in the Rose Hill shopping center and called Temple. He didn't answer. She finally returned all her friends' texts and got nothing back from them either. After about fifteen minutes she gave up and decided to be alone. She drank two milkshakes and thumbed through a discarded newspaper, reading about Aurora, Colorado. The kids behind the counter recognized her and whispered. A few customers noticed, too, but she ignored them, pissing everyone off, except for the workers who were enthralled by their proximity to fame. Full of milkshake, she called a Ryde for the three-minute drive back to her house and put in an appearance with her mother before going upstairs to prepare for the party.

She came down the stairs at fifteen minutes to eight, squeezed into the gifted dress that she was convinced made her look like a pudgy, rejected Bond girl. She had covered the top with one of her father's blazers that she had stolen years ago and worn throughout high school and an old waistcoat overtop of a torn white Bush tour t-shirt. Looking in the mirror, she felt like the bastard child of Debbie Harry and Boy George. But there was no one in the house to tell her otherwise. Both her mother and father had gone sometime earlier, leaving a note on the fridge to "Get in the car outside. And don't roll down the windows till you get there."

If the note hadn't been a big enough clue, she could tell just by the traffic and how long it took to get there, that her Uncle Luca's birthday was being held somewhere different this year. Context clues told her, this was the surprise. When she opened her door at the New York Botanical Garden, she knew it was. The Botanical Garden was her favorite place to escape to as a child. She had once skipped school in fourth grade and took the bus up from Long Island. There was holy hell to pay and she was banned from there, by her father, for almost three years. It seemed like either a slick joke or a snide comment that this was her big surprise.

Rondeletia made it into the party no problem. She successfully dodged and slipped around the press, who were more interested in her father and uncle anyway. The kid at coat check flirted with her and asked for her blazer. She turned him town with a sarcastic comment and went to the bar. The bartender in the back near the Perennial Garden, who was also about her age, flirted with her four about five minutes before she left and turned around directly into Temple.

"Where the hell have you been, you asshole?" Rondeletia yelled at him to fight the tears. As soon as she saw him, she felt the knot of tension in her chest unwind and begin to fall to her feet.

"Nice to see you, too!" Temple laughed and hugged her.

Rondeletia pulled away from the hug and stared Temple straight in the face, "Let's get the fuck out of here." She grabbed him by the hand and started pushing her way through the crowd.

Temple was a bit taken aback by Rondeletia's energy and behavior, but held on tight and followed her, "By the way, you look gorgeous as always! Are you wearing make-up?"

Rondeletia shot him a look over her shoulder. "Fuck you."

They finally stopped at the Reflecting Pool, both heaving and out of breath. Temple pulled off his jacket and threw it over his shoulder, sucking in the humid air of New York summer. Rondeletia sat down at the edge of the pool and kicked off her shoes.

"I didn't mean anything by it," Temple said, finally. "I just don't remember you having such full eyelashes before."

"They're probably full of the shrapnel from the looks I shoot at everyone," she said low, deciding not to beat around the bush.

Temple knelt down to be closer to Rondeletia's level and tossed his jacket on the ground, rolling up his sleeves. "What's going on?"

Rondeletia said nothing and stared at the pool for some time. "Why didn't you pick up when I called you today? And why do you never text me?"

Temple sat down with a grunt and took off his shoes and socks before dipping them in the pool. "It's been...a weird year for me."

"How so?" The knot Temple had unfurled in her chest had been replaced with the Rubik's cube Ludlow had handed her earlier. Examining it now, she was starting to believe he was right. Rather than unload with her problems, which wasn't in her nature anyway, she decided to put her Psych major to good use and listen.

"Ever since," Temple looked out at the garden beyond the Reflecting Pool and threw a pebble he found on the ground, "...Jaime...last year. And Riley. I've been getting...*hounded* about my relationship with her. And not just by my dad. He said Luca blamed me for a while for being too pushy. Wanting to marry her too quick. Said I was robbing the cradle and that's what drove her to run off with Riley. Then I started getting all these emails, in my *Harvard* account from some woman at Graphite offering me book deals and to grant her an interview."

Rondeletia's sense of vindication was outstripped only by her shame as Temple laid out, almost word for word, her life and verified Ludlow's theory. It had never occurred to her once that they both had gone through the same thing and she wanted desperately to go back in time and change it.

"I did love her," Temple added after a while, "which is the fucked-up thing. Because for a while...I can't even tell you where I was at I don't think," he turned toward Rondeletia and looked her in the eye in the dark, "I haven't talked with anyone, really, about this. I was in a pretty dark place for a while. When she died...when they recovered her body...I saw her. I didn't need to see that. And I was afraid that was going to be the lasting image I had of her. Then I realized that I would never see her again. Then, the fucked-up thing is," Temple chuckled, "a year later. I don't want to see her ever again," he laughed, "I'm fucking sick of seeing her face. How fucked up is that?"

Rondeletia cried quietly next to him. She put her hand on his shoulder and squeezed gently. It was the way they had communicated as children. When the room was full of adults.

When children were to be seen and not heard. It was the way they let each other know they were there.

"Well, if you think that's fucked up," she laughed but couldn't hide the tear in her voice, "do I have a story for you."

Breathe Through This

Northwest of Phoenix, near Six Mile Crossing, between Bagdad and Nothing, there's a place called Suicide Wash. Less of a migrant town and not exactly an outpost. It was once home to place where undesirables went to hide. Criminals too afraid, too feeble, or not enough of the two, to make it to the border. Resident's called the place Cadence. It was named after Oscar Cadence; the first and longest residing resident of the "town". He was dubbed the de-facto mayor, though he had no interest in politics and even less in leading anyone.

People came and went. Only two people besides Oscar stayed and no one else ever stayed for too long. Just long enough to stuff cardboard in their shoes, bandage their wounds, check the wind direction (with the windsock on Oscar's Airstream trailer) and blow.

There was a sign posted on the edge of the camp, distinguishing the town and population (which never changed, "Fourteen was better than thirteen," Oscar said, "and more believable.") and the town motto underneath it all.

Breathe Through This

The phrase came from a story that no one knew if it was true, but they told it with such zeal you would have thought it happened to them. The only standing explanation for who the near mute Oscar Cadence was and how he came to Suicide Wash. What went from hearsay, to legend, to gospel, to assumed documented and notarized fact. They said Oscar was a hell raiser, once upon a once, known to creak many a back-porch door during business hours. Said one day, (the closest anyone was ever able to peg down was somewhere in 1965) a husband came home early and caught him in the act. Kicked him to his knees, put a .38 special in his mouth and told him, "Breathe through this."

How Oscar got the barrel out of his mouth and his ass out of the house was never explained or established. Suffice it to say, Oscar had a .38 special and was rumored to be wanted for murder. If the crowd was cool enough, on a given night when someone decided to tell passers-through the story around the fire, Oscar would pull a brown paisley bandana out of the inside pocket of his denim jacket and let it be passed around. A snub nose with a four-leaf clover etched into the side. There were words wrapped around the clover that no one was ever able to read, but everyone theorized their origin from French, to Esperanto, to extra-terrestrial. One time in '83, a man from Killarney blew in for a few days. He was on the run after a series of liquor store and diner holdups; most recently, The Downwinder Café about a half hour outside Phoenix. When the pistol was passed to him, he read the inscription by the firelight and laughed. "Don't fuck it up," he said to Oscar, with a grin, and passed the relic back.

There was a brief period of time where people considered changing the town motto, but the man from Killarney left and the motto remained unchanged. It had become a mantra, almost an invocation of one's inner strength and too important to be fucked with. When someone would blow into Cadence stressed out and bleeding, or a wild card was dragged into the desert by Oscar and another with ball bats, when things got too heavy, someone would invariably sigh the town motto.

"Breathe through this."

Breathe through this and everything else will be cake.

Intermission at the Velvet Curtain Bar & Lounge

The eight-hour layover in Chicago is what kills me. Especially between two big gigs. A one-night stint in Boston, followed by a three-hour coach flight to O'Hare in the June heat and eight hours to kill on a downright balmy fifty-eight degree Chicago summer night before another coach flight, this one six-hours, still in the June heat, to the Reno desert. All this, and a paycheck too. If I was moving it would be different. But now I have to drag ass through an empty airport in the middle of the night with nothing but Dave Pike echoing up and down the hallways to keep me company. And the Sbarro was closed. As was the Hanrahan's, the Orange Julius, the Cinnabon, all the royal family and the Scottish barony. Not that I was hungry, but buying something sometimes gets me out of my head.

When I got my residency at the Velvet Curtain, I didn't think that I would have to travel this much. Not that it happens very often, just more often than I would like. I had travelled for years doing gigs as an open contract lounge singer, but getting signed was supposed to change all that. Maybe if I had become a piano player I wouldn't have to move around as much. And those guys seem to be pretty happy. Relatively so. Or maybe a bartender. But they move around a lot too. And I'd need an eighteen-month course in mixology, minimum. Lounge singers are jacks of all trades, and there is an appeal to that, it means steady work, but it also means more and closer contact with the audience.

I was stuck in a loop, thinking about the gig a few hours prior and wondering how long it would take me to get the black from under my nails. I looked around in my bag for a scrub brush, even a toothbrush but came up short. My girl in Nebraska always had one. One of those little nail scrub brush things. She was the only one I knew who did. But she wasn't a torch singer, so that might have had something to do with it. All the torch singers I knew were just as narrow-focused as the lounge singers, which is to say extremely. My girl in Colorado being about the only standout. She had all the charm and cool of a civilian coupled with all the skill and proficiency of a career torch singer twenty years her senior. I found a payphone and decided to call her up for something to do. It was about two o'clock in the morning there, so she was probably asleep. Or at work. Or out of town. It was still disappointing when she didn't pick up. I dropped another dime and called my girl in Michigan. She is a civilian, but she's cool. Neck and neck tie for favorite with my Colorado associate. But she didn't pick up either. I slammed the phone harder than I needed to and pulled on my jacket to fight the Chicago summer chill before I started walking the big empty airport.

Even if there was an arcade, I would have taken it. Stuff the opposing slot on the air hockey table with napkins or a tourist visor and play myself. Anything. Instead, every loud slam and echo that rang through the airport caused me to jump and reminded me of work. It made me wonder what it would be like to be a light and sound man. Those guys are always screwy, though. They make war veterans nervous. And most of them are half deaf. All of them are scatterbrained.

I smelled the industrial cleaner in the urinals and thought about my girl in New Hampshire. When I put two and two together it made me laugh. Then it made me ashamed. I shouldn't lead people on sometimes the way I do. It's part of the business, in a way. In as much as you never form any strong or lasting bonds with anyone, so you're always on the make. A look in the mirror put me on a different train of thought; maybe I should shave. I reached for my real shaving kit and thought of how I fucked up a few hours ago. I didn't have proper information from booking. That was my problem. And that's not passing the buck either. It was supposed to be a private show and I wound up bombing harder than I had in recent memory. My glove ripped at the end of my first set and the second set I just couldn't find my footing. The audience wasn't very receptive. It wasn't one of my better performances, either. I was first gig sloppy. No mic control at all. And I kept tripping over the cord. Some guy walked into the airport men's room and caught me staring at my hands. I quick sucked a back tooth and looked thoughtful, before I set to scrubbing my hands real hard with the Lava.

Maybe I should quit, was my next thought. I looked through the gate of the gift shop and scanned all the books and magazines on the racks. I had signed a NDA with management when they picked me up at the Lounge, so I couldn't turn around and write about it after I retire. But maybe I could be a consultant, or do something out in Hollywood. My girl, my first girl, from Phoenix had moved out there a few years prior and I'd never heard from her again. She was worth giving up the limelight for, to be sure. And if I was feeling a big enough push to get out, maybe my time on the stage was up. I was sure I could get a job working at a movie studio or on a tv show or something. I may only be a lounge singer, but I know a lot of things. You meet people when you travel. But I didn't think she would feel too good about eating food off a table bought with money made from lounge acts or even consultation jobs on night club operations. She also hated show business and all people involved. Especially me. So that ship had, more than likely, sailed.

I walked through the cemetery of empty airport seats, past my luggage and around the plastic potted plants. Every couple of laps, I would glance over at the line of payphones and jingle the change in my pockets. I hadn't heard from anyone in days. Just people at the club, bossing me around, telling me about shows booked. No one I wanted to talk to had called me. They hadn't even left a message on my machine. And now I was stuck in fucking Chi-Town at three in the morning with nothing to think about but my luggage and work. Part of the appeal for me about lounge singing was getting to work alone. But I didn't think that I would have to live alone, too. I thought about my girl in Nebraska and riding bikes with her in the summer when we were kids. A long ways away from where I was pacing now. It didn't seem real that the dumb ass with skinned knees would grow up to be an unknown touring lounge singer. I just thought I would be unknown and not much else. But at the same time, I knew the story of my career too well to know how and why I came to be where I was, pacing around the airport in the middle of the night in an Illinois heatwave that felt like mid-October.

The sound system was on about its fourteenth Dave Pike track. It made everything feel like a big joke. Back at the payphone, I started dropping dimes and dialing numbers. Michigan, Colorado, Nebraska, New Hampshire, PA, Phoenix, LA, Seattle, Kansas City, Houston, Detroit, Memphis, New York, Wyoming. I emptied my pockets down to lint and slammed the phone. It was only when I was out of change that I thought about hitting a vending machine. My singular saving grace being the fact that there weren't any.

Laying on my back across three chairs, I finally decided to quit. My toe tapped the side of a large wooden box planter and I started to think about what I was going to tell my booker when I got back to the Lounge…when the payphone rang. Not just any payphone, the one I had dumped about five dollars worth of dimes into what felt like twelve hours earlier. Looking around the empty mall of an airport, I decided no one else was going to answer it, and picked it up myself.

"Trainor?" I knew the voice.

"Yeah, boss?"

"What are you doing calling all over tarnation in the middle of the night from an airport payphone?"

I went cold. This was the first stanza to a song that could end in only one of a couple ways. "I, uh…"

"New York, Texas, Missouri, Washington state, fuckin'…Tahiti…" He ran down my list like a high school principal. "Are you looking to farm yourself out to another club?"

"No," I was sloppy, "I was just trying to call up some old friends to pass the time, you know. There's no one here but me and the night janitor. And I think he may be a rumor."

"How many friends do you have Trainor?" I was fucked.

"You know I get around," I tried to laugh.

"Uh-huh. How do you think the show in Boston went?"

"It uh…," I looked around for someone to answer besides me. Only Pike and his back-up band responded, "It, you know, wasn't my best gig, but I've seen worse. I've had worse."

"Really? Because I'm sitting in my office right now with a

very unhappy promoter who is demanding full refund for his ticket.”

“I would advise you tell the promoter that I played the shows as planned. It was his set sequencing that was off, not the performances. But everyone left the stage in the order they entered it.”

“Uh-huh...” There was a very long silence where I didn’t know what to do. “Are you still heading to Reno?”

“Whenever the plane decides to arrive. I’ve still got,” I checked my watch against the wall clock, “about six hours or so before they start boarding.”

“Good. Do you think you’ll make it?”

“I don’t see why I wouldn’t.”

“Uh-huh. I don’t see why you would have botched last night’s show either, so I guess we won’t know until it happens.”

“Look, boss, do you want me to come back or---”

“No! *Trainor*! I want you to stop costing me money!”

“Costing you money? Fuck you, costing you money! That refund wouldn’t come out of your pocket and you fucking know it!” My voice almost drowned out the jazz quartet, “Put the fucking promoter on the phone. Right fucking now, D'Angelo, put him on the fucking phone."

"Yeah?" His voice was as weak as his spine.

"You think that you can just come in there and shake my boss's fucking tree while I'm out town? No dice, asshole. I don't work for fucking free! I'm not gonna spend the next two days scraping fucking blood out from under my nails and waking up from screaming nightmares and not have a fuck-ing penny to show for it! You want to put on a show for free? Then put it on your fucking self. I'm tired of you fucking lowlifes thinking you can have your cake, eat it too and fuck the baker's daughter on your way out the door. Threaten my livelihood a-fucking-gain and I'll show up with a light man and a bartender and go to work on your wife and kids be-fore you get home from work and leave them conscious long enough to watch *your* fucking encore! Eat shit and die, Stre-semann! You now, by law, owe me a fucking tip. Leave it with D'Angelo and I'll be calling you if the count's off." I damn near broke the phone and walked away.

My adrenaline was back. It pounded in my chest for a few minutes while I waited for another phone call. There wasn't one. D'Angelo knew what I would do when he picked up the phone. He could have handled the promoter himself, but he needed an excuse to check up on me. Which means I had a closer tail than I thought I had. I kicked around the idea of skipping the flight and getting on another one. Maybe ex-changing my ticket for the seven o'clock to Los Angeles to pick up where I left off. Or maybe the eight thirty for Denver to pick up where I never really started. I fell asleep across the chairs knowing that I wouldn't do any of the above. I had paired down my life options a long time ago and none of those choices were anywhere in the cards. When I got back from Reno, I'd stop off in Michigan and spend a few days with a soft-faced civilian, then get back on the road and start touring again.

That's show business.

Holliday Transactions

Holliday Woodlock idly stirred her ice tea with one hand while she pretended not to notice me. I had been inside her house almost twenty minutes already and not a word had been spoken since I greeted her at the door of her Seattle home. Her silence was not maleficent, just unsure. There had been several previous conversations over the phone, but she still had reservations. Finally, she held her finger over the tip of her straw, pulled it out of the glass and leaned her head back.

"Where do you want to start with all of this?" she lifted her finger from the straw and let the tea run into her mouth.

"Wherever you want," I adjusted in my seat to show I was listening, "If it's easier to start in the middle or the end, go for it. We can always work back."

"To be completely honest," she turned toward me and moved stray dark brown hairs out of her grey eyes, "Legally, I don't know how much I can disclose. And I don't know how much of that I would want to in the first place."

She watched my thumb as I clicked on the recorder, "How

about the stuff at Michigan State? That was pretty widely covered in the news at the time."

"That's really old hat at this point, though," she squinted her eyes and looked at me with her head cocked, doubtful.

"For some. I mean, do you know how many remakes there are of Beau Geste?"

"You've got a point," Holliday rolled her eyes and looked out the window at the Pacific rain. It was a moment that her fans and devotees would have killed to see: Woodlock dressed in men's camouflage cargo pants and a thrift store Pearl Jam concert t-shirt, relaxing on an overstuffed sofa, her legs crossed and resting atop a glass top coffee table covered in expensive art books and science journals. The Dead Kennedy's tattoo on the inside of her right wrist still clear and unblurred. The immaculate living room inside the silver and white house that sheltered us from an early evening thunderstorm.

She turned to me and noticed a few drops of tea on the stomach of her shirt and brushed them off, "Well, I mean, it wasn't like I started doing it as soon as I got there. It wasn't like I unpacked and then immediately started cooking mephedrone."

The rain picked up outside. She diverted her attention to the window then looked back at me with just her eyes, asking if I had rolled up the windows in my car. I said I had. After a few moments of quiet second guessing, she moved her iced tea from the side table to the coffee table, setting it down on a copy of *Inorganic Chemistry*, before motioning to push up her sleeves (giving a quick flash of the Marie Curie portrait on her left bicep), brushing back her hair with her hands and clearing her throat with a sigh.

"Leary and Kesey," she stared down her nose at the coffee table, her hands gripping the back of her neck, "Hiskey and the Brotherhood of Eternal Love, specifically, those guys just fucked everything up, really. And their work, their whole philosophy was never anything I had any interest in. Now, when people think of underground chemists they just think of some *Nutty Professor* hippie elbow deep in bathtub acid or something and that couldn't be further from the truth. A lot of the underground chemists I meet have a lot more in common with, like, HAM radio operators or people that paint ceramics. Not much really gets past their own labs and if it does it's with other enthusiasts and in very small controlled environments. And within those groups, there are the ones that are trying to push forward and do something new, and there are the ones that want to go back. That are trying to replicate and break down some of the original formulas that guys were coming up with back in the early 1900's. When people didn't know what they were doing. That's sort of where my interest began.

"I had been reading about these early experiments that this guy Sanchez had done in France back in the late twenties and early thirties where he was the first one to synthesize mephedrone. First, he synthesized methcathinone, I think, then mephedrone. But it was the first time anyone had ever heard of it and it got mentioned in this one French journal and that was it. I was really interested in chemical history then, the more obscure stuff specifically. When I first cooked it, it was just on this little two range camp stove in my dorm. I just wanted to see if I could do it. And that first batch, I just tested it then flushed it. It really was just one of those dumb dorm room experiments. I didn't tell anybody about what I did. That was around...Christmas? '03. My first semester at Michigan State.

"All of the research that I did after that kept coming up pretty much empty," she took a deep sip of her iced tea then leaned back in the couch, her feet returning to the coffee table. "Everything said that after Sanchez's work, nothing was really done again until the sixties with Leary and Hiskey and all of them. I'm sure now if you looked it up, it would say nothing had been done with it until the stuff I did, which just goes to show you the unrecognized short-term memory of certain parts of the internet. In reality, in the late nineteen forties up through the middle sixties, there was this drug called Nymphetamine that was being made and sold out of go-go bars and gentlemen's clubs in at least Chicago, Detroit and Los Angeles, I know. Amphetamines, for the most part, weren't really that big on the East Coast until...well. But Nymphetamine was just mephedrone, nothing fancier than that. And it didn't take much to cook, so people were just cooking it up in, like, the dressing rooms of these go-go bars and selling it to the patrons out the back door. And they would package it, in these little glass vials called *nymphs* or *nymphos*. And once Leary and the Merry Pranksters rolled around and LSD and amphetamines became stronger and easier to procure, the whole underground mephedrone market sort of dropped out. But mephedrone is really about the purest amphetamine that you can get, because it's not cut with anything or mixed with anything to make it stronger or the effects more long lasting. Like, bath salts, that shit has been stepped on more times than a high school basketball court, it's ridiculous. And, like, the *True Detective*, *Breaking Bad* set ups people have to cook it... Like, I just told you I made it in my dorm room!" Holliday leaned forward and clapped, holding her hands in her lap, "I mean it's crazy!"

"But my roommate," she cleared her throat, "was dating this guy that worked at a bookstore or something in Lansing, East Lansing. He, apparently, when he was coming over to fuck her, was stealing my experiments and snorting them with her. Then he started selling it to a few people he knew. But, see, the thing about it is, mephedrone doesn't really get you high for all that long. It's a quick spike and then you sort of come down over about a fifteen-minute period. I have not done it, mind you. But my roommate, who shall remain nameless, came to me...or maybe it was him...or maybe both of them together, anyway, they came to me and started asking me to refer them to my buyer. They thought they had been raiding my stash and, like true junkies, didn't cop to it. They were just pissed off when it was gone. When I told them it wasn't my stash, but my experiments, they both sort of freaked out, thinking that they had been snorting some weird chemical compound, which they were in a way. But my roommate had been running this racket where she was selling her used panties online, passing them off as belonging to some underage girl. Way before that sort of thing was popular. Yeah, it was fucked up. But she and her boyfriend offered to set up a system where I would cook it, he would sell it and we would split the money fifty-fifty. To which I said, bullshit," missing her tea, she picked it up off the coffee table and held it on her stomach after she took a drink, "you're already running your own thing, there's no reason for me to split money with you. But as I was telling them this, I truly had no intentions of selling it, let alone making large enough batches to warrant anything more than experimentation. The appeal for me lied in touching science history. Here I am, some little nothing white bread Irish girl from Factoria, and I was able to successfully replicate a chemical formula first synthesized by a man almost a hundred years ago. How fucking *cool* is that?"

Holliday's big disarming smile spread across her face and filled the room. She wiggled her bare toes and let out a chuckle that echoed through the house during the lull in the storm. In many ways, she still was the girl she had described from her youth; surrounded by books on chemistry and history, the walls covered in band posters and high-quality replicas of fine art. A small original Van Gogh sneaking away at the top of the stairs to the second floor. But there was a beleaguered air about her, of a woman who had put in too many years in too short a time. Barely into her thirties, a weariness hung around her eyes and in the motions of her hands, offset only by the youthful energy of her body language, her mouth and the words that came out it.

"But that was when the school got involved. My roommate reported me to the RA. The RA reported me to the dean and less than a week later, they drag me into the dean's office and start soft soaping, then flat out interrogating me about what I had been doing in my dorm and that they had reason to believe I was a drug addict. I was scared. I was really scared, because here was this thing that I had worked so hard to get, I got this scholarship that barely got me in the door, but I was in. And now my fucking burn-out roommate and her waste of space boyfriend were going to rip it away from me. I started crying and told them that I was just making fondue," Holliday laughed the laugh that can only be had looking back on years in the rearview mirror. "They gave me a warning and took my little camp stove away. Then they made me do a piss test, which it took me a few years before I realized how fucked up that was, but I wanted to stay in, so I did it. I passed, of course. But my roommate didn't. That's when I started getting nervous." She flexed her toes a few times and gave me a look of fear and suspicion over her glass. "And it was shortly thereafter that I dropped out and went back to Factoria."

"What made you drop out?"

"That's some of the legal stuff that I'm not sure I can get into," she sat her glass of ice down on the table next to the couch and rubbed her hands together to deal with the condensation. "But suffice it to say, it was best for me that I did. The alternative wouldn't have been very good for me, in many ways. But I got back to Factoria, I'm fucking depressed. My family is disappointed in me, my friends are disappointed in me, *I'm* disappointed in me. I got this job at this athletics club in town, doing the fucking laundry. And my smartass, bacon-neck boss, this fuckin' guy from Texas with an attitude like a thirteen year-old girl, asks me one day while I'm dumping sopping wet towels in the washing machine, '*What did you learn in college, huh-huh.*' And the only thing I could think, but didn't say, was I learned to make mephedrone.

"That was when it clicked. And not in a, I know what I'm going to do with my life kind of way, but a, wouldn't it be funny *if*...kind of way. But I didn't do anything with it. I was still living at home, I'm working this slave labor job at a cut-rate, low end Y, and I'm pretty much feeling lost and alone. I still had the computer my parents bought me for college and late at night, I would go onto all of these underground chemist chatrooms and message boards and talk to people, just to not feel so alone. And this one guy is talking about setting up a sort of meet and greet type thing. In the kink community they call it a munch, where people get together out in the world and hang out and just feel less alone, kinda. But he's saying he's going to do like a theme party, you know. He has this rental space in the basement of a department store and he's going to set it up like one of those clandestine labs from the sixties. Those underground chemist labs for like the Weather Underground. And for people to bring what they're working on and sort of show off, you know? So, I had been reading about Sanchez and knew a bit about Nymphetamine and all of that, and like I said, I really wasn't about that stuff, which is why I went in costume as like this…*weird* Marie Curie ala John Waters. It was messed up. I didn't know, I seriously thought people were supposed to come in costume. And I brought these little glass dollar store vials of mephedrone. Most people there were pretty unimpressed, but there were a few people that were chem history nerds like me that thought it was really cool and we started talking about it. And to make a long story short, that was sort of the beginning of Thanks Nancy Fashions."

I casually checked the time and battery on the recorder. "How did you come up with the name?"

"I came up with that one. We all threw around a bunch of ideas, but that one that I threw out stuck. It was supposed to be a comment on what we were doing and a sort of fuck you to everyone else. You remember that whole '*Just say no*' thing Nancy Reagan did? It was sort of a sarcastic rebuttal to that, like, *Yeah, thanks, Nancy* and then the Fashions part was just a twist on designer drugs, so…That was all there was too it. And it sort of had a *Hello Nasty* type vibe to it and everyone was into that."

"And what was the point of Thanks Nancy, because that's something that hasn't really been reported on or discussed that I know of, and if it has it must have been lost in the shuffle."

Holliday leaned her head back on the couch and locked her knees together, rocking them back and forth gently,

"Thanks Nancy was just supposed to be like a club of underground chemists that wanted to do research and experimentation related to illegal and outlaw chemical compounds and formulas. None of us did drugs, none of us wanted to do drugs, we just had an interest in chemical history and wanted to try to replicate and synthesize early forms of illegal substances to see if we could do it and try to replicate and improve original experiments. Like I said before, it's that whole thing about touching history. There are these long nights and days that you spend beating your head trying to come up with or get different recipes to work and then one day there's that eureka moment and everything falls into place. Looking back on it now, I was a kid. I wanted a fast track into success and to feel like I had actually accomplished something. It was stupid, really. I was like eighteen. Nineteen, twenty? I hadn't done much with my life and I felt like a failure. So, there was something to taking other people's past failures and twisting them just enough to improve them and make them work on the first try. And there was the whole angle too of what we were doing was illegal and that made it feel dangerous and like we were way cooler than what we were. But it wasn't all drugs. There was this one guy who was obsessed with, like, mustard gas and chlorine gas, white phosphorus, napalm. All of those outlawed military chemical weapons. He even tried making a full set of rainbow pesticides, too, but I think he only made, like, three. And he was constantly looking for old recipes for Greek fire, but could never figure it out."

Holliday sat up and ran her fingers through her hair, shaking it out. She looked off into the hallway just in time to see her cat, Catalyst, pad down the stairs toward the kitchen. Catalyst looked over briefly when Holliday called to her, then turned away uninterested and kept walking.

"There was this one girl, that was part of what was left of the Cacophony Society. And she would make this Industrial Revolution-era adhesive, it was like rubber cement but worse. Way stronger with a hellacious smell."

"Was that Rose Trumble?"

"Yeah. I guess that made it into print somewhere?" she turned toward me from where she was still looking out in the hallway and spoke from under her eyebrows.

"She did an op-ed piece for Graphite a few years ago."

"Yeah, do it while I'm in prison so I can't kick your ass," she said under her breath in a pitched character voice. Holliday leaned back in the couch and adjusted, looking up at the ceiling. "But, yeah, she would take this glue out and smear it all over, like, park benches at the beach, or all over a parking lot, or glue the bathroom doors shut at bars or something like that. And then, we found out that she was stealing some of our experiments and selling them to the Cacophony Society. Did she tell you about that?"

"That she left out."

"Yeah, that's why we kicked her ass out. She was stealing

our shit and she was going to get us in trouble, because it was way too easy to trace everything back to us. We woke up to this news report one day, of an empty fast food joint that had been firebombed with homemade napalm and white phosphorus. And everyone got *really* scared. Understandably so. And we kicked her ass out. We broke up Thanks Nancy and a few of us went our separate ways. A lot of those guys I haven't seen since like '05, '06. But one day, I get a letter addressed to me at the athletic club, sent by the Cacophony Society, asking to solicit from us the materials that had been being provided to them by Rose. I took the napalm guy---"

"What was his name?"

"Not going to say," Holliday shook her head, still looking at the ceiling. "But went to a Hanrahan's and met with this dude that looked like Snidely Whiplash...and he offered to get the stuff from us in exchange for favors. We said money or nothing. He agreed and gave us a two-thousand dollar advance for three gallons of glue and a hundred nymphs of mephedrone. That's what put the ball in motion. Apparently, there were some real fuckin' old-timers that remembered actually buying Nymphetamine at strip clubs in LA back in the sixties and really got spun out on nostalgia and got a couple of other people hooked on it. After that, Thanks Nancy Fashions was a two-man operation run out of napalm guy's apartment garage. We started hustling, basically drugs and chemical weapons for the Cacophony Society for about two, two and half years. Their orders were small and we shared the recipes with each other so he knew how to make mephedrone and

I learned how to make mustard gas. It was a strange time. Part of me was a bit nervous, another part of me thought it was really cool and another part of me just felt dead and detached from everything. Like my life was a movie and I was just watching it play out from like a seat on a rollercoaster or something. Then napalm guy got this idea, he had been bobbing around on the message boards still and proposed the idea of selling our recipes online to people. I told him I wasn't comfortable with it and on top of that, they weren't really our recipes. We didn't come up with them. We just stole other people's and were just the only ones doing it anymore. I mean, he had a copy of the *Anarchist Cookbook* for Christ sakes. We were basically just tracing comic books at that point. And I guess that is what pushed me to come up with something myself."

"That was Baby's Breath?"

"Yeah," Holliday sat up on the couch and leaned forward, sitting on the edge of her seat with her hands together. "In all of the batches I had cooked, I wondered why no one had ever come up with an inhalable version of mephedrone. Or any other amphetamine or psychedelic for that matter. It didn't seem like it would be that hard. And with everything that was going on with weed vaporizers at the time…it just seemed like a no-brainer, like the next logical jump but nobody had done it. I guess a lot of people were just more interested in smoking and snorting things. And again, I can't say it enough…I'm a bad chemist," her laugh was a welcome comfort to the somber air of the room, "nothing I was doing was original or groundbreaking. And I also didn't have any interest in actually *doing* the drug. My brain had just discovered a pretzel and I wanted to un-pretzel it. So, I bought a bunch of asthma inhalers and cartridges offline and messed around for a few weeks and came up with an inhalable form of mephedrone. That became a big hit, to both my surprise and not surprise. The thing that surprised me more and really pissed me off, was I found that members of the *Cacophony Society* were selling some of this shit to people. So, we were making it for them exclusively and they were turning around and selling it to fucking junkies and bikers and gangs and shit. So that's when we cut ties with them. Stop all transactions, dropped all pending orders and just didn't make anything anymore. Which was kind of a relief, because...there's only so many clandestine labs you can set up and tear down and illegal substances you can cook in secrecy before it really starts to get old. I wasn't about it anymore, neither was my partner. We had both made, not a king's ransom, but a nice amount of money, which was way more than we ever had thought would happen and we were both just ready to hang it up. Then things really went south."

Holliday looked from the floor up at me. The light had dipped outside and we were sitting in near total darkness in her living room. The rain was still coming down and provided the only sound in the room during our silence. Holliday swayed back and forth on her knees looking at me with an intense look that I had never seen before, not even in photographs. After a few moments, she leaned over and clicked on the side table lamp.

"We were approached, again, by an organized crime outfit that shall remain nameless, to start producing again. We told them no. They told us in no uncertain terms, yes. They did something to my partner...that I still feel bad about today."

"What did they do?"

"They hurt him."

"How did they hurt him?"

"They. *Hurt*. Him." Holliday glared at me. Fearing she would stop the interview, I stopped my line of questioning.

"They paid us for our services, but they put us on an exclusive contract to cook for them and only them. Exclusive in as much as they would come after our families if we did it for anyone else. Or went to the police. Now...this is where things start getting a bit fuzzy, so you'll have to pardon me if I'm not clear on some details."

"That's fine."

"There was, quite literally, a new drug that was up and coming in Europe that I had been hearing rumblings about online for a few months. People had started whispering about it on message boards, which had now moved to the dark web. So even that had become illegal. This was also while Silk Road was still up and running. I won't tell you how I know this. But this new European designer drug, there had been reports that it wasn't really working out well for the people who took it. I contacted a chemist in Germany and conducted an exchange and got ahold of a sample of it. A few underground chemists were trying to reverse engineer this stuff to figure out what was wrong with it. It happens a lot more than you think. They usually use it as a bargaining chip to get jobs with the government or the police, even just on a contract basis. It's worked out a few times for people. But I figured out what was wrong with it and sort of...tucked that knowledge away somewhere. So, about a year or so after our reluctant alliance with organized crime, my partner and I caught word of an organization member going to Miami for an extended vacation. He put in a special order of nymphs and Baby's Breath---"

"I'm sorry to interrupt, you..."

"Yeah?"

"Uh...was it this...*organization* that gave you the nickname Nympho Nancy?"

"Yeah. That...thankfully didn't stick nearly as much as I feared it would. But, yes. If you would kindly not print that, I really don't want that coming back around for a second wave."

"That's fine."

"Off the record."

"Off the record."

"But my partner and I, we had to cram to fill this order before this person's vacation and…I don't know what happened. We must have been tired. We got sloppy. But for some reason, our recipe didn't turn out so well," Holliday shot me a look and held it. A small smirk crept onto her face in the lamplight. "And to top it all off, it was a really busy time for our associates, too. They were doing business all over the country and they were really starting to expand and get a foothold in different cities and parts of the country. And, I mean, I feel terrible about it, but I'll be damned if our batches just didn't keep turning up worse and worse. Every time we tried to make Nymphetamine we just wound up with Florida Man. It was a real shame. We thought we had lost our touch."

"And it was around this time that you and your partner's operation was discovered, is that correct?

"Yeah," Holliday sighed and clasped her hands together, looking back out into the hall, "it really was a scary time. But I think I only get scared when I look back on it. At the time it was just such a relief for everything to be over. And, I mean, prison is no fun, but at least there is some sort of structure and rules to what happens in your day. And for the most part, you don't really find trouble unless you go looking for it. I didn't go looking for it," she looked back at me, "I had had enough fun. Plus, it wasn't like I was a murderer or a child molester or anything. If anyone asked me what I was in for I just said drugs. Not really noteworthy in prison."

"I remember when I first read about your case in the paper, they were looking to charge you with twenty years for manufacturing and distributing illegal narcotics across state lines. I didn't follow your case that closely, though. What plea deal did you accept to get out in six?"

Holliday Woodlock smiled at me from the dark. Not an intimidating smile, or one of condescension. One I get all the time when a subject wishes to quietly tell me, we're done. Catalyst trotted out of the kitchen and into the living room, jumping up on Holliday's lap with a *prrt*. Woodlock nuzzled her and petted her head, talking to her in the secret language girls have with cats, before she kissed her on the head and sat her down on the couch. She stood up for the first time in several hours and asked me if I would like another iced tea. I shut off the recorder when she took my glass and walked into the kitchen. We talked for about an hour more, easily transitioning into the current Seattle music scene and upcoming shows and albums.

Finally, Catalyst came in again and began weaving through her legs. Holliday picked her up and kissed her head, using her long brown hair like a toy to brush her cat's face. Checking the clock on the microwave, I knew I had taken up enough of her time. Holliday's soft and delicate hands returned my firm handshake and her disarming smile thanked me for coming by to listen. I walked out the front door of her house somewhere around midnight and listened to the rain as it dripped off the eaves of the house that Nancy built.

The Other Side of the Fence

I don't have much to say for myself. Not that I would want to, or anyone would care to hear it at this point, but I suppose if I don't say it now, someone will just weave a yard a bullshit and print it somewhere, anyhow. The most important thing to know is that I really don't have an excuse. Aside from growing up poor, maybe. But I'm sure a lot of people would have a problem with that, too.

I was born and raised in Tennessee, about twenty minutes outside Knoxville in a town called Mascot. My parents loved me, and my siblings managed to stay sober and unimpregnated until well after high school. The only holy terror in the family, if you had to pick one, would have been me. I suppose someone, at the very least myself, should have heard the warning bells at a young age. But, most of the time, I had the uncanny ability to get into and back out of trouble faster than a reverend could slide his hand down your pants. I did my first B&E at 11 and turned it into a business venture by age 13. I hadn't owned it twenty-four hours before this kid in my neighborhood, Timmy Kerns, stole my basketball. The next day when he took off for the store with his momma, I snuck in through his bedroom window and stole it back. I also pissed in his bed and covered it up with blankets for good measure. It was pretty clear to all the other kids what I had done and slowly they started asking me to do the same for them. First my buddy Jerry. Then this girl I had a crush on who lived near my pappy named Janey Ripple. Needless to say, I went above and beyond for her (almost lost my leg to a rabid Newfoundland) and, based on my exploits, my services became more and more in demand. I decided I wasn't going to risk bodily harm and a possible stint in juvie for jackasses I didn't know if I wasn't going to get compensated for it in the end. I suppose that is where everything started to break loose. The way I look at it, I just followed the money.

You know that story Denis Leary told about the drug dealer trying to sell him the shit that killed Belushi? Well, I got the shit that killed Phillip Seymour Hoffman. No, really. I lifted a couple bags from his apartment and sold them for a nice chunk of change to a private collector in Seattle.

Every time a murder makes the news, or a celebrity dies, or someone is nationally declared missing, almost immediately there is a bounty set for their personal possessions on the internet. Everything has a price and everything will sell. From clothes to family photos, to half empty cereal boxes out of the cupboard. Usually, people are after women's underwear, sex toys, and children's bedsheets and stuffed animals. The child items sell for double the adult items. Triple if they are stained.

Last July, a girl in Indiana went missing after she went for an afternoon bike ride. Within 72 hours there was a thirty-nine item wish list with projected prices posted to the dark net site Barbary Coast. I trimmed the fat from the list and tacked on three chewed pens and a flash drive of family photos and private pictures from her laptop. The laptop was sold separately. Eight days after she went missing, she was discovered dead on some back road by a man walking his dog. As soon as the news broke, I posted the listings. My stock sold out within an hour. Barbary Coast caps all auction bids at three million. But, I do accept "tips" and "donations" through Venmo payments to an offshore account.

Since then, things had been pretty slow in national murder and missing persons cases. Except for the Mallory Winslow case. Back on Black Friday, a 15 year-old girl was abducted from her home in the middle of the night. Her parents were found shot to death the next morning, inside their car parked outside the Cinemagic in Merrimack, New Hampshire. Since that night, it had been impossible to get anywhere near that house. By the time February rolled around, prices were at an all-time high. Any longer and they were libel to drop as people started to lose interest. I had to move and fast.

I got in touch with a police dispatcher in Merrimack. I knew him from Barbary Coast as "ch0wderhead" from where I had hooked him up with the full lingere set of an O.D.'d porn star a few years prior. I went back and forth with him for a bit, then he agreed to do me a solid. So, I made a reservation, packed up my bags and mailed them to the Doyle Inn Merrimack before hopping the first flight to New Hampshire.

But when I got there, the Doyle in was closed for renovations. I was stuck in my rental car for over an hour arguing with my third-party booker before they told me my reservation had been transferred to the Holiday Inn Express, along with my luggage. That night, I checked in, made a sweep of the town and worked out my route. The driveway was roped off in police tape, but there was only one cattle car posted outside. I usually liked to have more time to think things through, but I was in a race against the clock. There was this little sushi joint in a strip mall not too far from the hotel and I decided that would be my reward after I finished the job. Drop in for some sushi, then book town bright and early.

The next morning, I stripped down my kit to just what I would need and a few just-in-case's and drove to my getaway location to wait. The Winslow house was in a cul-de-sac on Sawmill Lane. I pulled off the side of the road at a clearing and parked the car near the edge of the woods. I threw a cargo net over the back for camouflage and waited. Sitting there in the car, I realized I had forgotten my mask in Knoxville. I tried to work out something by tucking my nose in my shirt, but finally said screw it. At 10:15, a call went out over the scanner for all units to report to a suspected shooting at the elementary school on the other side of town. It was supposed to be an active shooter, but I guess old chowderhead chickened out and lived up to his name. I listened for the siren chirp to fade in the distance, then I made my move.

I cut through the woods and made my way to the back of the house. It was cold and the snow had melted, but the whole place was a mud slick. After I passed through the back yard, I dropped my boots in a garbage bag at the edge of the rear patio and slid on a pair of no-soles before I cracked the lock on the rear sliding glass door. The alarm didn't go off, which didn't surprise me too much. The place was still an active crime scene. I figured I had about an hour or so before my piggy friend would join me again. As long as I kept quiet, and didn't make some rookie mistake like run out the front door, he wouldn't have caught me anyhow. But I don't like cops and the less time spent around them, the better.

I cut through the kitchen at the back of the house, through the main hall and up the stairs to Mallory's bedroom. Her door was open, but with police tape criss-crossed over it. I Catherine Zeta-Jones'd my way through it, pulled out the list. Three pairs panties, current bedsheets, diary and a chewed pen from her dresser. I took a quick dig through her nightstand and found her vibrator and a small bottle of lube, half empty. I snatched the most well-worn stuffed animal from her bed, then ran down the hall for her toothbrush. Just as I stepped out of the bathroom, this ear-stabbing, shrieking alarm started going off. I instinctively dropped my duffle and got on my knees, hands behind my head. Finally, it occurred to me it was the smoke detector. For my own safety, I reached up and turned it off, then went back to work. At least I was the only one around to see it happen.

I skipped down the hall to the parent's room. My run in with the alarm made me jumpy and by that point, all I wanted to do was get out of there and fast. I checked the bounty again and snatched the mother's hairbrush, lipstick, two sets of matching bras and panties and a pair of expensive looking shoes. There was a request for the current book from her nightstand, which I grabbed at the same time I found her cell-phone charger. Now, I know next to dick about jewelry, but I sure have stolen a shit ton of it over my career. My saving grace was the fact that the necklace and earrings that were requested had been shown in the photo that the news had been flashing of the mom and her husband at a family reunion the previous summer. It took a bit to dig them up, but I found them. I knew that even if they didn't sell in a lot, I would be able to hock them somewhere. Hopefully, at least reimburse me for my airfare. There were four pre-rolled joints and about an ounce of weed in the underwear drawer and I threw them in with the stash. (A thankyou gift to the dispatcher. There was no way I was gonna ship that shit across state lines.) No one had shown any interest in any of the father's shit and my jump scare didn't have me feeling too good about dicking around to look, so I did one last once over of the list and went downstairs.

Thankfully, I hadn't cracked the lock on the sliding doors (like I did this one time) and stopped on the back patio to switch to boots before I headed off for the woods. It was around that time, that I got that eerie sense that someone was watching me. I slowed down tying my boots, but never stopped, and did my best to be casual about looking around. I didn't see anyone. I hadn't heard any cars. My finger itched to check the scanner on my phone, but I didn't feel like hanging around any longer and high-tailed it back to the car.

When I got back to the hotel room, I sat down on the bed and crashed for about three hours. I hadn't even changed out of my gear. Sometimes, you don't even know how stressful a job is until you get out on the other side of it. After I got scrubbed up, I spent the rest of the afternoon posting the listings to Barbary Coast. The sales drug ass a little bit but sold out in about two hours. Once the last lot was marked as sold, then I took off for the sushi joint around seven o'clock.

Maybe because it was February, maybe because it was Tuesday, I don't know what the reason was, but the place was packed. Thankfully, just as I stepped in a couple cleared out and I got a place at the bar. The food was better than I had expected, and I actually got into the crowd for a little bit there. No one knew who I was, or what I had gotten away with that afternoon.

Until the eight o'clock news came on. Lead story that night, Mallory Winslow had been found. She had managed to escape her captors and was discovered walking down the middle of the road in some neighborhood called Montpelier upstate. Unharmed, but frail and a bit dazed. If I had been chewing at the time, my food would have hit the table. The story of Mallory's return dovetailed nicely into the story about my B&E. And I learned who had been watching me. Turns out, the family had one of those new home security systems installed that looks like a doorbell, posted in the front and back of the house. And guess who was shown, full face on the evening news breaking into, then leisurely tying their boots on the back patio of the poor Winslow girl's house. I don't think anyone was watching, but I did get a lot of weird stares on my way out the door. Or it could have been because my phone was going off like a slot machine. I had a lot of unhappy customers that wanted immediate refunds.

Thrill Seekers Wanted

Coming out of the Isles in East Fort Lauderdale, for a time there was a sign stamped into the ground near the intersection of South Gordon Road and East Las Olas Boulevard. A plastic sign shoved into the grass with a wire H-frame. Harold Rocksmith was on his way to work when he saw it, picking his breakfast out of his teeth with a sterling silver toothpick he kept in the glovebox of the Mercedes for such an occasion. His wife, Debbie, couldn't stand the sound of his fingers in his mouth. The sign caught his eye and he did his best to remember the phone number. Harold had a track record of positive omens and good fortune throughout his life. It was just uncommon they occurred this early in the morning.

That night on his ride home, Harold had a notebook ready on the seat next to him and copied down the number. Later, over dinner he slipped the note to Debbie. She was just as excited as he was. After that, there was little other to talk about between the two of them than the sign.

Debbie nibbled her French manicure as she sat on their brand new white leather couch and glanced from the phone, to Harold, and back. Harold stood in the door to the living room, beer can in a company coozy, smiling at Debbie, his right hand jammed deep in his pocket. Debbie smiled nervously behind her blonde Farrah Fawcett hair and watched Harold with slow eyes as the phone rang in her ear. An answering machine took the call, a nice sounding young man was the voice of the prerecorded message.

"This is Cole, I cannot come to the phone right now, but if you are calling about my sign, I wish I could. Please leave your name and number and the best time to call, and I will get back to you. Very, very soon."

Debbie laid it on thick. Harold stopped drinking and focused on the hand in his pocket. When she hung up the phone, he drained his beer and left the can and coozy on top of the cable box on the Panasonic. Coast Guards patrolling off the shore of Alice Town in the Bimini Islands could hear the Rocksmiths that night.

The next day, Debbie called Harold during his lunch hour to report they had received a callback. Harold closed the door to his office and listened as she whispered him the news. They were to meet the man called Cole at the Hanrahan's bar of the Doyle Inn & Suites in town that night. Harold told her not to wear panties. Debbie told him she was ten steps ahead of him. He stopped at home after work and changed into a clean baby blue Polo, reapplied his English Leather and swapped out his khakis for off white beach slacks. Debbie finished applying her makeup and teased Harold that, in her sundress and pearls, he was wearing more clothes than she was.

The Rocksmiths floored it into town. Weaving through traffic with the top down, laughing at the horns of pissed off drivers. Debbie placed Harold's right hand between her legs and he dropped his foot on the gas. They got to the Hanrahan's bar twenty minutes ahead of schedule. Debbie started drinking screwdrivers to get into the mood. Harold pressed his back against the bar and looked across the room, out the bank of windows onto the street. The man they were meeting was supposed to be in a pink and black striped polo with blond hair.

"Can I buy you a drink, miss?" A man slid up next to Debbie and pressed into her. She recognized the voice immediately.

"Cole?" She said slyly.

"None other." The young man took Debbie's hand and kissed it before offering Harold a shake. The party was underway and the Rocksmiths had no idea what to say.

"You guys already started without me, I see," Cole chuckled, brushing his feathered hair back out of his face.

"You've got a lot of catching up to do, my friend," Harold gave the man a wide fatherly grin. "What are you having?"

"Oh, just club soda for me," Cole held up his hand and laughed, "I'm the designated driver tonight."

"Oh?" Debbie felt a bit stung. He hadn't mentioned coming with anyone. "Did you bring your girlfriend, your wife?"

"Nothing like that," Cole had a smile that never stopped, and Debbie never wanted to stop looking at, "I just drove myself. My girlfriend had to stay late for work."

Harold adjusted his belt, "I can't wait to meet her."

Debbie held her straw between her teeth and gave Harold an unapproving smile before edging closer to Cole. The young man grinned and wrapped his arm around the woman almost old enough to be his mother and began stroking her bare freckled arm with his thumb. If Harold had had a cigar, he would have puffed it.

The rest of their conversation proceeded in the same tone. Debbie flirtatious as a pubescent girl, Cole an obliging heart-throb and Harold playing the role of father and chaperone. Over time, however, it became obvious to Cole, faster than it did to Harold, that all Debbie was looking for was flirtation. She just wanted to be idolized and fought over and nothing more than that. It didn't stop Cole from sneaking a few kisses and letting his hands wander to places inappropriate to touch anywhere outside of private quarters. Debbie got what she wanted, while Harold was counting on their next excursion to get his.

The three parted ways a little after eleven thirty, Cole helping Harold walk a stumbling Debbie to the convertible. They talked briefly at her window about their next meeting and shook hands. Debbie clumsily kissed Cole's arm and smeared what was left of her lipstick on his wrist. Cole passed a note, before Harold and his wife sped off into the night, leaving him to wave from the summer-busy sidewalk.

It was a blur for the Rocksmiths until the weekend. Debbie nursed a hangover for most of the next day, then set to planning her outfits for their weekend with Cole. Harold touched up his John Oates mustache and perm, but did little else. His wife, among other women, idolized him as the pinnacle of masculinity, he could see no room for improvement. On Friday night, they watered the plants, took out the trash, and locked the house for a long weekend. They told their neighbors they were going to Key Largo for a few days and to watch for mail and prowlers.

In reality, they traveled an hour and a half north from their Idlewyld home to the South Star Motel in Belle Glade. The town and the motel made Harold a bit uneasy, he was always happier in high-class hotels, but the seediness of it all did nothing but excite Debbie. After her head in his lap going down US-27, Harold would have accepted a dog kennel, as long as her mood would maintain.

They rolled into the parking lot when there was still light, but it was fading fast. The a/c portion of the neon sign out front flickered. Harold rolled his eyes and felt his stomach turn. Debbie commented on how wet she was. Cole answered the door of number 8, holding out chilled Seagram's wine coolers for everyone with his big college smile. Harold carried the bags into the room, annoyed at how small their quarters were. Debbie asked which bed was Cole's, he told her whichever one she was in. She ran to the far bed at the back of the room and dove onto it like a little girl. Harold asked about Cole's girlfriend. He said she wasn't able to make it, but she did send something along. Harold became furious, but remembered Debbie's attitude in the car and commenced to getting drunk. His temper cooled out quickly thereafter.

Several drinks later and the Rocksmiths were into it. Debbie was on top of Cole in the bed, her hands, that were only just beginning to show veins and age spots, climbed up and down his chest, as she looked over her shoulder at her husband in the corner. Cole pulled himself up into a sitting position against the wall, under the fire sprinkler, and held Debbie by the chin, propositioning her for a blowjob. Debbie looked over at her husband, who was pink faced and drooling with a smile. She stared him in the eye as she took Cole into her mouth, who began talking casually.

"What do you do for work, Harry?"

"Tele---," he cleared his throat, "Telecommunications engineer."

"No kidding?" Cole chuckled, "Wow. I've never met anyone who's done that before. What's your company?"

"Crystal Communications," Harold's red eyes were beginning to leak as he smiled at his wife.

"Huh," Cole looked straight ahead at the curtains in the closed window. "I've never heard of them."

"They were started," Harold cleared his throat again and sucked the alcohol out of his mustache, "by Barry Anslow. He was the chief electrical engineer for the...Disnee...the Dinsee property."

"You helped build Dinsee World?" Cole asked in a sarcastic tone with a wide smile.

"Well...sort of," Harold struggled to set his bottle down on the television, but it slid off and spilled on the floor.

"Do you like that?" Debbie smirked up at Cole.

Cole glanced down at Debbie, "Shut up." He wrapped his legs around her back and locked his ankles together. She squealed.

"We, uh," Harold watched the last splashes of Mango wine cooler spill out onto the carpet, "we just finished a big bid with   the   uh...Dinsey...working   on...Ipclot, err...Ep...uhm...Epcut."

"Huh." Cole stared at Harold deep in thought. "Small world." He looked down at the woman in his lap and pulled her away by her hair, as he reached into his pocket with the other.

"Hold on, baby," she moaned, spit dripping down her chin. More from the alcohol than anything else. "I was just getting started."

Cole took a three-inch-long glass test tube topped with a rubber cap out of his pocket. Even through his drunken state, Harold could see it was full of liquid. The young man tipped back the housewife's head and poured some of the contents in her mouth.

"Don't," Cole said sternly, staring into her glazed eyes, "swallow."

Debbie returned to her work, smiling at being told what to do. Cole dropped the vial on the bed and turned back to Harold, who was pulling out his cock. The young man paid no mind and turned back to the woman in his lap.

"What've you got coming up next there, Harry?"

"Hm?" Harold was doing too many things at once to carry on a conversation.

"At work," Cole looked at him, "You said you were just finishing up Epclot or whatever."

"Umm," Harold licked his lips and ran his tongue through

his mustache, "Didney is looking to uhh...they wanna make a channel station...for kids...you know."

"A tv channel for kids?" Cole was incredulous. "No."

"That's what they say," Harold sweated, "What's in the bottle?

"Oh, this?" Cole held up the vial, then turned back to Debbie, "My girlfriend couldn't be here, so she gave me some spit for me to use when we play. Teeth." He grabbed Debbie by the head and held her in place. "*Teeth. Teeth.*"

Harold rocked forward in his seat and grabbed at the vial with one hand. Cole looked at him like Secret Service spotting a rooftop gunman. He yanked the vial away and threw it on the pillows on the far side of the bed.

"What are you doing?"

"I wanna use...s-some," Harold couldn't understand, "I'm dry over here."

"I don't care," Cole shook his head.

"Now, look," Harold stood up and his pants began sliding down to his thighs.

"No, look here," Cole pulled a .9mm from under the pillows and aimed at Harold, "I said, *no*."

"Wait. Wait a minute." Harold held up his hands as a knee jerk reaction.

By then Debbie sensed the change in the room and looked up at Cole. Seeing the gun in his hand, she pulled back away from him, letting out a quick inebriated scream.

"I don't remember telling you to stop," Cole pointed the gun at her face, still staring at Harold.

Instantly, the tears came. Debbie looked from the gun to her husband. Her face crunched, she shook her head, tears streaming, but she made no motion to move. Harold wasn't quick enough to look at her, and as far as he figured, she was on her own.

"Get. Back." Cole looked Debbie in the face and pressed the gun to her forehead. "Or I'll put something else in your mouth."

Harold finally found his spine and let out a sound like a high school football coach.

"Whose got a gun to whose wife here?" Cole cocked the pistol, still staring down Harold.

Debbie shook her head at her husband before dropping her head into her hands, sobbing. Harold stood in flaccid silence, his socks soaking up spilled wine cooler. Cole grabbed

Debbie by the back of the head and pulled her toward him, the gun still pressed into her forehead. "And not just those kisses you were blowing before." All the youth and vivaciousness had fallen from Cole's face. He still looked like a young man, but one that had seen war and the hardships of life.

Debbie's cries were muffled in his lap, "You--- b---."

He pulled the gun away long enough to conduct Harold back to his seat, then returned it to her head. "I want a long, glowing love letter your mother would be proud of." Debbie's shoulders shook as he pressed her head deep into his lap.

Harold stared at Cole, his drunk too strong to shake off. He adjusted in his seat and felt the sweat of his shirt peel and rip against the Naugahyde as he turned. The box air conditioner in the window kicked on, but did nothing to chill the room.

"So, tell me, Harry," Cole stroked the gun he held to Debbie's head, "If you were to be found, dead, alongside your wife, in a Belle Glade roach motel, obvious evidence of a three-way tryst, do you think that would be very becoming of an employee who works providing television programming for children?"

"No." Harold slurred, coldly.

"No. Ok," Cole rocked his head back, leaning on the wall

and looking up at the ceiling. Seconds later, he turned back. "Then why take the risk?"

Harold said nothing. Debbie's sobs pitched. Cole reminded her about the gun.

"I mean, I was just thinking, when I first got your guys' call, and when we met at the bar, you seemed real gung-ho about this whole thing. Like you'd done it a few times. And now here, to find out what you do for a living...help me out here. The two just don't seem to mesh."

"No." Harold admitted, "they don't. But everyone has their dark side. We," he nodded towards his wife, "Debbie and I, we explore ours together. The way normal people do."

"Normal people?" The youthful vitality returned to Cole's face. "You're letting your wife blow a stranger at gun point in some shitty motel. Does that sound normal to you?"

"I'm not letting her." Harold tried to growl around his slur, "You're raping her."

"And you're doing a damn fine job of stopping me, too." Cole ripped Debbie away from his lap and kicked her in the chest towards the opposite bed, before walking over to Harold. "See, this is what I can't *stand* about you people. You're so quick to point the finger at others, but you don't do a shittin' thing to change it. She's your wife! Act like it!"

Debbie sobbed in the corner. Harold watched as she climbed to her knees and began crawling towards Cole. He tried to direct her to the bottle on the floor, but broadcasted with his eyes loud enough for China to hear.

"What? This shit?" Cole looked down at the bottle and kicked it away. Before he could turn back to Harold, Debbie had clutched onto his leg.

"Please," she cried, "You're...*beautiful*. Take me with you."

Cole slowly turned toward Harold, then cut his eyes to look at the sobbing woman on his leg.

"I have---never," Debbie said between gasps for air, "met a man, who's as much of a man---as you---in---my---*life*. You're *beautiful*. I love you. And I will always love you...forever. Please---don't---leave---me---with---*him*."

"What the fuck kind of household are you running, Harry?"

Harold sank into his chair, his pants still unbuttoned and exposed. Debbie pressed her face into Cole's leg, smearing her makeup. The room stood in silence for a moment, like a twisted moment in a Tennessee Williams play. Harold thought about his job and seeing the sign on his way into work. All of the young women he had helped move up the ladder. All the college-aged secretaries and summer interns. He thought about his wife and how all their gettogethers had been at her suggestion. She always wanted these more than him. He was content to plow the copy girl in the downstairs storage room on lunchbreaks. It wasn't an impossible situation to get out of, he just wished it had never come to this.

"*Hello?*" Cole snapped his fingers, "Earth to Andy fucking Capp!"

"Take her," Harold shrugged, fumbling to zip up his pants. "Take the car, too, I don't give a shit. I'll mail you the papers." He was stopped in standing up with a sharp crack to the face.

"What the fuck makes you think I came here looking to shack up?" Cole pressed the gun between his eyes. "I *kill* people, asshole. This is fun to me."

Harold looked up at Cole from the chair, his vision distorted by the pressure between his eyes.

"And you're fucking dumber than I took you for in the first place," he shook the leg Debbie had glued herself to, "and she's crazier. You two are a fucking pair and a half, I swear to god."

"What if you let us go?" Harold bargained.

"Why?" The youthfulness only returned to Cole's face when he laughed.

"You've proven your point, alright? We get it. We have a lot of things to work out between us. But there's no reason to kill us. We won't tell anyone…and you can just let us live."

Cole grabbed Harold by the back of the neck and squeezed, shoving the gun in his mouth. "You still don't fucking get it, asshole. You and this little wife of yours are *going to die*. This isn't some business opportunity you can bargain yourself out of. This isn't Aesop's Fables. And it sure as shit ain't the god damn Twilight Zone. I don't *like* you. You people are scum to me. You don't have a snowball's chance in hell of walking out of this room alive. Your wife, ditto. You think you can sit in judgement of me for who I am and what I do and then go back to making rat cartoons for kids? Uh-uh. Your ass brought you here, which makes *you* no better than *me*. You could have stayed home, fucked your wife and counted your Disnee Dollars, but no. You like to pretend you're something you're not. And I like to use people like you, to remind the other villagers that there are dark and scary things out in the woods. And if you want to run with the wolves, you better not be a fucking sheep."

Cole stepped back from Harold, pulling the gun out of his mouth, and lifted Debbie to her feet. He barely had to indicate, and she began kissing and licking his face as if it were the Fountain of Youth. The gun was kept level at Harold's eyes as Cole returned Debbie's affection like a starving man. After a minute or two, he pulled back and spit in her face. She begged him to continue, reassuring him that he could do anything he wanted. Hit her, anything, just take her away from her life.

Harold sank deeper into his chair. He watched for hours as Cole violated his wife, never fully convinced he wouldn't survive and be fucking his secretary within the week. When dawn broke, he didn't think about it anymore. Or anything else, for that matter, Cole put a pillow over his face and fired a round into his head after he nodded off. Harold never even made an attempt to run.

Debbie never heard a thing, either. She passed out at some point, too, but Cole didn't stop until he was finished. Once he had, he shook her awake with his foot on her face. She looked up at him with eager doll eyes and reached out for him. Cole pressed the barrel to her cheek and told her to spit, holding the vial to her mouth. Debbie let out a sigh of pleasure when she felt the steel and happily obliged.

"You never asked for a divorce, did you?" Cole seethed.

Debbie looked up at him with hurt puppy dog eyes, her face pressed to the bed, and shook her head.

"Are you afraid?"

"Uh-uh."

"Does he hurt you?"

"Uh-uh," she cleared saliva from her lips, "he barely touches me."

"Then why do you stay with him?"

"Because he has money," she smiled, "and I get to meet guys like you anyway."

Cole saw that the vial was nowhere near full and pressed it to her lips. "You do realize that makes no sense at all."

"The notches in my Tiffany bedpost say otherwise." The woman Cole always knew he was dealing with finally appeared.

"You are the most disgusting thing I've ever stuck my dick inside of." Cole spoke plainly, his eyebrow raised and nodding.

Debbie moved to get up from the bed, "I've got a lot more tricks up my sleeve."

"No, you don't," Cole shook his head. "You've been married to *that* guy for how many years and you're trying to tell me you're some kind of French courtesan? Bullshit." He pressed her back down to the bed with the barrel to her cheek. "I'm more concerned with the *spit* in your *mouth*."

Debbie smirked the whole way back down to the mattress, until she saw the powder burns on the pillow over Harold's face. Only then, did she really start crying.

"You killed him?" Her face flushed and tears slid sideways down her face. "Oh my god, why did you kill him?"

"Spit."

"What are we going to do? I was going to leave with you! You didn't have to kill him."

"I said," Cole pressed the gun past her lips to the back of her throat, "spit."

Debbie gagged and choked, saliva flowing from her mouth in thick gobs of foam. Cole slid the vial around on the sheets, collecting as much as he could. He held the tube up to the early morning light streaming through the crack between the curtains and saw a tinge of pink floating in the bubbles.

"I got more out of you than I thought I would."

Debbie burst into tears. Not of a woman in fear, of a child used to getting its way. Cole ushered things along and called it quits when the vial was three quarters full. His ears couldn't take the whining.

He hung the *Do Not Disturb* sign on the door and took the Mercedes north towards Tampa and beyond. It was three days before the Rocksmiths' bodies were discovered by a maid. By then, the man name Cole was long gone.

A new sign was stapled to a telephone pole in Galveston.

LOV[E] + Life

Scott Murphy was having a hard time with his bag as he walked through the parking lot of the Bedford Hills Correctional Facility. He thought that after all these interviews he would have had his system down pat, but there wasn't anything that was going down without a fight that day. He hoped his subject wouldn't be the same. Cassie Grunwald had seemed aloof and, at times, antagonistic in the interviews he had seen with her. He had dealt with both before, but he would also take a pass on both if he could.

The guard searched his bag at sign-in. They left him his pen, notebook and recorder, keeping the bag and the rest of its contents there. He had to fight to get that much, even after he showed them his Princeton student ID.

Scott had planned out his senior thesis before he graduated high school. He was going to interview women convicted of violent crimes, then do a detailed analysis of what unified them all. Little to no legitimate scholarly documents had been written on the subject at the time of his graduation. Since then, there had been several half-assed tv shows and documentaries on the subject, but nothing of real substance. It wasn't a topic he had a profound amount of interest in, but it was an angle he didn't see anyone else exploring. And until recently, he thought he was surefire destined for greatness, before a girl in his class changed her thesis to *Grief, Mourning and Obsession in World Entertainment Media*, based on her real-life connection to the Moretti-Campione tragedy a few years back. As soon as she announced the change of her senior thesis topic, Scott felt sunk. He needed to do something real flashy and groundbreaking to get his professors' attention and garner the grants and praise he was looking for. He just didn't know what it was yet.

As the guard was walking him to a visitation booth, Scott realized his questionnaire was in his bag at sign-in. Then he remembered the copy he had folded into his jacket pocket back at his dorm and breathed easy. He was still setting up when another guard walked Cassie over to her side of the glass. She picked up the phone and stared at Scott. Not menacing, but definitely not inviting, either.

Scott absently picked up his phone and spoke as he flipped through his notebook. "Thank you for agreeing to meet with me, Ms. Grunwald."

"What's your name again?" Cassie's voice had a natural purr, but her tone was stand-offish.

"Scott," he picked up his wallet off the ledge and held his student ID to the glass, "Murphy."

"That's right," she remembered, "College boy."

"That's me," Scott had gotten used to this treatment and let it roll off his back. He looked up from his notebook and at Cassie for the first time.

She was cuter in person, which he didn't expect, and easily twenty years younger than all his other subjects, which he already knew. Since she had been incarcerated, Cassie had been forced to start wearing large, thick, horn-rimmed men's glasses, instead of her usual contacts. Her jaw length bob of strawberry blonde had grown to shoulder length and was permanently tied up in a bun. She had been raked over the coals by the media and people online for being ugly. Scott felt that was beside the point. Sitting face to face with her now, he was inclined to disagree.

"Well...*Scott*," Cassie didn't move, but something in her behavior changed, "what do you want to know?"

"I was hoping to get a bit more of your side of the story," Scott rolled into his routine, "I'm not looking for any specific angle and I'm not gonna spin your story into some news article. I just want to hear the case from your point of view, front to back, as much as you are willing to share." He continued, "I know it's a lot and we don't have to dive into everything right off the bat, but that's my main goal with our conversations. The truth. As best and as much as you can remember it. From your side."

A smirk crept across Cassie's face as he spoke, "You've practiced that a lot haven't you?"

"I've said it a few times," Scott decided to go with truth. If this interview was going to be a bust, he needed to know as soon as possible, so he could cut bait and find a new subject. Her difference in age, and the details of her case would help flesh out his paper and not make it so lopsided and one note. It would also make it more relevant, due to how recently it had been in the news. But if his subject was just going to jerk him around, he had better things to do on a Saturday.

"Who else have you interviewed?" her delivery was comfortably interrogational.

"That's confidential."

"Confidential? I thought you were writing some essay, not a New York Times article."

"That's why it's confidential," Scott said plainly, "News outlets must disclose who they are writing for and subjects they've interviewed, if they have agreed to be on the record. This is a scholarly publication---"

"Scholarly, now," Cassie mocked.

"---so, all subjects remain confidential during the interview process, until the time of publication."

Cassie squinted her eyes and fought a smile, "Why does this sound like bullshit?"

For the first time, Scott noticed the Midwest lilt in her voice. He had also been caught. She was smarter than he originally took her for. "Because it is," he couldn't fight the laugh, "It's not entirely wrong, but it's by no means a rule. It's just my personal preference. Subjects know only that they are interviewed, no one else. I don't want to instill any sense of competition. I will tell you all other subjects are women who have been convicted and incarcerated for violent crimes and that's all."

"So, I'm a subject now." Cassie's tone had officially shifted from antagonistic, to teasing, "An interview subject in a scholarly publication. If my father could see me now..."

Scott knew her father was a touchy subject. He had molested Cassie as a child and beat her mother and older brother, forcing them to move across country from Cheyenne, Wyoming to live with Cassie's maternal aunt in Wyoming, New York. (Wyoming, as it had been noted ad-nauseum in the media, is located in western New York state, only 16 miles east of Attica Correctional Facility and 5 miles south of the defunct Rolling Hills Sanitarium. Neither of which had any bearing on Cassie's case, but the news outlets loved saying it.) Scott made a mental note of her comment, but ultimately took it as turn of phrase and let it slide. "That's right."

"I could get a degree, you know," Cassie spoke in a way

that reminded Scott of girl's he went to middle school with. "What's your major?"

"Psychology."

"Wouldn't that be funny? A girl in prison for a murder she didn't commit with a degree in psychology she got while she was locked up. Earned off the state's dime no less. If that's not poetic justice, I don't know what is. Maybe I should go for a law degree," Cassie looked off into the distance and tucked her tongue into the corner of her bottom lip as she thought.

"Did you have any college aspirations when you were in school?" Scott asked as nonchalantly as he could.

"Are we starting the interview, or are you asking out of curiosity?"

Scott plugged a cord into the microphone jack next to the phone and hit the button on the recorder, "Maybe a little bit of both."

"Can I ask you something?" Cassie leaned into the glass, her arms folded across her chest, propped up on her elbows.

"Sure."

"Does this get you off?"

Scott said nothing, but his reaction was enough.

"Because, ever since I got your letter I've been wondering why some college boy like you would be running around to prisons interviewing female murderers and convicts. That whole thesis thing is just bullshit, right? This gets you off." Cassie held the receiver closer to her mouth and talked huskily into it, "You record your meetings so you can listen to them at night...take out your cock and dream what it would be like to fuck one of them... Tell me I'm wrong."

"You're wrong."

"That was quick," Cassie raised an eyebrow.

"The truth usually is," Scott's face had gone hard. He was rapidly losing interest in the interview.

"Burn," Cassie sat back on her stool and unfolded her arms. "That was a pretty solid burn, college boy."

"If you're not interested in doing the interview, we can stop right now." Scott gripped the mic jack and glared at her through the glass.

Cassie stared at Scott's hand on the jack, holding her mouth open as if she were about to speak. Her green eyes searched for a quick answer as she twisted her finger around the metal phone cord. "Maybe it would be best if we did," she panned her eyes to look at Scott.

Scott immediately pulled the jack out of the wall and pressed stop on the recorder. He was ready to be gone.

Cassie talked over the shuffle as Scott put his things in order, "Sorry to make you come all this way. I'm just not up to it today. Red tide," she tucked her chin and looked up at Scott, "You understand."

"Thank you for your time," Scott spoke without looking at her and hung up the phone. Cassie was still sitting when he gathered up his things and walked to the guard at the door.

He spent the rest of the week forgetting about Cassie Grunwald and searching news articles for women who had committed murder. All he could find were stories on Snowden, Ariel Castro and Flight 363, which didn't do him any good. When he conceived the idea for his thesis, he never thought that he would actively be hoping for someone to be murdered just to maintain his GPA.

Tuesday of that week, he was sitting in a morning lecture when his phone started to buzz. He didn't recognize the number and declined the call. After class, he saw they had left a voicemail. He included the transcript in his thesis:

"Hey, Scott, it's Cassie. Um...I was thinking about you. [laughs] Well, I was thinking about your interview and...I know I was sort of rude to you and we didn't get to talk much about my case. And I kinda feel bad about it and I kinda feel like I wasted your time, so...I know you kinda left in a rush and

I don't know if you were wanting to come back up or not, but...If you want to...You can come at me a little harder... I'll answer whatever questions you have. I'm sorry I was mean to you before. You're good people. You're not like those reporter assholes. I trust you...Anyway, I hope to see you around. By-e!"

The decision to go back to Bedford Hills was not an easy one. Scott spent most of the week with his head in his hands, kicking around whether or not to go through with it. But his thesis, his graduation, hung in the balance. That was the sole spark that took him two and a half hours into upstate New York for the second weekend in a row. Friday at noon he made the appointment and left early Saturday morning.

Cassie was in much better spirits this time around. They managed to get an open meeting space in a mess hall (at Scott's insistence, hoping the more open environment would make her feel less hostile, something he had learned from previous interviews) and Cassie greeted him with open arms, like classmates at a high school reunion. They talked for about fifteen minutes, off the record but on mic, about childhood, school and growing up. Cassie frequently referenced missing Wyoming, saying: "What's the point of being in New York if you're locked up?"

She also introduced Scott to several new articles of prison slang, most notably *zoom-zooms* and *brake fluid. Zoom-zooms* being any sort of pastry, snack cake or baked good and *brake fluid* being drugs such as thorazine that are administered by staff to "chill out" unruly inmates. Scott had been deeply entrenched in prison slang for the last couple of years, it being almost a pre-requisite to communicate with inmates. However, the older inmates he had been interviewing, mostly stuck and referred to more legal and day to day slang regarding parole, sentences and sections of the prison. Cassie, being younger, was dialed into a much different part of prison life, with a more childish outlook on values, points of note, and interest. This caught Scott off guard at first, until he put two and two together; Cassie was a kid.

Cassie Grunwald was arrested in 2009 at the age of seventeen for the murder of her boyfriend, Luther "Buck" Smithson. She was convicted in 2011, at nineteen, and started serving her life-sentence at "the same prison as the Long Island Lolita". Now, two years later, she spent her twenty-first birthday in prison and was talking to a college student two years her senior about how to make desserts in your cell using mashed up lunch cakes and non-dairy creamer. At the beginning of their second session, the person Scott had met during their first interview was a distant memory. It also seemed hard to imagine a girl that reminded him of one of his classmates had stabbed a guy twenty-eight times in the chest with a hunting knife. But she had.

On the evening of Tuesday May 12th, 2009, Buck Smithson, 22, came over to Grunwald's Wyoming, New York house at around 8:15 PM. The only two people home were Cassie and her brother Chris, then 19. Their mother, Valerie Grunwald, 42, was working at the Dollar General six miles away in Pavilion. Somewhere around ten o'clock, Chris left for a friend's house, leaving Cassie and Buck in the house alone. At 10:37 PM, Cassie sent Chris a text message asking him to come back to help her "clean up a mess" she had made in the kitchen. Chris returned a little after 11:00 to find Buck stabbed to death on the kitchen floor, a knife stuck in his neck, his left hand partially severed and his genitals sliced from his body. Cassie was nowhere to be found. Rather than call the police, Chris called Cassie. Their phone call lasted only nine minutes and they did not contact each other by phone or text until almost an hour later. In the meantime, Chris Grunwald wrapped up Luther Smithson's body in a painter's drop cloth and buried him in the back yard, under the floorboards in the shed. Somewhere during this time, Cassie came home and helped clean up the kitchen before their mother returned. Little did they know, their mother would not return until late the following morning, having gone over to the house of her boyfriend, Tim Lawrence, after her shift. Buck Smithson was not reported missing for two weeks. After that, it was short work for the police to find his body and the evidence of who murdered him. The Grunwald siblings had burned their clothes on the charcoal grill in the backyard. Cassie maintained that she had nothing to do with Smithson's murder. She said she stormed out of the house after the two had a fight and went for a walk to clear her head. She claimed the mess she referred to in her text to Chris was a bottle of Jack Daniels that had been smashed during their argument. She said that she was anemic and feared picking up broken glass. Medical records confirmed her anemia, but there was no evidence of broken glass anywhere in the house. Chris Grunwald pled guilty to assisted manslaughter and received fifteen years incarceration and five years parole. Cassie pled not guilty to first degree murder. She will die in prison.

All of this rushed through Scott's head as he watched Cassie laugh and reminisce about growing up in Cheyenne. She talked about a pet hamster she had for a brief period of time, named Toby, and cooking with her grandmother. Scott steered the conversation in the direction of her crime and Cassie followed amicably. Her story remained the same. The Jack Daniels bottle, the argument with her boyfriend, and a story she didn't tell until she was on trial, that her brother killed Smithson when he came home during her walk. Scott listened dutifully, but he still didn't believe a word of it. He did, however, feel bad for Cassie. When he spoke, her green eyes listened intently. When she spoke, her gaze never strayed. Scott breathed a quiet sigh of relief that Cassie had agreed to speak and, in turn, saved his paper. But he was a bit crestfallen when he had to leave.

Scott returned to his dorm that night and began transcribing and shaping Cassie's portion of the paper. He didn't go back to Bedford Hills, but he did make a few phone calls to clear up and elaborate a few parts of her story; something he had done with every subject. After about a month of sporadic phone calls, their communication stopped altogether a few days before Christmas.

New Year's passed and rolled on through January into February. Scott had moved on from interviews and contacting inmates all together. He was now in the home stretch of his thesis and beginning to contemplate turning it in early. "Campione's paper is a half-assed glorified memoir," he thought to himself, "This has legs. And opportunity for expansion." Such became his mantra and he would repeat it to himself in times of self-doubt. But there was something in him that he couldn't rest easy. He thought, frequently, about the women he had interviewed. How their opportunities were lost and, while they lived on the same planet, their worlds were entirely different from his. Every time he snuck extra food from the cafeteria, or a look at Rondeletia's ass when she took the desk in front of him, he thought about how simple it would be to lose it all. One fit, one moment of uncontrollable anger, a period of time lasting no more than a few minutes at best, and he would be an interview subject in someone else's paper. While the most punishment he would receive from stealing from the cafeteria would be a reprimand and to pay for the food, his much personally resented growing sexual attraction to his main competition caused him much more grief. Every fantasy and fleeting daydream he had about her was always interrupted by Cassie Grunwald. The wide-eyed enthusiasm she listened to him with, even the callous, prostitute-like bitterness she used to tease him during their first meeting, was still a level of attention that his sworn enemy and object of affection had never shown him.

Scott was brooding about this, and other short-comings of his short life on the evening of Sunday February 10th, 2014. His roommate was giving him an unwanted impromptu narration of his *BioShock 2* gameplay, when his phone rang. The number had no contact, but he still knew who it was.

"You are being asked to receive a call from an inmate at the Bedford Hills Correctional Facility. The inmate's name is *Cassie Grunwald*. Do you accept the call?" The message was delivered by a robot, but Cassie's name was spoken by the woman herself.

Scott died in the game. He dropped the controller on his chest and stared through the screen. His roommate snatched it away.

"Yes," he said wide-eyed.

There was a beep and a click before a familiar and flirtatious voice answered, "Hey, there stranger."

"Cassie? Wha-...what's goin' on?"

"*Noth*ing," Scott could almost hear her curtsey, "I just figured I'd call and ask how your paper went. Did you get an A?"

Cassie's tone was not of a convicted murderer spending life in prison. It sounded more like an old girlfriend calling for sex when she gets lonely. Scott got up out of his chair and left the dorm room, looking for a quieter place to talk. "Uh...I actually...uh," he pushed past a group of people walking through the hall and made it to a window at the end, "I haven't finished it yet. Well...I have finished it, but I haven't turned it in yet."

"Oh," Cassie sounded a bit deflated, but recovered quickly, "When is it due?"

"End of the semester. It's a...it's a course grade. An overall project of my major."

"A thesis!" she said, happy she remembered.

"Exactly." The hallway was colder than his room. Scott held his arms close to his chest and looked out over the quad as the New Jersey light faded.

There was a bit of a pause before Cassie said in her playful tone, "What do you think your professor will think of the part about *me*?"

"I don't know," Scott laughed, "I'll have to ask him when he reads it."

"It would probably help if you included pictures," Cassie said thoughtfully.

"That's called a magazine article," he laughed again, "not a paper. Otherwise, a thesis would be, like, a million pages long.

"Do you think I'm pretty enough to be in magazines?" Cassie's voice was almost a pout.

Scott froze. His brain took in no other information than what was in his direct field of vision. It scrambled for a few seconds, looking for an answer. "I think there is a niche for *everything*," he chuckled low.

"Even girls with no make-up in prison blues?" Her voice was still at a near pout, with an uptick of hope.

Something about her comment, or maybe it was her tone of voice, or maybe something he could not comprehend, excited Scott in a way that both exhilarated and terrified him. And the terror, excited him even more. A warmth spread through him and he leaned against the cold sill of the window with his bare arms. "I think you could find a market for that," he said more cavalier than he intended or expected.

Cassie giggled and let out a tomcat sigh. "I was thinking...I know that your paper is done and all, but...if you wanted to come back *up*, you know...I wouldn't be opposed to it. I really liked hanging out with you last time and...I would really like hanging out with you again. It would be nice to get visits. And have someone to talk to."

Scott thought it over in his mind. His eyes started darting over the cars in the parking lot, doing math and weighing options. He clucked his tongue as he thought before finally saying, "Sure. I have some things to take care of this week for class. But I can wrap them up before the weekend. How's Friday sound?"

"Saturdays are better," she said calm, but with a smile in her voice. "We could get more time then."

"Sweet, yeah, I'll be up there then," he smiled back.

"Awesome! I can't wait."

"Thanks for calling," his mouth spoke faster than his brain could process the words, "It was...it was nice hearing from you again."

"It was nice hearing from you, too." There was a long pause over the line. "I hate to cut it short, but I gotta go."

"No, I understand," Scott's romantic sex-soaked day-dreams came crashing down under the force of harsh reality. "I'll, uh...I'll see you Saturday."

"Yep! I can't wait."

"Bye."

"By-e!"

Scott waited for the line to click. He looked at his phone in disbelief, then walked on air back into his dorm, a thousand pounds heavier. That night he tried to sleep, but couldn't fig-ure out what he was going to do, or even how he got into this situation. He watched in his mind's eye as Rondeletia slipped away and was replaced by a twenty-one year old murderer in prison issue shoes. A part of his life felt like it was ending, but he couldn't shake the excitement of seeing Cassie again. Or the thought of how to ditch her. Being that she was in prison, it shouldn't be that difficult. But he felt indebted to her and in a way he didn't to the other women he had interviewed for his paper. He also couldn't deny himself the chance to see those eyes look into his again.

The weekend came quickly after that night. Scott busied himself with work and school work in between getting ready for his visit with Cassie. It seemed only right to bring some sort of gift. After a few days of thinking, he finally settled on one and walked through the parking lot back into Bedford Hills with a large Tupperware container.

Cassie was like a sugar-high teenage girl when she saw him. Her hair was down and her green eyes were wild with excitement. Her mood was only amplified when he showed her what he brought.

"Scotcheroos! Oh my god, how did you know?" Cassie smiled at him and he couldn't have been happier.

"I just Googled 'midwest snacks'. They were pretty easy to do after that." Scott watched her dig into the container, happy to see her happy.

"Have you tried one?" she looked over her glasses and offered one to him.

"I was waiting to try them with you, actually," he took a square from her hand, brushing a finger in the process.

They ate in silence for a minute, with nothing more than smiles and sounds of appreciation.

"Thank you so much for these," Cassie said with her mouthful, "That was so sweet of you. And makes this all the more appropriate." She picked up an envelope off the bench seat next to her and handed it to Scott. "I had to save up and get it mail order."

"Oh, wow," Scott said genuinely surprised, "You didn't have to do anything for me."

"I wanted to. It meant a lot to me you actually listening to my story and coming to visit me. And now these...I'm gonna have to fight bitches off to save these," she laughed.

Scott opened the envelope and pulled out a greeting card. The front showed two animal looking cartoon characters jumping in unison and slapping a high five. When he opened it, the card began to sing, and stars popped off the cardstock with springs and danced. He read the long message Cassie had written all over the inside, down to the very last *xo* in her signature.

"Thank you," Scott smiled, "This is...this is very nice of you. You didn't have to do this."
Scott looked from the card to Cassie, who smiled back at him with a slight blush. He turned back to the card and saw a small flap of paper that hadn't fully come off the card stock

when it was cut. When he shifted the card in his hand to swipe it away, it shifted along with him. He felt something inside the card slide and noticed that the paper didn't match the rest of the cardstock. It also looked less like cardstock and more like the edge of a Polaroid. And the card suddenly seemed much heavier than other musical cards he had encountered. Slowly, he pressed his thumb against the edge of the unknown object and slid out a self-shot nude Polaroid of Cassie, clearly taken in her cell. He looked up from the photo in shock to see Cassie smiling at him with chocolate in her teeth.

"I never got a solid answer on if you thought I was pretty enough to be in magazines," she said low but casual, "I thought this might help change your mind."

Scott carefully looked under the flap of the greeting card, into the inner workings of the sound device. There were easily three photos inside. He looked down at the envelope and saw another sliding out at the edge.

"Where did you get a camera?" A rush of panic and excitement shot through him. The only thoughts in his mind were getting caught and Cassie taking the pictures.

Cassie held up a finger to her lips and smiled, "Tuck those in your pocket. Or else they'll find them when they search your card."

Scott did his best to inconspicuously hide the Polaroids in his pockets. He glanced over at the door a few times. The guard stood with his hands gripping his belt buckle, eyes dead ahead, looking bored and stoic.

The rest of their hour-long visit was much more reserved. Cassie snacked on Scotcheroos, licking and sucking her fingers and brushing her hair out of her eyes. Scott felt tortured. He adjusted in his seat and leaned in close to listen intently to what she said, but all he could hear was his heartbeat and all he could see was her naked. When their time was up, Cassie made a big production of kissing him on the cheek. She looked down at his pocket, then back up at his eyes and gave him a wink.

"Have fun," she smirked. "Thanks for the zoom-zooms."

They hugged, for a shorter length of time than Scott would have preferred, then parted ways. As he signed out at the visitor's window, the guard told him he had chocolate on his face.

The rest of the weekend and most of the next week barely happened for Scott. He spent every waking moment reliving his visit with Cassie. Not even fear of his work slipping could snap him out of it. He did, however, several times consider re-writing her section of his paper, but he wasn't lovesick enough to know that it would completely sink the importance of her story being included at all. Instead, he reworked a few sections to show Cassie in a less monstrous, if not sympathetic, light.

Thursday he called her again, hoping to set up another

visitation for the weekend. The secretary that answered the phone told him that Cassie would have to call him back on Friday, she wasn't able to come to the phone. Scott's heart broke and sank into his stomach. He flipped through her photos repeatedly, pressed into the corner, sitting on his bed and waited for Friday. When he finally reached her, it was less than stellar news.

"Yeah, you can't come up for a while," Cassie said with a disappointed sigh. "I got LOV because they caught me with a dot machine."

Scott was familiar with the term LOV. It stood for *loss of visitation*. Dot machine, however, was a new one on him.

"It's a homemade tattoo gun," Cassie explained, "I needed to borrow it from a girl so I could put a little thing on my wrist."

"I don't think you need anything on your wrists," Scott tried to chuckle to cover his earnestness, "You have very fetching wrists."

"I think you'd like this though," she purred thoughtfully into the phone, "It's a *tiny...little...S....*For *Scott*."

Scott had never done any hardcore drugs while at college, or any other point in his life. But in that moment, he knew none of them could ever touch the way he felt.

"Then I got a ticket for gunning in front of the guard while they searched my cell."

Scott had to ask about that one, too.

"Let's just say, it involves my fingers and a little man in a boat."

Scott was absolutely dumbfounded.

"Are you still there?" she squeaked.

"Yeah, I'm here," Scott coughed. "I'm definitely here."

"Good," Cassie said contentedly, "I was scared I stopped your heart there for a second," she giggled.

"You did for a minute. But you started it again seconds later."

Cassie laughed. Scott floated.

"I hate to cut us short, but I can't stay on long. The only reason they let me use the phone is because I told them it was for your paper."

"When can I see you again?" Scott couldn't fight his panic.

"Write me," she smiled.

"Cassie..."

"Huh?"

"I...I think I'm in love with you."

Cassie laughed an almost villainous laugh that transitioned into a giggle then a torch singer-like purr, "Talk to you soon, babe."

Lock, Stocking &
Barrel

Raff Hanrahan enjoyed sunsets, particularly when his hands were dirty. It was the sign of another day's hard work done for the books. He didn't like to track grime and steel into the house, but he would always stand in his West facing front door at the end of the day and watch the sun dip behind the mountains. His blue healer, Beacan, would sit at his feet and tolerate it. He knew when the light was gone, food would come shortly after.

Cool down that night, however, would have to wait. Beacan lifted his head and looked off into the distance. Just then, Raff saw a dust cloud rise about five minutes down the road. His closest neighbors were eight miles away and no one came down his road accidently. They would have to find it first. But that never hurt business. Knowing it would take some time, he stood in the door and waited.

After a few minutes, he could tell it was a car. There was something written on the side in white letters that he couldn't make out until it pulled up into the dirt patch in front of his porch. It was Western Union. Western Union usually made deliveries on Wednesdays and Fridays. Today was Saturday. When the driver hopped out of the front seat, he knew they weren't delivering a check. They were delivering trouble.

A woman about twenty years younger than Raff in a strange combination of men and women's clothes stomped around the front of the car to the base of his porch steps. She was wearing a torn bright red dress over a pair of men's pin-stripe trousers, a corset covered by a Western Union delivery driver's jacket and a cap.

"Are you a smithee?" Her tone was demanding, but only because of her nerves.

"Yes," Raff said in his even-tempered way. Beacan looked up at him. Raff made a slight gesture with his hand, pointing at the floor and the dog laid back down.

"Good."

The woman walked to the rear passenger side door of the car and yanked it open. Raff couldn't get a very clear view of what she was struggling with in the dim light of the oil lamps, but it looked like she was going to lose the fight. With a groan, the woman finally gave up and walked around to the other side of the car. She held onto the doorframe and used her high-heeled boots to push a safe out onto the ground. Raff did not move.

"I'll give you half of what's inside," the woman panted,

walking around the car, "I just need it cracked and I'll be out of your life forever."

"Wrong type," Raff stood motionless in the doorway.

"What?" The woman moved closer to the base of the steps.

"What you're lookin' for is a locksmith, not a gunsmith," Raff said coolly, "Furthermore, that there is a combination lock, so I don't think a locksmith would be of help anyhow. Further still, I don't touch nothin' that ain't above board. So, you can pack up your things and if anyone asks, I won't say a word and you can be on your way."

The woman stepped closer to the porch and into the full light of the lamps. Her lipstick was smeared and blush had started to rub off. Raff could also see that her face was polka-dotted with blood.

"I'll give you half of what's inside," she said desperately.

"I heard you the first time," Raff said with a nod.

The woman turned back toward the road, then looked around the property with the expression of a rabbit caught in a snare. "It looks pretty lonely out here," she said in a voice that belied her panic, "You all cut off."

Beacan watched her with his eyebrows raised. Raff continued to say nothing.

"When was the last time you had company?" The woman began to climb the stairs, her heavy soled boots thudding against the hard wood with her high-class sashay. "A friendly voice around the house? A woman in your bed?" The woman took off her cap as she reached the top of the steps and let her long blonde hair fall down around her shoulders as she breezily slid over where to Raff was leaning. "I could compensate you for your troubles." When she smiled, her eyes glittered in the lamplight underneath the blood droplets. "Plus, half of what's in that box. You'll make out like a bandit."

Raff sucked on his mustache as he listened. He waited until she finished before responding, "That's the problem right there, ma'am. I don't particularly want to. And by the looks of your current situation, you already made up your own bed. You don't need mine. Now, if you would kindly leave my property. Or I'm libel to start getting orn'ry."

The warm softness of the woman's face was replaced by cold hard edges. "Nothing like Rocky Mountain hospitality."

"The Rockies are about a hundred miles thataway," Raff pointed southwest, "You might find a locksmith with a feather bed somewhere in between."

The woman followed Raff's hand as he pointed. When she turned back to face him, there were tears in her eyes. A single one escaped and rolled down her cheek, taking mascara to join the raid on her fading blush. "You *bastard*."

Fighting full-blown tears, the woman stomped off the porch down into the dark to begin the struggle of putting the safe back in the car. Beacan looked from the woman to Raff without lifting his head. Raff didn't move from his spot in the doorway. The woman struggled and screamed, trying to lift the safe, her back arched and straining. She managed to slide it less than an inch through the dirt then collapsed, sobbing, on top of it. Beacan lifted his head from his paws and looked up at Raff, who continued to stare at the woman. Finally, Beacan let out a whimper, getting Raff's attention.

"You go help her then," Raff gestured.

Beacan turned from Raff, to the woman and back again. He whimpered as his front paws slid across the porch. Raff sucked in his cheek with a sigh and left his post at the door. The woman jumped when she saw his shadow over her shoulder. Raff held up his hands, then slowly knelt down to lift the safe. The woman wasn't so eager to let go of the safe, despite her earlier petition for help. Finally, she rolled off, leaving Raff to heft it himself. He got it up to knee level, but it wasn't high enough to push into the car. The woman hopped to, gripping the base with thin fingers. The two managed to return the box to the car, with no small amount of sweat and grunts.

"Thank you," the woman leaned against the door of the car, wiping tears from her eyes with the cuff of the Western Union jacket.

Raff pulled a bandana from his back pocket, wiped the sweat from his face and brow, and ran a hand through his long salt and pepper hair. He turned to the woman and saw the job she had to contend to with the jacket sleeve and passed her the bandana. She turned it away with a sniff and looked away from Raff.

"You're not gonna out glow the moon," he said simply, "No point in being miserable."

The woman shot him a look and held it. She crinkled her chin and pushed it out in defiance before snatching the rag from his hand. "It works for you." She looked for a clean spot in the lamplight, then proceeded to wipe the sweat and blood from her face.

"Rafferty Hanrahan," he said with his hand out, "Most just call me Raff."

The woman looked up from the bandana and stared at his hand for a moment before returning his shake. "Georgia Peach."

"That the name your mammy gave ya," Raff said slow, "...or your madam?"

"Father, actually," she shot him a look to go along with her words, "...but it *is* good for business." Georgia's voice trailed off as she looked down at the ground.

"Who are you running from?"

Georgia folded the bandana and handed it back to Raff. She opened her mouth to answer but was interrupted by Beacan barking from the porch.

Raff looked down the road, over the roof of the car. There were two large clouds of dust speeding down the road in the last light of the setting sun. "I suppose I'll be finding out here directly."

Raff turned back to Georgia. Her expression of jackrabbit fear had returned to her face.

"Do what I say. Don't argue," Raff never touched her, but his words felt like a hand on her shoulder. "We got about five minutes," he glanced back in the direction of the cars to clock their progress, "Maybe three at the speed their drivin'."

Raff opened the doors to the barn that sat about thirty yards away from the house. He and Georgia stood on opposite sides of the Western Union coupe and pushed it into the barn. In the near total darkness, it was too dangerous to risk taillights or engine noise. Raff then locked up the barn and led Georgia up the stairs and into the house. The first room off the front door was the kitchen. He knelt down in the dim lamplight and lifted a section of the floor out by a metal ring. He swept his arm and motioned for Georgia to go in.

"I can't see anything," she said scared.

"It's just a fruit cellar," Raff was calm, but confused by her reluctance. "Just follow the stairs till you hit bottom."

Georgia cautiously stepped into the black until she felt a wooden stair. Raff took a few steps into the sitting room and came back with a blanket, handing it to her. She looked from the blanket to him as if both were foreign concepts.

Raff shook the blanket gently, "I don't know how long you'll be down there. Just try and stay quiet."

Georgia cautiously took the blanket and held it to her chest like a little girl with a doll. She looked down the stairs into the blackness and slowly began walking. Raff waited until the footsteps became soft, then closed the door over her.

Beacan followed Raff out of the house onto the porch, confused that food wasn't being made now that they were inside. Raff reached into a canvas sack that hung near the door and pulled out a bone the size of a human forearm. He had picked it up at the butcher a few weeks before on one of his rare trips into Cheyenne and was thankful he had forgotten it until now. Raff held the bone down at Beacan's eye level and led him out to the porch. He dropped it in the spot where Beacan had been laying, then carefully walked over to his rocker on the other side of the doorframe. The cars were about a hundred yards away.

A black Ford coupe pulled in first with a dusty green pick-up in tow. The pick-up Raff recognized, the coupe, however, he had never seen before. Sheriff Matt Talbot stepped out of the driver's side of the pick-up, accompanied by his deputy Jakey Reeves riding shotgun. Talbot raised his hand to wave, but was cut off by the booming voice of one of the passengers from the coupe. They all three looked like G-men, in black suits and hats with long black trench coats. The man who stepped out of the back seat was holding a tommy gun. The man in the front passenger seat was holding a double-barrel shotgun.

"You Rafferty Hanrahan?" The booming voice of the driver demanded. He walked over to Raff's porch and put one foot up on the first step.

"Yeah," Raff croaked, looking down at the man and rocking slowly.

"You seen anyone drive through here with a Western Union delivery vehicle?" The man did his best to stare down Raff, but was too short to pull it off.

"No, sir."

"Raff," Sheriff Talbot started, "these men are with the---"

"*I* can handle this, thank you, Sheriff." The little man leaning on his porch didn't even bother to look over his shoulder when he spoke. "My name is Harry Kerns, Mr. Hanrahan, I'm with the Pinkerton Detective Agency. These men here are my associates, Tom Kunkle and Dick Rapoport."

Raff said nothing, just nodded. Kunkle and Rapoport looked around the property with shifty eyes. Talbot and Reeves stood a few feet away in front of the truck, looking bored and irritated.

"We're looking for a woman by the name of Georgia Peach," Kerns began, "about two hours ago she shot and killed three men then stole a Western Union delivery vehicle and fled city limits. She is believed to be armed and dangerous and we know she is on the run."

"With all due respect, Mr. Kerns---"

"*Detective* Kerns."

"---Mr. Kerns, why are the Pinkertons looking for a suspect in a Western Union robbery?"

"We shouldn't be, is my point, Mr. Hanrahan. We were called in to investigate a man by the name of Savage Tom Savage. Know him?"

"Can't say I do."

"Turns out Savage was---"

"Was he part of that Dillinger's gang?" Raff rocked gently on his heels, giving no regard to Kerns' impatience.

"Savage was a two-bit hustler from Mason City, Iowa. He's a small-time wannabe thug, pimp and all around bad news. Peach was one of his girls. He ran them out of a hotel on Seymour, near the Lakeview cemetery."

"You keep saying *was*."

"That's on account of he's dead, Mr. Rafferty."

"Hanrahan," Raff corrected.

Kerns straightened his back and stuttered a sigh, "There was a small convoy of Western Union vehicles, a car and an armored truck, knocked off on Pebrican about two hours ago. Then we find Savage's body, and what was left of his head, in a pool of blood outside Finnegan's pub."

The Pinkerton's attempt at making Raff uneasy wasn't working. He just rocked idly with one foot. Beacan hit a particularly juicy part of his bone and let out a growl.

"Then a woman matching Peach's description was seen high-tailing it out of town in a Western Union automobile," Kerns pitched his voice to sound angrier, "Now, neither of them may have been John Dillinger, but what we have here, Mr. Rafferty, is an armed robbery, theft of federal property, theft of private property, multiple homicides and disturbing the peace! Now that may not sound like much to a bunch of country bumpkins like you," he looked from Raff to the sheriff and deputy, "but where I come from that's not something to blow your nose at! This woman is *dangerous* and she must be brought to justice!"

Sheriff Talbot held up his hand and stepped into the light of the porch. "All we're asking, Raff, is if you've seen anyone come 'round here in the last hour or so. You're the farthest person away from town, so I thought---"

"*You* thought?" Kunkle didn't look like the youngest one, until he opened his mouth. He stared at Talbot and adjusted his grip on the tommy gun.

Talbot glanced at Kunkle, then back at Raff, "Maybe she might of come by here. Asked for a place to stay. Maybe even just passed through."

"Nobody been by here in a few days," Raff shrugged. "Lynch's boy was here a few days ago to pick up an order. Ain't seen nobody since then. I was thinkin' on goin' into town tomorrow for a few things, but with an active police search goin' on, I think that just about puts an end to that."

"What about that there?" Rapoport piped up and pointed toward the barn with his shotgun.

Kerns turned in the direction of the barn, then slowly swiveled his head back toward Raff, "What've you got in the barn there, old man?" his voice seethed with imminent victory.

"Tools."

"What kind of tools?" Kunkle stepped forward and bobbed his weapon.

"The kind someone could commit robbery with?" Kerns added.

"Now, I told you fellas," Talbot stepped forward, "Raff here is a gunsmith. Over there in that barn is his shop."

"I want to see inside," Kerns stood up and straightened out his shirt with a smirk.

"You ever seen a workshop before?" Raff was statue still, except for his rocking heel, "Now, imagine it inside a barn."

"Sounds to me someone here is interfering with a police investigation, doesn't it Dick?" Kerns continued to glare with his short man smile.

"Sure does, Harry."

"Tom," Kerns tucked his thumbs behind his belt buckle, "shoot it open."

"It's a shop, fellas," Talbot said frantic.

"It's just his shop. You don't need to shoot it up. He'll be out of a job," Reeves added.

"Or," The Pinkerton turned toward the small-town sheriff and deputy, "he could be harboring evidence. Or our perpetrator."

Raff rose from his chair and began walking down his stairs to the posse of cops at the bottom, "I may be simple. But I'm not stupid. If you're looking in any official capacity, you're gonna need a warrant. Or a court order, before I let you look anywhere on my property. If not," Raff stood on the step above Kerns and leaned down into his face, "I'd like to ask why you're so nosy."

Kern's smile faded as he set his jaw, "If you wanted one so bad, then why didn't you just say so?" He locked eyes with Raff before calling out, "Tom! Dick!"

"Yeah, boss," they responded in unison, like a shared brain.

"Pack it up. We're heading out of here. We'll be back with a court order in the morning."

"I'll fix breakfast," Raff spoke without barely moving his lips.

After a few more intense moments of eye contact, Kerns peeled away from Raff's stare and walked back to the coupe.

Talbot remained where he stood until they passed and gave Raff a shrug and an apologetic look before returning to his truck with Reeves. Raff leaned against the post of his porch and watched the taillights fade into the night. Once he could no longer hear engines, he turned around and walked inside. Beacan did not follow, he was too engrossed in his bone.

Raff lifted the door to the fruit cellar and looked down into the blackness. "Are you hungry?"

There was a long period of silence before Georgia's voice echoed up, "I don't know. I wasn't really thinking about it."

"How about this," Raff adjusted to lean on one knee and talked down to the woman he couldn't see, "All things considered, we have maybe a few hours before those Pinkertons show up here again without the sheriff. Maybe with a court order. I can sit you down, scrape something together and get you one last home-cooked meal before you hit the road…"

Georgia waited for him to continue, "Or?" She slowly climbed out of the cellar enough for the hazy outline of her face to be seen.

"Or we can go out in the shop and get that safe cracked open for you."

Raff held out his hand. Georgia climbed the last remaining stairs and took it. Together they walked out on the porch and began making their way to the workshop. Raff let out a short quick whistle and Beacan followed close behind, leaving his bone on the porch.

The only electricity on the property was fed to the barn. It wasn't common that Raff worked into the night, but it happened often enough that he rather have lightbulbs than oil lamps to work by. It wasn't a large barn, maybe twenty feet wide. In the center was the Western Union car they had pushed in earlier. Raff tried to keep the center of his work shop open to move around. That night it came in useful for a different purpose. The two hefted the safe out of the back seat and onto a work bench. Beacan sat dutifully at the door as look out.

"I take it you don't rightly care about the shape of the thing when it's done." Raff sorted through his tools.

"All I care about is what's inside," Georgia stood next to him, running her fingers along a rack of unmounted rifle barrels.

"What is inside, if you don't mind me asking?" Raff picked up a twelve-pound hammer and a crowbar.

"I don't know, honestly," Georgia adjusted the blanket around her shoulders and continued to look at firearm parts. "I assume it's valuable, though. It was being carried by Western Union."

"Could be a lot of deeds and land grants," Raff climbed a small three step ladder and stood over top the safe.

"They must be worth something to somebody," Georgia turned around to see Raff in his pose. Her mind flashed on how difficult it would be to get into a safe with such primitive tools. It was not at all what she was expecting. And if what was inside was the same, she knew Raff must be worried that he wouldn't be compensated for his efforts. "But if that is the case, my offer still stands. I still owe you for saving me from those men."

"Let's just get this open first," Raff held the crow bar in place dead center on the dial. He brought the hammer down once with a loud *clink* and chipped a slice into the face. "This may take a bit, so keep an ear out."

Raff beat away on the safe for some time before he had fully smashed the dial. Once through, he beat out the lock bars and went to work prying off the door through the missing piece.

Georgia alternately watched Raff and slowly walked around the shop and looked at all the tools and gun parts. Each barrel, no matter how big or small, all had the same marking on it. Some boldly stamped. Others were intricately carved. But all were the same.

"What does this mean?" Georgia ran her finger along a stamped shotgun barrel.

Raff looked through sweat and hair over at where she was standing. In seconds, he saw what she was looking at and turned back to the safe. "It's a sort of signature. A stamp of approval," He pried a few times then dropped his tools in a huff, "You work on a firearm, more often then not build them from the ground up, you leave your mark, so anyone who sees it knows you were the one."

"How many different marks are there?" Georgia turned to Raff, "And what do they mean?"

"As many as there are gunsmiths," Raff dug through the drawers of his workbench, "It depends on the smithee as to what he wants it to be."

"How did you choose yours?" Georgia walked over and stood next to him.

"I didn't," Raff said thoughtfully, "Not really." He found a box of kitchen matches, took them out of the drawer and turned to Georgia, "My pop was a smith. And his father before him. Grandad came up with a shamrock. Pop added a leaf. I added the words."

"What does it mean?" Georgia followed Raff as he walked back over to the safe.

"It's a saying from the old country," he struck a match and used it to peer down inside the safe. "My pop used to say it to me all the time." He stared into the safe through the broken dial until the match burned down to his fingers. Just before it scorched him, he flicked out the flame with a quick movement of his wrist. Raff lifted his head and motioned for Georgia to come over, before striking a match for her to see down inside. "It means 'This is your chance'."

Georgia looked down inside the safe and felt her heart stop when she saw gold. And stacks and stacks of cash. She stood up from the safe and looked at Raff with a smile.

"And I guess this is *your* chance," he smiled back.

"How do we get it out?" she could barely contain her excitement.

Raff motioned for her to step aside, then stood up on the step stool and kicked the safe to the floor with one foot. When it hit the ground, the door flew off and exploded cash and gold all over the dirt floor of the barn. Georgia ran over to the mess of riches on the floor, crying with laughter. The barn was filled with a level of excitement that Raff had not been around in years. Like an infant with a pile of baby ducks. After a minute, Georgia grabbed a bundled stack of cash off the floor and sat back on her knees to hand it to Raff with a smile. She slowly held out the stack to him, then quickly pulling it back before her arm reached full extension.

"Unless..." she curled an eyebrow, "You want to come with me."

"I'm not the one on the run," Raff said flatly.

"You would be if I told," a mischievous smile began to move into the neighborhood of her eyes.

"You'd also be arrested." Raff punctuated his statement with raised eyebrows and a shrug.

Georgia looked Raff up and down, her eyes twinkling in the light of the bare bulb with evil thoughts.

"Please don't make me regret helping you," Raff's shoulders drooped and his face along with them.

Georgia let out a barroom laugh and dropped her head into her hands full of money. Her laughter trailed off into something like a sob. Raff began to chuckle along with her. Georgia let out a long squeaky breath then cackled again. She slipped on the money as she tried to stand up, but Raff caught her before she fell too far. Georgia gripped him tight and didn't let go for a while.

They weren't very judicious about counting out the money. Georgia split it down the approximate center and piled her half in the trunk of the car. Raff threw a bit of his in when she wasn't looking. He dug around on his shelves for a while before he turned up a can of black house paint. He quick dry brushed a few coats over the Western Union logos on the doors and threw handfuls of dirt and rocks on the car to make it look like a farm vehicle. It was early morning, but still good and dark when he finally slid open the back doors to the barn. Georgia patted Beacan on the head and jumped in the driver's seat.

"What are you going to do with the safe?" She asked as Raff leaned down into the window.

"What safe?" He stared blankly into her face and blinked a few times like a dumb child.

Georgia laughed, but she was tired. She turned to look out the rear barn doors into the black space of night, then back at Raff. "What are you going to do with your money?"

Raff cleared his throat and thought for a moment, "I've always enjoyed cooking," he said absently, "Maybe I'll take a run at opening a little place."

"I can be a waitress," she said eagerly.

"You've got a lot of big plans for someone on the lamb for robbery and murder."

"I only killed Tom," she said sadly.

"Hmm?"

"Tom Savage. He was the only one I killed. They're gonna

try to pin the Western Union drivers on me, but that was Tom, not me."

"Either way," Raff shrugged. "But...maybe a few years down the line, when things blow over, I'll see you for a blue plate special." He gave her a smile that crinkled at the corners of his eyes.

Georgia leaned in and gave him a quick peck on the cheek. She didn't even mind the sweat. Raff stared back at her before giving the door two quick smacks.

"Stick to the fence line till you hit the road."

Raff walked to the back door and swung his arm the same way he had when he introduced Georgia to the hole in his kitchen floor. Georgia smiled and waved, blowing kisses and even gave two quick duck honks of the horn. Raff watched the last set of taillights fade into the dark of the night. Once he could no longer see or hear, he stuffed his spoils into a potato sack, and walked Beacan into the house to stash it in the fruit cellar.

Happy Trails

I was boosting a car outside Portsmouth when they caught me. It had to have been a sting. To this day, I don't know who ratted me out, but the only person I don't suspect is myself. They dragged me into a building that looked like a bank and threw me in a cell. Never even booked me. Some dago cop took my wallet while I was pressed against the hood of the cruiser, then called me *fucking mick* for the rest of the night. Joke was on him. I'm not even Catholic.

I must have been in that cell for about twelve hours before they finally pulled me out. Two meat packers in police issue boots dragged me into an interrogation room and handcuffed my wrists to the table. There was a fat guy with a bald head and a pasty hairless face already sitting at the table with a stack of folders. You could smell the close shave on this guy. His hands were soft and his eyes were sadistic. I knew he was a fed.

"Wayne Garrety." He said my name like it was news to me, but not to him. "Twenty-five of Fall River, Massachusetts."

"And?"

"Oh, nothing." He dropped the file he was reading on top of the stack next to him. "I was just remarking on your impressive and rather colorful history."

"I'm a regular god damn rainbow."

"How long have they kept you in that cell?"

I said nothing.

"I can get the police to uncuff you, if you'd like."

"What would *you* like?"

"Do you know who I am?" He did that shrug thing with his hands folded that all pompous assholes do.

"Judging by the smell, I'd say you're some kind of narc."

"My name is Agent Taber Mitchum, I work for the Central Intelligence Agency." He looked at me like I was supposed to be in some sort of awe. I wasn't. "You have a rather impressive background yourself. Two years United States Airforce. Mechanic. I understand you presented a new design for Grumman F-14 landing gear. What became of that?"

"I was discharged."

"I can tell you what happened," he hunched his shoulders, leaned in toward me and whispered, "they *used it*."

I had nothing to say to this, because I didn't care.

"You're a rather bright young man, Mr. Garrety," he leaned back in his chair and folded his arms, "which leads me to wonder what you're doing stealing cars in Portsmouth, Rhode Island."

"Have you tried getting a job in the private sector after working in the Air Force?"

Mitchum looked up at the ceiling and thought for a moment. "No. No I haven't"

"You can't."

"Well," he licked four fingers at once and flipped open the folder he was just looking through, "it says here that you are currently employed at...Dulaine Auto Body."

"Yeah, you got my paystubs in there, too?"

Mitchum looked up at me from under his brow. I could tell he was getting sick of me and it didn't bother me one bit.

"Slackin' off over there in Langley."

His whole body shifted. Mitchum dropped the friendly, holier than thou façade and leaned in close to me with his fat Marlon Brando bravado. "Alright, Mr. Garrety, I can see you like to get right down to the point. Which is good. That's real good. I'm that kind of man myself. Right now, you're looking at fifteen to twenty years. Minimum, for your offenses. Third strike in three years for grand theft auto. I'm here to offer you a proposition."

"I'm not a rat."

"In my line of work," he pressed one chubby finger into the steel table, "it's called a *mole*."

I leaned in and mocked his conspiratorial tone, "Call it whatever the fuck you want, I'm not doing it."

"There is a gang," Mitchum ignored me, "in Portland. Oregon. Of outlaw van enthusiasts. I want you to infiltrate, subvert and expose their organization. And provide me with a list of any, and all known associates."

"And why would I do this for you exactly?"

Mitchum gave me a shit-eating, nut job politician smile. I could see the reflection of all the horrible things he was re-sponsible for flicker across his eyes like a tv screen. He didn't have to say anything after that. I knew I was fucked.

I had twenty-four hours to get my affairs in order. Pack my clothes, bail out on the year lease for my apartment, and make sure there wasn't anything that would make me have to leave Portland for Fall River in the foreseeable future. The

CIA gave me no money, no lodging, no cover. Just enough scratch for a plane ticket and a list of part stores and repair shops the "van enthusiasts" were reported to frequent. I only had two hundred some dollars in random bills and a duffel bag of clothes when I landed. Mitchum had given me a card with his contact information and told me to tell him when I got there. When I called him, I asked where the hell I was supposed to stay or how I was supposed to get in contact with these people. He just laughed and told me he had faith in me. That I would figure it out.

A travel brochure at the airport pointed me in the direction of some cheap motels. I caught a carpool with some Christian missionaries to the cheapest one, only so I wouldn't have to blow money on cab fare. One line into the first hymn and the twelve bucks would have been worth it. I caught a room at the Sweetheart Motel in an area called Boise and ate out of the snack machine.

The next morning, I started calling around the list of parts stores and body shops checking for jobs. Most of them said no, a few just hung up and two said that they recently had openings. One was a mom and pop parts store where the owner, who was about two hundred years old, kept falling asleep during my interview. If this van gang wasn't a figment of Mitchum's Agent Orange soaked mind, it was obvious to me why they would go there. It was far too easy to shoplift. The second on my list, was a body shop called Tom Cat's Rat Rods and Engine Repair. There was a hand painted cut out of that Rat Fink over the garage bays and AC/DC on the radio.

The owner, oddly enough named Tony, stood just inside the door to the office and looked me up and down.

He wiped his hands with a rag and asked, "What's the difference between a carburetor and a differential?"

I couldn't see my face, but I know I made one. "About forty dollars."

"Beautiful," he wiped the sweat off his face with a greasy rag and threw it in a bin full of others, "you're hired. Can you start tomorrow?"

"I can start today."

"See you tomorrow. Seven a.m." He dropped the door and walked back into the bays.

I held it down at Rat Rods (I refused to call it Tom Cat's, because I never met the son of a bitch) and sniffed around as much as I could in the general direction of criminal activity. There was a decent amount of it. One of the shop's specialties was outfitting cars with secret compartments for drug smuggling. I knew about it, but never was involved. Still too new on the payroll to be an active participant. Then one day, this guy came in. About my age, a few inches shorter than me, long red hair and a beard. He was wearing black jeans so dirty you could tell from a distance and a dirty white Mr. Horsepower t-shirt. A brown leather vest with a big patch on the back over a black denim jacket and old scratched black leather combat boots. He looked the way they described cowboys back in the day, only dressed out of the '80s. This guy walked into the office, talked to Tony behind the counter, then left with a big brown box without paying. I asked Tony later who it was.

"Oh, him? That's Torch."

"Dude's name is Torch?"

"Short for Blowtorch. It's uh...like a nickname."

"Not very creative. Who the hell gave him that one?"

"Some club he's in. They strip down and re-build old vans and stuff. Like Ram Vans and Tradesmen. Shit from the seventies."

"What's the club?"

"Uh...Bedouins, I think. I can't remember. Why, you lookin' to join?"

"I don't know. I didn't know there was anyone else around here into vans."

"Ask him the next time he's in here. He's a pretty friendly guy."

"Who wants to know?" Blowtorch stood in front of me,

tapping an envelope on the counter. He had a no nonsense look about him under his shaggy red hair.

"Me. Tony was telling me about your club. I didn't know there was anyone else around---"

"What do you drive?" He never stopped staring or tapping the envelope.

"Nothing right now. I just got into town not too long ago. Been lookin' to save up for this Tradesman I saw in a lot over on Going."

Blowtorch stopped moving. His eyes were fixed on a blank point in space and I couldn't tell if he was still breathing. "I'll think about it. Let me talk to Tony."

Something must have been right. When Tony came out of the office, he passed me note and gestured back to Blowtorch as he pulled out in the parking lot. His van had a white eyed wizard shooting lighting from a staff painted on the side. I called Mitchum that night from my motel room and told him I might have made contact. He told me to call back when I had.

Later that week, I did. Tony tapped me on the shoulder while I was under the hood of a Chevy Malibu and said Blowtorch was waiting for me on the bench outside the office. When I asked what for, he told me it was probably because of that club I was asking about. I leaned out of the bay and saw him sitting there with one foot cocked out, staring west. Blowtorch noticed me like a cat and motioned for me to come over. He said he had talked to the club and they were interested in meeting me. That they wanted me to join them for a party that night at Popcorn Park. Torch stood up, pulled a set of keys out of his leather vest pocket and spun them by the ring before catching them in his palm. I told him I would have to wait until quitting time. He told me I could go now or forget about the whole thing. I excused myself to get my things out of my locker and left a note for Tony on the register.

The ride out was interesting. *Fighting for Madge* was in a volume competition with the engine. Blowtorch's intensity never faded. He stomped pedals and glared at the road like he'd been fucked over by the world and wasn't going to take it anymore. We listened to *Then Play On* two times through on the way up. I tried to talk to him about music. He didn't make any indication that he was listening, but he was.

"You like Fleetwood Mac?" I sounded like one of my old girlfriends.

"Real Fleetwood." He stared out the windshield as the sky got dark. "That Stevie Nicks shit can eat a dick."

And that was the extent of our conversation. We traveled almost an hour outside of the city, down NW 53rd Drive into the woods. There was a dirt road that cut down over a hill we followed to a clearing that looked like an old abandoned logging site. There were five other vans with various flamboyant paint jobs, circled in a loose wagon train fashion around a sizeable fire near an old construction office trailer. You could occasionally see shadows of people weaving in and out and around the scene. Blowtorch pulled his van up near the office trailer and parked.

"We're here." He jumped out of the van and closed the door without waiting.

I milled around the outer edges of the fire, not out of sight, but not forcing my way in. There was a stream somewhere nearby, but you would never know it to hear it. Black Sabbath played loud and echoed through the woods, covering all other noise. Occasionally there was a laugh, or maybe a scream of some variety, but mostly it was quiet. Aside from the music. Four other guys with long greasy hair, in relatively the same get up as Blowtorch ran around making general fools out of themselves and torturing these three girls who barely looked old enough to be out of high school. They sat on log benches near the fire and tried to laugh off the guys drunken groping. The men seemed to be more obnoxious than harmful, but I still wouldn't want it if I was a girl. I looked around for Blowtorch but couldn't find him. One of the men walked up to the cooler I was standing a few feet behind and tried to stare me down as he pulled out a beer. He ripped off the tab and threw it in the fire.

"Who are you?"

"Blowtorch brought me."

"Who's Blowtorch?" He shrugged and looked around.

"The guy that brought me."

"I don't know any Blowtorch." He turned around and yelled at the rest of the group. "Any you assholes know anyone called Blowtorch?"

The men said no. The girls pointed at the office trailer.

He turned back and shrugged again. "Sorry, pal. You're S.O---"

The door to the office trailer was kicked open from the inside. A short man that looked like the nephew of Dennis Hopper strode out. He had a long Civil War era mustache and fluffy blonde hair that fanned out from his head in a lazy pyramid. He looked dangerous, only because he wanted to be so badly. There was a large Bowie knife strapped to his left ankle in a sheath that he pulled out and flashed as he walked toward me. The rest of the group stayed where they were and watched. Blowtorch stepped out of the trailer and leaned against the door frame, hands in the pockets of his vest.

"You like Sabbath?" The knife-wielder's eyes were cocaine-wide. He scraped the tip of the blade against his thumb.

I looked around, trying to guess the right answer. "Yeah. Yeah, they're pretty great."

"I fucking *love* Sabbath, man!" He grabbed the back of my head with his free hand and pressed our foreheads together. There was a fog of Hai Karate that surrounded him like Pig-pen. "They're my shit! What's your favorite album?"

My mind raced to think. I was more into hardcore punk bands like Black Flag and Dead Kennedys. But my high school days rushed back to me and I pulled one from the air. "Master of Reality."

"Good!" He pushed me away, still holding onto the back of my neck. "But...is it better than Sabotage?" The blade spun slowly in the air between my eyes.

I was glad he was pointing me in the direction he wanted me to go, because I really wanted the blade out of my face. "No. Man. Sabotage is way better."

As fast as it started, the knife-wielder spun around to the group and held up his arms in victory. "We have a winner!" His voice was shrill enough that it cut through the music and echoed through the valley.

The group by the fire cheered, but did not come over to join me. My blade flashing indoctrinator turned back to me and pulled a small plastic bag out of an inner pocket of his vest. He stuck the edge of the blade in the bag and did a long, obnoxious snort, vacuuming about a quarter tablespoon of white powder off the steel. "It's not champagne, but it does in a pinch." He held another mound up for me.

"No, thanks, man."

"C'mon! You're a Sabbath man! I thought you liked to party!"

I shot my eyes around the camp. The group by the fire was ignoring me. Blowtorch was still standing in the doorway. Realizing I had no choice, I thought of the CIA crest and hummed the national anthem as I did my first hit of coke. It fucking sucked. I instantly had cotton-mouth and spent the next two hours grinding my teeth, wishing I could chew through a log.

"God damn the pusher man, huh?" The knife-man holstered his namesake and ran over to the fire to steal a beer.

Blowtorch came down after a while. He was quiet, but sort of introduced me around to everyone. The guys goofing off by the fire were Bull, Doc, Otto and Yankee Dan. The man who questioned me about shit music was called Dusty, for obvious reasons. He was the leader of the outfit and bank rolled the whole operation with his daddy's money. Torch said he grew out the mustache to hide scars all over his upper lip from insisting on snorting entire cartels worth of cocaine off his blade for the last four years.

Despite the antagonistic introduction, the entire group

pretty much seemed to be a joke. There was van customization and restoration for sure. Most, if not all, of the parts were hot. There was a penchant for alcohol, cocaine, weed, and LSD, and a vast number of girls of questionable age. But most of what was going on the group wasn't anything you wouldn't find outside of a frat house or a bachelor party. The meaning behind the name Popcorn Park became evident when, on my third visit, Doc, Otto and Bull were firing shotguns into the air for no apparent reason. In the daytime, you could see hundreds of shotgun shells littering the ground, some half buried in the dirt like fossils. The Bedouins also shunned, criticized, and made fun of bikers and motorcycle clubs, calling them faggots, all the time emulating them at every turn. Their leather and denim colors were chosen to be in direct opposition to the uniforms of gangs like the Hell's Angels, but just made them look like contrary wannabes. They also quoted and cited *Easy Rider* constantly. *Just like Easy Rider* was a phrase commonly smiled at one another after seemingly any occurrence or event.

The most dangerous and rage-inspiring member of the group was Dusty. And it wasn't just because of the mustard gas cloud of Hai Karate that followed him everywhere like a shadow. He possessed the holy trinity of dangerous personality traits: violent, mean and stupid. No one claimed to know his name, who he was or where he came from, except Blowtorch. Dusty was born Chet Puckles to a family of prominent Republican politicians. He had spent his entire life doing drugs, fucking off and raping underage girls. Which happened more than once during my time with the Bedouins. If there were screams from inside the office trailer, or his blue dragon airbrushed '77 Dodge Ram Van, you knew better than to stop it or ask what was going on. I daydreamed many times about pinning his balls to his desk with his coke dusted knife, dosing him in his toxic aftershave like lighter fluid and setting the whole god damn forest on fire around him.

I would make weekly, sometimes daily calls to Mitchum about what I was learning about the group, which was a whole lot of zilch. He accused me of not digging deep enough and more than a few times, danced around reversing his offer and sending me to prison anyway. Talking with Blowtorch, I learned the things that were holding me back. I needed a van. And a nickname.

The first was much easier to achieve than the second. I finally bought the Tradesman I bluffed about earlier and worked with Torch for weeks to get it to something like street legal, but acceptable to the rest of the club. I opted to skip the airbrush dragons and wizards and shit and went for flat black with olive green accents. I was proud of it, in a way. Mostly, because it put me one step closer to the end.

The nickname was another story and I kind of stumbled into how I got it. Talking to Blowtorch, I found out that the whole Black Sabbath thing was all Dusty. He was obsessed with the band, specifically, *Sabotage* which was played on a near constant loop when he was around. Paused only briefly to play a different Sabbath album, or at times the *Easy Rider* soundtrack, then put back on again. (If one day, some futuristic alien-robot archeologists discover my bones in a mass excavation of Earth, they will find the cord progression to *Symptom of the Universe* and the lyrics to *Born to Be Wild* etched into them somewhere.) Blowtorch joked quietly between us that Dusty probably lost his virginity to it. There was no other reason a guy would be so obsessed with a single album. The musical taste of the other club members deviated from Dusty's, but only slightly. Bull was an AC/DC fan, Doc was into Pink Floyd (hence his name), Otto was into Zeppelin, and Yankee Dan was into Skynyrd. The one unifying band was the Allman Brothers. All of this, did nothing but make my job much more difficult. Blowtorch claimed (early) Fleetwood Mac and called it good, but outside of the group he had a broader spectrum of musical tastes. He knew some punk but wasn't into it. One night when we were installing panels in the back of my van, I played him some Motörhead. That he enjoyed. From then on, I claimed Motörhead as my favorite band, which scared some and intimidated others. Dusty did not approve, but he was too scared to do anything about it. I began wearing t-shirts with the skull and sewed a patch on my patchless brown leather jacket. One night, Otto, the second most obnoxious member of the group, was giving me guff about the progress I was making on my van. He took a stick out of the fire and started to scrape FAG onto the side in charcoal. I punched him in the face and kicked him back towards the flame, bloodying his nose and setting one pant leg on fire. In retrospect, what I did was a bit over the top, but I hadn't blown off any steam since I had started this whole bullshit undercover work and it was a long time in coming. After that, everyone called me Teeth. I had a nickname and I was fully brought into the fold.

The night I was given my back patch (which looked like a cross between the poster for that movie *Wizards* and Frazetta's *Death Dealer*), Dusty called me into his office along with Torch and Bull. He said they were going to go on a run to Seattle to steal a large batch of weed from some small gang outfit. Apparently, he heard through the junkie wires that a gang had more than they could handle and he was more than willing to take it off their hands. I called Mitchum that night and told him what was happening. He sounded fat G-man pleased. I asked him if there was anyway he could guarantee me safety or immunity if I got arrested for criminal activity while working for the CIA. He told me not to get caught and hung up the phone.

By the time I got my backpatch, I had been with the Bedouins for nearly six months. I rode with them for another twelve, gathering information and siphoning it back to Mitchum. I had no idea what he was looking for. As best as I could tell, it was normal gang shit. Drugs, guns, robbery, rape. The only thing off the table was murder. But it seemed the more I reported back, the less interested he became. Finally, I didn't even talk to him anymore, I relayed all of my findings and information to his secretary. First in code, then finally just flat out, figuring if she worked for Mitchum none of what was going on would damage her sensitive ears.

Almost two years after Torch drove me to Popcorn Park, I

felt the kite string was about to snap. Dusty's cocaine intake was reaching Scarface proportions and his criminal-master-minding was starting to show it. All in all, it wouldn't have been a problem if it hadn't been my ass that was going to get caught in a sling. We had just come back from a long run, from Portland to Sacramento, to Seattle, a quick stop back in Portland, then Detroit and home. Everyone was beat. Even Otto wasn't running his mouth. All the vans needed oil changes and new tires, and people in general just needed time off the road. Then Dusty rocks us with the news of a big score "that would change everything". He separated us into teams. Me, Torch, Dusty and Yankee Dan were to go back up to Traverse City, while Doc, Otto and Bull went to Montana. That was as much as he told us before we hit the road again. When we finally got to Michigan, he told us the plan was to rob a police armory while cops were moving stations. No one was about it. It had all the trappings of a suicide mission. I tried to get in contact with Mitchum beforehand, but came up empty. We pulled off the job, with no small amount of guts and managed to make it back to Portland, rattled but unscathed. Otto, Bull and Doc were already at Popcorn Park, having ripped off thirty pounds of cocaine from the Butte chapter of the Galluping Gooses. It was then that Dusty told us his plan. We were to drive to the Sierra Army Depot in Herlong, California, "steal a bunch of shit" then break for Mexico. Right then I knew, this whole thing was almost over. All I had to do was somehow manage to survive it, and I would be home free.

Every stop we made on the way down to California, I tried

to make a call to Mitchum. I never got an answer. A few blocks away from the base, we pulled into the parking lot of a diner called The Downwinder II and split up into two vans. Otto hopped into the shotgun position of Dusty's van, while Torch and I rode in the back. Doc drove his van with Bull next to him and Yankee Dan in the back. Everyone was nervous. Even Dusty, a little bit. We had loaded the vans with M-16s and AK-47s before we left Popcorn Park and everyone grabbed a piece. A few months earlier, I had punched out some pusher outside of a local bar and stole his sawed-off shotgun. I brought it with me everywhere I went and claimed it to be lucky. This was supported by the four-leaf clover etched in the steel and everyone accepted it as my talisman. In reality, I was just limiting the number of illegal firearms the police could attach my prints to. Dusty said there was no time for chicken shit and told me to leave it in my van. So, I picked up an AK and left the safety on.

It was dark, but we didn't know what time. No one wore a watch, not even Dusty. Which was weird, because so many of his hairbrained ideas relied on what he called "perfect timing". Instead, he cranked *Sabotage* and we rolled in a two-van convoy to the gates of the Sierra Army Depot. I couldn't see much from the back of the van and could hear even less. Ozzy Osbourne was begging to be taken to heaven as *Hole in the Sky* shook the guards on duty awake. Doc, Bull and Yankee Dan jumped out of the van behind us and opened fire. I saw at least one guard go down, but I didn't know if he was dead. Another guard returned fire from behind a guard shack and the shit was on. Within seconds, red lights began to spin over the gates and more men in green fatigues came out of nowhere. Otto stepped out his door and barely got off two shots before he went down. The windshield broke and red exploded from Dusty's head and chest making the shattered glass even more impossible to see out of. The music kept blaring over the gunfire. I could hear screams and shots pop off outside of the van. The van rocked as heavy rounds started knocking dents and blowing holes into the walls around us. I screamed but couldn't hear myself. Finally, one of the soldier's bullets took out the radio and left nothing but the sounds of war. Blowtorch kicked me and made his way for the back door. There wasn't anytime to break the news any softer. I told him I was an informant. That I had been working with the CIA the whole time. If he surrendered with me, I would be able to get him out of this. His blue eyes glowed under his red hair. Every muscle in his body clenched and I could see his jaw grinding underneath of his giant biker beard. He punched me in the face with his weaker left hand and, for a second, I thought I had died. There was a flash of white light and a crunch, then the world came back in Technicolor with theater surround sound. I was in the Battle of Khe Sahn, only I was in a van in northern California. I sat up from where Torch had knocked me out and looked out the back door of the van, just in time to see him catch almost a dozen rounds to the chest. There were explosions up and down his body from his knees to his collar bone. Parts of his vest and jeans flew off. I instantly smelled blood and knew it was his, hot splatter hitting my face from a few feet away. Torch stumbled back a few feet, then lifted his M-16 with one hand and started walking forward. He held his left hand to his chest and it turned to pink spray in seconds, leaving a balled fist of red meat and exposed bone. He squeezed the trigger in a short, controlled burst and I watched his face disappear like an asteroid shower pelting the surface of the Moon. Torch was dead before what was left of his body hit the ground.

I don't know how long the shots went on for after that. All I know is I waited for them to stop before I stepped out of the van. I left the AK inside, not wanting to give them any confusion as to if I was armed or not. When I stepped out of the van, I held up my arms and kept repeating:

"My name is Wayne Garrety, retired US Air Force. I'm working with Agent Taber Mitchum of the CIA. I'm an informant."

The soldiers dropped their weapons and told me to get on my knees. Two MPs that looked like the twin brothers of the meat packers that hauled me in to meet Mitchum the first time, handcuffed me and dragged me into the compound. Being that I was a civilian and not active military, they had no jurisdiction and transferred me to the local police station. With my hands in cuffs, I reset my nose in the back of the police cruiser from where Torch had broken it. The cops thought that was funny. They threw me in the office of their Chief Officer, Capt. Earl Peach, and explained who and what I was. The door had barely closed on us and I became a motormouth. I explained about Portsmouth and Mitchum and Portland and the Bedouins. The whole plan and my involvement with it all. I must have said I worked with the CIA about a million times. I pulled the business card out of my wallet and gave it to the cop, begging him to call Mitchum. He stared at me, bored, rubbing his silver mustache, then took the card. Turning it over in his hands, he gave it more examination than a business card is worth, then tucked his chin and looked at me over the desk. When I finally ran out of breath and felt I was digging myself into an even deeper hole, I stopped talking. Without a word to me, Capt. Peach picked up his phone and dialed Mitchum's number. It rang several times before I heard an answer. He repeated my story, briefly and with substantially less expletives to the person on the other end. Then came the sickening part. He just stared at me, rolling the card between his fingers on the arm of his leather chair, saying *uh-huh* over and over and over again. In the middle of his Gregorian chant-like mantra, a message came in over his shiny new Champion fax machine. Peach glanced at it as he continued to drone into the handset, then hung up with a twangy *g'bye*.

"Well, Mr. Garrety, I've got some good news and I've got some bad news." He turned his chair a few degrees in my direction and read the fax. "The good news is, your story checks out."

"And the bad news?"

"The *bad* news...," Peach laid the fax down over the nameplate on his desk for me to read.

OPERATION: HAPPY TRAILS – **TERMINATED**

I felt my stomach drop and all my blood drain out onto the floor. Instantly, I wished I had ran out into the hail of bullets and turned my head into a Jackson Pollock painting all over the side of Dusty's van.

"Your outfit closed up shop almost two months ago. Meaning, any and all illegal activity you have taken part in since the 9th of May, 1985 was not, and will not, be protected by the Central Intelligence Agency."

I dropped my head in my hands and let out an extended *son of a bitch* that put some Grateful Dead guitar solos to shame in its runtime.

"I don't like you, Mr. Garrety," Peach continued, "You're young, smart-ass and have a rap sheet longer than the Appalachian Trail. *Despite* having an honorable discharge from the United States Air Force. But, you do have one thing on your side," he pulled his finger away from his mustache and held it in the air, "Which is, I believe you. So, for that, I will ignore this." He crumpled up the fax with one hand and tossed it in the wastebasket next to his desk. "And give you exactly three hours," he punctuated with more fingers, "to get the hell out of California. Which shouldn't be too hard, being that we are thirty minutes from the state line. I won't arrest you. And I won't charge you, but whatever happens to you once you leave this state, is *your* ass."

I barely had my cuffs off, before I was head and shoulders out the door of his office. He was kind enough to give me directions back to The Downwinder II before I hightailed it out of there. The cops in the station gave me funny looks, but no one came after me. The cool dry California air cut through my lungs like a bag of straight razors but I could still smell cordite and blood. I was happy to find my van in the parking lot untouched and in the same place I left it. I fueled up at a gas station just down the street and took off for Portland. There was little I needed in my apartment. Mostly just clothes and a once over to make sure I wasn't leaving anything incriminating behind. I caught a look at myself in the bathroom mirror and thought I had seen a ghost. I looked like my smack addicted older twin brother. But, while I looked like an outlaw, I knew that chapter of my life was over for good. I threw my things in my customized van and went the fuck back to Fall River.

Evening Stock

Business was slow and the muggy air made it worse. It had been most of a month since my last big case and I was starting to worry about how I was going to keep the lights on. I cleared out my fridge at the trailer, shut off all the power and moved into a backroom at the office. That way I would cut down on gas and other extraneous expenses like having a/c at my house and siphon my piddlely little stream of cash into keeping the business open. For what little time I had left, anyway.

I had *The Black Cat* playing on the desktop monitor and my laptop open to Twitter, just in case someone would try getting ahold of me that way. But at 9:30 on a Friday night in June, it wasn't looking good. The damp evening air was thick and cold whenever it decided to blow up off the river, but mostly it was just hot and stale in the office. I had taken to cutting a/c in the evenings and opening the windows to save on cash. It didn't really help, because there was hardly ever a breeze. But it gave me an excuse to drink a gallon of Lemon Blennd a night, so it wasn't all bad.

At some point, I had tuned out of the movie and started spinning a quarter on my desk, trying to see how fast and long

I could make it spin. It was only after I became wholly devoted to the cause, that I got a *ping* on my Twitter. It was some guy named fishEYE96 sending me a private message.

"are you awake?"

"Only physically." I typed back before I thought it through. There were a few minutes of no response before I remembered that people don't usually find me funny and I gave a straight answer. "How can I help you?" I capped it off with a smiley face for good measure.

"my friend is gone I think she might be in trouble and I think she might hurt someone."

I directed the loquacious Captain Descriptive to the phone number in my bio and asked him to call me to discuss his case further. It took longer than I had expected, but I picked up the phone on the first ring.

"Shamus O'Malley Detective Agency." I couldn't find the cursor to mute or pause the movie.

"Are you who I was talking to on Twitter?" There was nothing special about his voice. He just sounded like a guy.

"Yes, this is Hannah Brennan." I finally gave up and turned off the speakers.

"Oh...I was...I kinda thought you were a guy."

What I had once thought to be a clever business name, had now become a gigantic pain in my ass. "You're not the first," I held the phone between my shoulder and my cheek and spun the quarter, "You were telling me something about your friend?"

"Yeah," he sighed like a girl and put his thoughts together. "Yeah it's...it's kind of a long story."

"Lucky for you, I'm not going anywhere," I picked up the quarter off the floor and spun it again.

"Well, my friend, see...is an actress, right? I'm a...I mean you've probably never heard of me, but I'm a director."

"Do you and this rising star have names?"

"Well," his girl sighs were really starting to piss me off, "her name is Ingrid Winterbottom, but...she goes by the name Phoenix Vesper."

"Not much of a trade-off."

"Yeah, well," he didn't get it, "It's a name I kinda gave her, right? See, we were making this movie last year up in the Poconos and...something happened."

The quarter spun and took its sweet time laying down flat

on the desk. I could tell Cecil B. Demille was waiting for me to be astonished. I wasn't. "I'm listening."

"Well...it was this vampire movie we were making. Ingrid was the lead and...I don't know, she just like, slowly started changing, you know? Like, slipping away? I mean we had worked on things before and...she, like, could *sometimes* go method? Like, it wasn't an all the time thing? But this one, she really went for it and...we tried talking to her. We tried, like, getting her to snap out of it and, like, be Ingrid again, but...she just slowly became Phoenix."

I rested my chin on the desk and gently tapped the top of the quarter as it spun. "Still listening."

I could hear the guy chew his nails over the phone. "I don't know, I'm just, like...really scared."

"This was last year you said you shot this magnum opus?" I leaned back in my fake leather gaming chair and spun it back and forth in a semi-circle with my feet. "Why didn't you do something then? I mean, it seems a little late to be this bent out of shape about it."

"Have you heard about those killings on the news?" For the first time in the entire call, his voice trembled.

"A few, yeah."

"I think that's her."

I rolled the quarter across my knuckles and watched out the front window of the office as someone snuck their boat out onto the river for a late-night cruise. "And what led you to that conclusion?"

"They said the murders looked...ritual. And that the victims had had their throats slashed."

"And this all came out of your movie, I'm assuming?"

"The ritual did." He sounded guilty.

I pulled up to the desk and followed his Twitter direct message back to his account. Matt Roust, indie-filmmaker, horror lover, world conqueror. Or so said his bio. He hadn't been active in a while. A few things here and there. A full scroll back on the wheel led me to his posts from the previous summer, talking about the beginning of production for his new movie *After Sundown*. A photo showed a group of about twelve kids, standing in a cluster like they were leaving for summer camp; tongues out, wide smiles, the obligatory girl on a guy's back. Standing off to the left of the frame was a girl that looked to be about nineteen, black dyed scene hair pulled back into a ponytail, black lipstick and a small heart drawn on her cheek in black eyeliner. She was looking at the camera from under her emo peekaboo, holding up a peace sign, in a Marilyn Monroe t-shirt and black leather jacket. She was tagged as @wyntrbuttom. I followed the tag to her account, but it was private. Typical kid shit. But at least now I had a face to a name. "When was the last time you talked to her?"

"A few months ago. But I haven't seen her since last August when we wrapped."

"So," I shut my eyes tight and pinched the bridge of my nose with my free hand. For the first time all night, I felt tired, "you shoot this movie last year in the Poconos where your 'friend' plays a vampire. She starts acting whacky, thinking she *is* a vampire and you and your crew just let her go and now almost a year later, a few months after she stops talking to you, a couple people wind up dead and you think it's her that did it? Not trying to point fingers here, but if your theory is true, don't you think what you did was a tad irresponsible?"

"I love her." He wasn't crying, but he did sound earnest about it.

"I kinda figured that, but that wasn't what I asked."

"I know! I know, it was really f-ed up what I did!" What passed for vitriolic with Matt, would come across as disingenuous from most. I couldn't wait to see his movies. "But, like, I don't know who to turn to. I don't know where to go! Ingrid's out there and she's in danger! I don't want her to get hurt."

"Based on what you've told me, she's the safest thing in the woods, at the moment."

"Can you find her?"

I had been doing an internet search for the "ritualistic" murders in question. I found an article, forty-eight hours old, talking about an old man that had been killed in an "occult fashion" in the Beaver Cemetery. A quick scan of the text said police felt it was linked to a recent string of deaths that had started in Flatwoods, West Virginia two months ago. All elderly, all with throats slashed, left surrounded in "cult paraphernalia".

"Where is she from?" I could feel my face contort as I scrolled through the article.

"West Virginia."

"Uh-huh," I thought with my tongue in my cheek. "Do you have a number for her parents?"

"Why?"

"I don't know, I just want to talk to someone who remembers Black Monday."

"She's *twenty-four*."

"And I would imagine for at least a few consecutive hours of those years, the two gene donors of her DNA spent some time around her. It's a stretch how much they might now, but I want to take a shot anyway."

Roust rattled off a few names and numbers for me. Before he hung up I asked him which parent's card he was going to be using to pay. He told me he was using his. I had caught a glimpse of his new car and excitement about his trip to Cabo San Lucas on his Twitter feed and bumped up my price by two hundred dollars. He didn't seem to care. He sounded like he was ordering a McFlurry.

I spent the next hour getting my ducks in a row for the next morning, then went looking for any evidence of this movie. It took less time than I thought. He had posted the whole thing to Viddy back on Halloween. The timing was so cute I could have just died. And the movie actually didn't look that bad. The editing needed help and the script and the acting, effects and music were for shit, but it was a nice-*looking* movie. I gave the Oscar to Roust's equipment. The thing that jumped out the most, though, was Ingrid. Not for how good she was, but how all over the map she was. I chalked this up to shooting out of sequence. In some scenes, she looked like an awkward emo kid that just lost its braces, in others, she looked like a strung-out dope fiend out to reinvent the acting wheel. Her nail polish chipped, her make up smeared and her roots grew out. From a better actress she would have come across as a convincing modern vampire, a la *Near Dark*. Instead, she looked like someone halfway down the funnel of a deep, dark, personal spiral.

I got some sleep and called her parents in the morning. They didn't have much to say. They hadn't seen much of her since she moved out at seventeen and didn't know where she was or what she had been doing. They said she moved out of state after high school and hadn't come back to visit but a few times. Her mother called her quiet, her father called her serious. She had always had an interest in scary movies and Halloween as a child, taking a particular shine to folklore, ufos and "crippids". The Flatwoods Monster being something of a local mascot, they weren't too concerned. Before I hung up, they said they didn't know she had been in any movies and wanted me to send them copies. I remembered a few key scenes of her face covered in red corn syrup looking like a methadone addict and said I couldn't make any promises.

Next calls were to morgues. I had had a few run-ins with cops and local police stations. If I wanted to cover any ground, it was best to just mosey around them and then claim ignorance if I was caught. I also could feel a trip to the Poconos looming in my future. A yo-yo trip from Bridgewater to Flatwoods to the Poconos didn't sound like a good time to me. So, if I could clear some things up on the phone, I would. The closest hospital to Flatwoods was in Braxton. The coroner said some extended family had picked up the remains of Peter Jones earlier that week for burial. He didn't feel like telling me much after that. And this attitude followed for all other calls I made from Weston, to Morgantown, then finally Beaver. That made four bodies in two months time.

No one was outwardly copping to the ritual angle. Then

again, they barely wanted to discuss deaths at all. Accepting there was no choice, I got gas at Sheetz and grabbed a milkshake from Bruster's before heading off for West Virginia.

It was three hours to Flatwoods. Rob Sonic and *Failure Is An Option* kept me company on the ride down. I passed a sign declaring the town the Home of the Green Monster. Barring that, there was nothing to differentiate it from any other eastern town. I thought about getting in touch with her parents again and maybe checking out her house, but if she left right after high school, there wouldn't have been much reason to. Instead I opted to find the area where the "ritual homicide" occurred.

The article had been fuzzy on the details, but the accompanying video gave a pretty clear idea. There was a small white house on WV-4 just north of town, with a detached two-story garage. The police tape was still over the door. I did my best to hide my car behind the garage. Anyone northbound wouldn't see it, but if they were southbound I was screwed. I took the cement steps up to the front door of the quaint little country house and slipped inside. I could smell the blood before I closed the door. The evidence markers were gone, but I could still feel the presence of the police everywhere. There had been a struggle in the living room, a blanket was hanging over the side of a brown suede La-Z-Boy and a green plaid slipper was left stranded in the short hallway leading to the back bedroom. I tucked my nose inside my shirt and did my best to not make noise as I walked. The house was empty and no one was expected home, but I can't ever fight my inner ninja creeping tactics when I'm somewhere I'm not supposed to be.

The blood was contained mostly to the bed, but there was a lot of it. An amorphous blob about four and a half feet in diameter browned the mattress. There were candles that had been left to melt on the headboard, footboard, floor and nightstands. Something had been written on the wall above the bed in blood, but there was no telling what it was. It kind of looked like what the Hitchhiker smeared on the van in *Texas Chain Saw*. I snapped a few pictures with my phone and left. The news hadn't been wrong, it was ritual.

In *After Sundown*, the vampires were created as the result of a blood ceremony. As best as I could understand, because Captain Descriptive's stellar script hadn't bothered to explain it, vampires didn't need other vampires to turn them, necessarily. It was a transformation that happened as the result of ritual. The only thing they needed from another vampire was the mumbo-jumbo they had to say. This was passed along in some scroll and written in mock latin. I looked it up, there were no real words spoken, English or otherwise.

I took off from Flatwoods and headed north to Weston. Lynne Oster was sixty-two and homeless. News reports said they believed she had broken into Trans Allegheny and was squatting in one of the far wings of the asylum. When I got there, they wouldn't let me in. It wasn't tour hours and I didn't have state or Federal police license, so I wasn't allowed. Which wasn't all bad, because the must and mold was killing me just standing in the entry way. I still needed inside, though. The soccer mom working the front desk was an ego-tripper, but a smile at the security guard got me some place. Flirting was not my preferred method of getting information, but if it works, it works, and I will use it to my advantage. I asked if he would take my phone up to the crime scene and take pictures for me. At first he resisted, but I did my best Rita Hayworth (which I'm sure was convincing with my messy hair, lack of make-up, boots, jeans and oversized cardigan), then offered him twenty dollars. He took my phone when the soccer mom left and waved off the twenty when I handed it to him. When I got out to the car, I saw that he had entered his phone number into my contacts. Slick move, but I wasn't interested.

The scene looked much like the one in Jones' house, but slightly more developed. The effort was taken to draw a pentagram on the floor in orange construction spray paint and more candles at the tip of each point. Bloody footprints spread out from the massive puddle on the floor. There were no symbols, aside from the same one smeared on the wall that had been over Jones' bed, that now looked somewhat like I C. This told me, whoever was doing this, wasn't working from some text, even something as juvenile as the *Necronomicon*. Everything they knew about "ritual" came from movies. There hadn't been a pentagram in *After Sundown*, though there had been candles. Mostly the scenes where Phoenix Vesper was supposed to be tying people down and eating them, Roust had focused on Ingrid's bad fangs and contacts and the corn syrup dripping down her cleavage.

It was while I was looking at the photos in my car and eating fistfuls of peanut butter M&M's that I got another direct message through twitter. This was from @moonandstars. I checked out their profile before I looked at the message. It was a girl from Morgantown that fancied herself a hippie.

"r u looking 4 Ingrid?"

"Yes I am. May I ask who you are?"

"i was Ingrids roommate b4 she wnt missng. matt told me 2 tlak 2 u"

We arranged to meet at a coffee shop on Van Voorhis Road. She was sitting at a window seat in her flipflops and crystal cruncher getup, staring at her phone when I got there. It was late, I had been on the road for about six hours already and hadn't ate since breakfast, but I didn't feel like diving into a reheated sandwich or overpriced coffee shop muffin in front of this woman. Instead, I bought some boxed brown sweet water advertised as chocolate milk and nursed it while we talked.

She said her name was Mithril Tatton. She had met Ingrid when she moved back to West Virginia after things didn't work out in PA. They had met through Mithril's Craigslist ad for a roommate and Ingrid moved in with no money and no possessions. She said they got along, but Ingrid was prone to mood swings and disappearing for days at a time. Her excuse was she was off making movies, and Mithril's snooping through her Twitter and Instagram confirmed this, but only about half the time. Tatton described Ingrid as "lost and misunderstood soul that is just looking for a place in this world." She thought Ingrid had found it in Roust, but their relationship was never anything serious. Roust was too awkward and flighty to formally ask for a date and the rest of the time he spent filming and going on vacations. Tatton said she managed to convince Ingrid to take her along on one of her disappearing acts. She said they just went out into the woods, listened to music, drank cheap wine and talked about going out west. After one night of sleeping out in the woods in a sleeping bag, Tatton said she bailed. When she offered to drive Ingrid back, she said she wasn't done yet and would just hitch back. Said that's how she traveled all the time anyway.

"What did she mean she wasn't done yet?"

Mithril shrugged her sunburned shoulder's and rolled her eyes. "No clue. I mean, I love being out in nature, but she wasn't doing anything. When I go out camping I go hiking or drop mushrooms or something. She was just sitting around and, like, meditating and getting drunk. She never took off that leather jacket, either. She would stare off into space and sort of do this, like, chant under her breath."

"Do you know what it was?"

She shrugged again, "It just sounded like noise."

"What do you know about when she went to make After Sundown?"

Mithril rolled her eyes and dropped her head into her elbows where her arms were outstretched on the table. "That *fucking* movie." Her voice was muffled and buzzed against the table. She lifted her head again, "Have you seen it?"

I nodded.

"It's so stupid. Like, I don't even know why Ingrid hung out with that guy. My cousin could make better movies and he's two."

"I'm more interested in what you know about what happened during filming. And where she went and what she did afterwards."

"She packed up her stuff one night and said that she was going with Matt and some other friends to some place in Pennsylvania. She said that they were going to make some vampire movie that might take all summer and she would be back when it was done."

"That was it?"

"Until about six weeks ago, yeah." She nodded, frustrated and sick of it. "I tried texting her, I tried calling her. She blocked me on Insta and Twitter and I had no way to get ahold of her. I packed up all of her shit and stuck it in a closet.

I had to get another roommate to just pay the rent, but I kept her stuff in case she came back."

"What happened six weeks ago?"

"I came home, after being out with some friends, and there was this person skulking around outside the apartment. I had my boyfriend stay with me and he went up to see who it was and it was Ingrid. She said that she was sorry and that she wanted to go in and get her stuff back. I couldn't see her in the dark, but I recognized her voice. Then when she walked up to the porch light, she looked different. She looked, older and, like, her eyes were sunk back into her head. She kept staring at me like this," Mithril dropped her head and did a Kubrick stare at me, "and, like, she was looking at me through her hair, which was all grown out and greasy, you could see her blonde. And, like, she hadn't done her make-up, she usually did like this really heavy wingtip eyeliner. She hadn't done that at all. It was just, like, you could see the fallout from some mascara and that was it. And she was wearing the same clothes she was wearing the last time I saw her and they looked old, like she'd been living in them. When I opened the door, she just stood outside and asked if I would invite her in. Chris stood there with me and we both just looked at each other. She wouldn't come in until we invited her. Chris knew where I had put her stuff and I just had him get it for her so I wouldn't have to be around her. She kept shifting her eyes and looking around, and had this, like, permanent, really creepy grin. Not like a full out smile, just this, like, smirk, that never changed."

"What happened after she got her stuff?"

"She came out and hugged me. She told me it was nice living with me, but she had to move on and maybe we could hang out later. She was really cold and she hugged me for a really long time and I felt her, like, nuzzle into my neck and she did this purr like a cat. I looked at Chris and he, like, reached out and pulled her off of me. I'm so glad he was there, because I don't know what would have happened. Ingrid never told me that she was bi or anything, but she was talking to me and looking at me in a way I'd never seen her look at me before."

"Like she wanted to eat you?"

"Or fuck me," Mithril held the back of her neck and bobbed her head. "Which, I don't know that I ever *would* have done that with her? but I certainly wasn't feeling it then."

I couldn't tell if she was trying to be funny or not, but it didn't matter. She gave me her contact information and we parted ways shortly thereafter. The sky was just starting to turn peach and purple. I asked my phone to do a search for milkshakes and it found a Carvel somewhere in town. That was enough to hold me over until I got back to the office.

Everything I had to go on was old news, but it all certainly seemed to be pointing in the direction that Ingrid, if she was in fact the one committing the murders, was heading north. The logical destination being the Poconos. Whatever had happened that made her go screwy, happened while they were shooting After Sundown. And while it was a longshot to check, it was the only way I knew to stay ahead of her and anymore killings. The next morning, before I took off, I checked the news while I was still at the office. There had been another murder yesterday, in Bellfonte. A seventy-one year-old man on life support in his home. Police suspected foul play. I suspected Ingrid Winterbottom.

It was a five-hour trip out to Mt. Pocono. When I got in the car, I messaged Roust and asked him to send me all the shooting locations they had used for *After Sundown*. He sent me a list and said most of their shooting was done primarily in and around the Penn Hills Resort. I put on *Are You Gonna Eat That?* and went wagons east for the Poconos.

It looked like a small-town Vegas casino lost in the bush of Saigon. The sun was hot, the bugs were loud, and green grew in places it shouldn't in and around graffitied resort walls. A basketball court grew out of the woods and chain link fences cut off wild undergrowth from other wild undergrowth. There were no trespassing signs posted, what seemed, every fifteen feet. A section of chain link and a jersey barrier blocked off the entrance to the main part of Penn Hills, a small pile of fresh potting soil dumped just outside a path cut around the blockade. The most surreal part of the whole place was how obtuse its presence was, divided down the center by PA-447. Traffic zipped by regularly, windows down blaring shitty pop and country music.

There wasn't any secret or hidden place I could store the car to look around. And I wasn't too jazzed on the idea of stumbling around there in the dark. I asked my phone to find a local hardware store. I bought a pair of bolt cutters and drove back to the hidden driveway that was chained and fenced off from the road. When there was a lull in the traffic, I cut the chain, pulled in and placed the chain link wall back to keep up appearances. As long as I wasn't stupid, I had free roam of the entire grounds.

The side of the road I had picked was mostly bungalows. I recognized them from the movie. They looked more like something out of *A Boy and His Dog* than a vampire flick, but I wasn't there to judge. It was kind of cool in a sad, lonesome way. But the place didn't seem like it would have been that good of a time to stay at back in the day, either. Every room I walked past, I could of swore I heard the sound of drunk couples fighting and make-up sex. Some stuff I had read online said it was "heartbreaking" to see this place in ruins. I thought it seemed appropriate.

There was a scuttling sound above me as I entered one of the buildings. I looked up in time to see a dumbass squirrel scurry up an eave. Inside, the smell was putrid. It smelled like mold, death and inebriated promises. I pulled on the respirator I bought at the hardware store and added the smell of rubber and plastic to the mix. But it comforted me some that I wouldn't be breathing in some sort of *Invasion of the Body Snatchers* microbe or lung melting fungus. I tiptoed around obvious soft spots in the floor and checked the building from top to bottom. No luck. When I stepped outside again to breathe clean air, I took in how many more buildings there were to search and knew that I didn't feel like sticking around there all day. So, I waited for a lull in traffic and skipped across the street to the main resort. My cardigan caught on the chain link and ripped. I made a mental note to fix it and pad my bill to buy a new one.

This building was bigger, and while I wouldn't have wanted to live there, it would have been preferable to the bungalows if those were my only two options. There was a wall of tvs stacked up in the lobby. The carpet had either once been green or once been yellow, I couldn't tell. It was at a draw at this point. Large chunks of plaster had fallen off the water damaged ceilings and littered the floor like a poorly graveled driveway. Big skylights let in the late summer afternoon sun, enough that I didn't have to strain my eyes or drain my phone battery for the flashlight. As I walked through the halls of the resort, I recognized areas used in the movie. Little set ups here and there. For as much production value as this place had, Roust sure as shit didn't utilize it. But it did tell me that I was more than likely in the right place.

I turned off the main hall into blackness and felt my breath and heartbeat catch in my throat at the same time. It didn't feel right. There was the unshakeable sense that I, suddenly, was not alone. The walls felt as if they were breathing and there was a general feeling of *not welcome* to the entire wing. The windows of every room had been blacked out with sheets and blankets, leaving, at best, ambient amber light spilling out into the moss carpeted hallway. I wished I carried a gun. I wished I hadn't come in, or at least told someone where I was going. I had a feeling that I had only had a few times in my life, the feeling that I might not walk away from this alive. There was a solid wood handled broom leaning against the wall at the end of the hallway. That and my pepper spray were my only lines of defense.

The smell of must and mold came in strong through my respirator. I tried to focus on knowing I wasn't breathing them, only the fumes, and began my ninja creep down the hallway. The breathing motion of the walls became amplified as I walked. The window in one room had been smashed, leaving a pink bed spread to blow limply in the breeze. I checked each room individually, to no avail, and was beginning to think it was all in my head. Then I found it.

The outside wall of a large suite had been tattooed with markings all around the doorframe. The room itself was black and seemingly infinite. I held the broom handle in one hand and my phone's flashlight in the other and cautiously crossed the threshold into mid-summer afternoon blackness. There was a path kicked through the debris on the carpet, signs of at least moderate foot traffic. Roaches and rats saw my light and scrambled off into the dark. I could feel my chest get tight and the pulse in my head strain against the straps of the respirator. A sense of claustrophobia set in in the dark and I wanted to rip the mask off my face, but in my fear, I predicted certain and instant death. The heart shaped bed was empty, under a lean-to of gilded mirrors that Liberace would be proud of. My flashlight beam bounced back at me, creating a shadow behind me that almost made me scream. Once I finally managed to control my own breathing, I heard the breathing of something else. And whatever it was, it was bigger than a rat. I eased over the soft spots into the bathroom, until the breathing got louder. Nothing was obvious, which only made me more afraid. Then I saw a slick black mass with a rise and fall that matched the rhythm of the breaths. And it was laying in the heart shaped tub. The floor creaked as I crept over to it. When I fully had the mass in my beam, I saw that it was Ingrid, asleep on top of a pile of pillows and bedspreads. She was curled up, on her side, her breathing labored and wheezing. She looked dead, and sounded to be on the brink of it, but when her eyes shot open, the look they gave me told me she was very much alive.

"You...*dare*...disturb my slumber?" Ingrid rolled over in slow motion and clawed her way out of the tub with skeletal, spider-like hands.

"Ingrid..." I held the beam directly in her face, the broom handle out in front of me for protection.

"*Do...not* call me that. You haven't earned the *right*." Her voice sounded like she had spent the past twelve months smoking three cartons a day.

"Your parents have been very worried about you. And Matt and Mithri---"

"Those swine are not my parents. I am not of this world. I am a creature beyond your comprehension. I am a child of darkness. The daughter of The Man That Smiles." She pulled back her lips and revealed bleeding pink and white gums over yellow teeth. Her jaundiced skin was contrasted by dark sunken eyes, set into a face of odd angles, like thin skin stretched over animal bones. "He waits for me. And when he returns, we will return together to the place below the earth called Bleak."

She was gaining on me and I didn't like it. I could see her Andersonville thin body move under her clothes and it made me wince. Her knees would knock together, struggling to hold up the weight of her emaciated body. I tripped over a nightstand and crashed to the floor. My phone disappeared somewhere in the dark. The only light in the room came from the dim amber light in the hallway. I turned onto my stomach and lifted myself up to make a run for the door. There was a thud as a hundred and fifty pounds of human bones fell on my back and knocked the wind out of me. I heard a snap in my ribcage and knew that I had broken a floater.

"Unless..." Ingrid's voice wheezed in my ear. She was stronger than I had taken her for, "You are my test. He has sent you to me to prove I am finally worthy. Worthy to return home."

I managed to pull my left hand out from under me and found the broom handle in my hand, cracked in half. The pink light from the hall glistened off the smooth wood and I took it as a gift. One blind swing over my shoulder cracked Ingrid in the head and she commenced to screaming. I saw the glow of my phone behind the door and snatched it up before I slammed the door behind me, taking off down the hall. The respirator made me feel like I couldn't breathe. Against my better judgement, I ripped it off and was hit with the full spectrum of toxic and potentially lethal smells of Penn Hills. They nearly dropped me. But the sound of Ingrid's inhuman shrieks kept me going. When I reached the main lobby. I stopped in a beam of light from a skylight and turned back to face the hallway. Thudding footsteps echoed out of the blackness down the hall. The black leather clad scarecrow form of Ingrid Winterbottom flew out of the amber dark into the bright lobby, a savage, rabid animal look in her eyes, mouth impossibly wide and screaming. She made it a few feet before she hit the first beam of light from the ceiling, at which point her scream turned from rage to fear. She collapsed to the ground, kicking her legs, trying to cover her greasy hair with her leather jacket.

I snapped back into reality after a few seconds, realizing I had been standing with the broom handle in my hands like Crash Davis. Ingrid kicked dust and mold spores into the air with her feet. She spun in small circles and writhed on the ground, screaming in agony. Still holding the broom handle, I grabbed her by the collar of her leather jacket and dragged her out of the sunlight.

"Who are you waiting for?"

"I can't tell you," She tried to cry, but her body didn't have enough moisture to pull it off, "If I tell you, I won't pass the test and I can never return to Bleak."

I shook her by the collar and gritted my teeth. "You already failed the test, remember? I am the test. Now tell me who you're waiting for."

Ingrid's face approximated something akin to human. She turned away from me and looked out from under her grown out emo peekaboo with one eye. A bloody tear formed in the corner and ran down her face. "I can't."

I threw down the broom handle and pulled out my pepper spray. Her face flashed with fear and her eyes went wide. She tried to kick me with her feet, but I was kneeling on her legs.

"Were you sent to kill me?"

"Yes. And I will. If you don't tell me who you're waiting for."

"Please don't use the garlic," Ingrid's raspy voice cracked and another bloody tear dripped down her face. "I'm already weak from the sun and may not survive."

"Then tell me who you are waiting for."

She breathed deep and didn't look at me. "The Man Who Smiles."

"Who?"

"My father. He was the first of our kind. He abandoned me as a child until I could prove I was worthy to return home. I did everything he asked, but I've failed. Now I can never return home." There were mere seconds of rational thought before she collapsed into my arms and began sobbing.

I didn't know what to do. She felt as strong as a cancer victim and as distraught as a orphan, but I couldn't reconcile it with the Sleestak of a person that, moments ago, was threatening to kill me. It took me a minute to shift my position and hold her so I wasn't still sitting on her legs. She didn't last long after that. Ingrid passed out from pure exhaustion and I left her asleep on the dirty carpet of the lobby floor. I took a few minutes to search her room, until I found what I was looking for. Then I decided on a believable sanitized version of the truth and called 911.

I went to her parents first. I called them from the hospital waiting room. They weren't footing the bill, but I figured they had more right to know about their daughter than Roust. They asked me to wait, but I told them I couldn't stay. Just left them with the information of the hospital and doctor treating her and went back to Bridgewater. I left out everything I had learned while I was in the waiting room and decided to pass off not giving them my find as a slip of the mind and mailing it back. The psychiatrists were definitely going to need it.

The Y across the river from the office was open late for summer hours. I stopped in to get a hot shower and change out of my musty clothes, then went back to the office to get a fitful night's sleep. I hung out and wasted away the morning through to the evening, just to get another full day on the bill, then called Roust. He was asleep before he answered the phone, but he after what I was about to tell him, he would be wide awake for days. I held the line while he transferred the money, then laid into him.

"Why didn't you tell me all this shit about Indrid Cold?"

"Who?"

"Fuck you. I really should be reporting you to the police."

"Who...who is Indrid Cold?"

"Oh, you know, this delusion you helped your so-called love foster that she was the offspring of a vampire-alien hybrid?"

There was silence from the other end of the line. He knew he was caught.

"Uh-huh. I found her, by the way."

"Oh my god, is she ok?"

"Well, if the doctor's fix her body, she may spend the rest of her life in a psych ward. How would you rank that on your scale of 'ok'?"

More silence. The only sound was Roust chewing his nails. "I...really didn't expect it to get out of hand. I mean...everyone thought it was a joke. We all thought it was a joke. We thought she did, too."

"At what point, *exactly*, did you realize that she didn't think it was a joke? Was it when she stared losing her shit while you were filming or was it when your ass puckered at the first report of a body in Flatwoods."

"Probably then, yeah."

"Really? Cause I have something here that says different." I flipped through Ingrid's leather-bound sketchbook diary on my desk. "She says here, on August eleventh of last year, that you and the rest of your little film school buddies cut her out of your lives completely. Couldn't get ahold of a single one of you, she says."

Roust didn't hang up. But he didn't say anything either.

"I'm not the one that should be talking here."

"She..." Roust gave one of his girl sighs and whined, "It's not my fault! I didn't come up with all that stuff about Indrid Cold, she did. She's been talking about it since I first met her.

She said that people had it wrong, that he couldn't be in alien, he had to be a vampire, based on the way they described him. And she kept emphasizing that his last name was Cold. She said that could only mean one thing. Look, Ingrid didn't like who she was and she hated where she came from. She was convinced she was from someplace else. We talked about it one night and she said that she wished she was a vampire so she could die then live forever. And, yes, I was the one that made the connection between her name and Indrid Cold, but what I said about her being his kid was just a joke. She ran away with it! And you don't know Ingrid. You don't know how she can get. She gets an idea and she just won't let it go."

"Then why the fuck did you plant that idea in her head?" I felt like I was reprimanding a child. "By all accounts, from what I'm seeing, Ingrid is not mentally stable. I think you knew that. I think you liked that about her. And I don't think you ever loved her at all. You saw her as a toy. Something you could fuck with. Download a whole hard drive of bullshit into her head and watch her spin out with it like a battle top. But you being you, had no fucking clue what you were doing and it spun out of your control."

"Yes! Exactly, I---"

"That's not an excuse! And I am not letting you off the hook! Neither should anybody else! You took an easily manipulated person and fucked their head until they broke and damn near killed them! You knew exactly what you were doing. You just thought you could pass it off as some sort of Daniel-Day Lewis trip gone wrong and walk away scot free."

"I'm sorry." His voice was low.

"You don't need to apologize to me. You and your little fucking film crew need to apologize to her, because based on what I'm reading," I flipped through her journal for a specific passage but couldn't find it, "you are all equally responsible. You're just the only one that broke. And quite frankly, could have probably pulled this whole scam off if you hadn't called me. But pride is a son of a bitch."

"I do love her."

"Bullshit. You have a bridge you want to sell me, too? Cause I'm not buying it either."

Roust whimpered into the phone and started crying. Also, like a girl. "Is she ok?"

"She was breathing when they took her to the hospital. But that was about eighteen hours ago."

"I don't want her to die."

"You should have thought about that before you filled her head with bullshit."

"What..." Roust sucked back a nose full of snot, "What happens now?"

"I mail Ingrid's diary to her parents and recommend they get her serious psychiatric help."

"What do I do?"

I seethed. "Well, as detestable as this whole situation is, it's *de rigueur* for Hollywood. It might even be considered bush league. So, I don't think it will negatively impact your film career."

"This isn't about my career." Roust sounded agitated.

"Really? Could have fooled me." I hung up the phone and dropped it on my desk. The slam made me cringe. My disgust had gotten the better of me.

I sat at my desk for a little while before I went into the kitchen and fixed a Lemon Blennd with heavy ice. It was cooler in the office than it had been on previous nights. And while I wasn't out of the woods, the knot of financial tension wasn't twisting in my stomach for the first time in a long while. I put on some music and stepped out onto the front deck of the office that looked out over the parking lot and down on to the river. There were no boats on the river and traffic was summer easy. I hummed along with *Creep On Creepin' On*, breathing in the small purple flowers that grow at the base of the stairs and thought about evening stock. The night people we are warned about as children and the real-life monsters we encounter when we become adults. They are far more dangerous than things you see in movies, but nowhere near as obvious. That is the great trade off; you can have something obvious and harmless or you have something inconspicuous and lethal. My mind spun back to Penn Hills and Ingrid wheezing in a heart-shaped bathtub. I knew if my job was to track down Universal monsters on the reg, I'd hang it up and find a new job. I'm not cut out to be Buffy. But while people like Roust looked and sounded milquetoast, they still have all the capabilities of the most nightmarish creatures imaginable, sans supernatural powers. But you don't need superpowers to crack someone's mind. All you need is the desire.

I hit the ice at the bottom of my cup and stood up from where I was leaning on the railing. A chill had settled in and I decided to call it a night. I went back inside, logged off, and put on an old episode of *Mystery Science Theater 3000*, before drifting off to sleep.

Raistlin Skelley lives somewhere in Pennsylvania.
He is also the author of *The Five Year Trip*.

www.ingramcontent.com/pod-product-compliance
Lightning Source LLC
Chambersburg PA
CBHW061917130726
47908CB00017B/1661